WRITERS' RENDEZVOUS ANTHOLOGY 2017

Writers' Rendezvous Anthology 2017
Copyright © 2017 USA
All rights reserved. This book, or parts thereof, may not be reproduced in any form without permission. All content is owned by the authors.

ISBN 9781977990921

This anthology contains works of fiction. Names, characters, places, and incidents are either the product of the authors' imaginations or are used fictitiously, and any resemblance to actual persons, living or dead, businesses, events, or locales is entirely coincidental.

Writers' Rendezvous, Bloomfield Township, Michigan USA
www.btpl.org/writers-rendezvous

Anthology Team

Writers' Rendezvous Facilitator	Tim Patrick
Editor in Chief	Phil Skiff
Contributing Authors	Peter Banks Diane VanderBeke Mager P.L. Middlebrook A.J. Norris Tim Patrick D.M. Patton Theresa Shen Phil Skiff Anthony Stachurski
Manuscript Editor	Diane VanderBeke Mager
Design Committee	Peter Banks Diane VanderBeke Mager Lorenz Mager A.J. Norris Theresa Shen
Graphic Design	Lorenz Mager
Publication Support	Don Skiff

Dedication

I would like to dedicate this first anthology to the hundreds of people who have been a part of Writers' Rendezvous over the past twenty-two years. Many went on to become successful published authors. Some even made it onto The New York Times best-sellers list.

None of this would have been possible without Ann Williams, head of Adult Services at Bloomfield Township Public Library, who in 1995 had the foresight to set aside a block of time and a room for local writers to meet and exchange ideas. Thank you for providing us with a safe haven to share our innermost thoughts and ideas with our peers.

Special thanks to the founding members of the group who helped hammer out the format of our writers' workshop and turn it into a unique venue:

- Robyn Clariday, whose frustration with her lack of progress on a work of young adult fiction led her to throw the only copy of her 75,000-word manuscript into the back of the garbage truck as it drove away. She went on to sign a book contract with a major publishing house and to write several successful novels.
- Rowena Cherry, a sci-fi romance writer, who left us doubled over in laughter when she unrolled a poster of mammal sexual appendages, hoping we could help her choose the proper one for her protagonist. She has since published several books and hosts *Crazy-Tuesday*, a radio talk show.
- Marilyn Spencer, a talented artist and writer, who had one of her short stories chosen as a finalist for the nationally recognized Pushcart Prize. Marilyn's insights and patience helped us learn the art of storytelling. Sadly, pancreatic cancer took her from us.
- Kari Cimbalik, whose creative energy and ideas never ceased to amaze. Her book was the first one published by a member of Writers' Rendezvous.

Dedication

Additional thanks to the following people who contributed to my aspiration to be a writer, to the group, and to this anthology:
- My late wife, Barbara, whose encouragement and support helped me pursue my dream of writing.
- Distinguished Professor Jane Eberwein, who provided me with the opportunity to become a published author.
- Mark Kelly, whose material helped keep the group together during the lean years, when we had few members and scant material.
- A.J. Norris, a talented and successful writer, who has had to endure my constant mispronunciation of her first name. And, despite her growing success as an author, did not abandon the group.
- All the current members who have helped advance the group and its impact on the community.
- Diane VanderBeke Mager, for her tireless efforts to edit the anthology, despite the tragic loss of both her parents within two months.
- Lastly, Phil Skiff—THANKS for patiently shepherding this project through to completion.

Tim Patrick
Facilitator, Writers' Rendezvous

Foreword

Dreams, we all have them. They are daunting and often terrifying.

Writers' Rendezvous is a workshop focusing on long and short works of fiction, non-fiction, memoirs, and poetry. The purpose of the group is to help people reach their goals as writers. Be it the person who dreams of becoming a published author or one who writes for the sheer joy of sharing a story, we offer a safe environment.

Writers take turns presenting their work to a group of peers who provide respectful insights and constructive feedback on all phases of the process. Many of the authors are members of additional writing groups that reflect their particular genre. Several enter competitions or find inspiration in online writing prompts.

Writing is easy. Writing well is difficult.

Carving out time early in the morning before work, losing track of entire afternoons, or seeking isolation late into the night after the world has fallen silent, writers ply away at their stories, essays, and poems. The authors in this book have dedicated countless hours of their lives to the craft. Some are new, others are veterans—all have the burning desire to continue perfecting the art of storytelling.

Some stories and poems flow on to the page. Others do not. Legend has it that Ernest Hemmingway rewrote the ending to *The Sun Also Rises* ninety-nine times. Writing is not for the faint of heart.

The authors herein have dared to dream and to publish.

Come travel with us into a world filled with brilliant imagery, quirky characters, and thought-provoking essays, poems, and works of fiction and non-fiction. Whatever your genre, there is something for you. Dive in and enjoy.

Foreword

Writers' Rendezvous Anthology 2017 excerpts*:

A man with dark glasses and a sexy scruff looks up at the sound. Shit, I think he sees me. I drop the curtain and race back to bed, torn between utter embarrassment and a burning desire to meet him.

I force myself to close my eyes, restarting my earlier tale of romance in my head; but it no longer appeals. My thoughts wander. I imagine myself joining the party outside . . . escaping responsibility . . . relinquishing control. Senses heightened, a new bedtime story takes shape in my mind. . . .

■ ■ ■

Rejoicing in the autumn aesthetics, it would have been easy to miss the body lying in the sand near the water. Just above the reach of the lapping waves, half blending in with the beach, she was nude and unmoving. Unsure at first, he paused a moment before acting, afraid he'd stumbled upon another lost soul seeking solitude or a late season nudist just catching some rays. The cove was perfectly concealed with only the sun and sky bearing witness. Despite the scenery, the figure in the sand became the new center of the universe; it was all he could see and ponder. Human beauty trumping nature's sublime bounty.

■ ■ ■

My father and I were strangers. When I was a child and busy with fairytales, my father was actively involved with the politics of the Republic of China. He never had any time to converse with me and my other siblings.

■ ■ ■

Foreword

Vadim had never experienced pain like this before in his life. When he was thirteen, one of his uncle Dzhey's plow horses had kicked him right in the chest when he'd gotten too close. He'd rolled around on the ground unable to draw a breath, terrified he was going to die. The pain from two cracked ribs had been excruciating. But even that paled in comparison to this.

■ ■ ■

When I was ten and my sister was eight, our parents divorced. It was the summer of 1973. Divorce was still considered a shameful event, especially for us Catholics. I was in 5th grade. As my father was leaving my life, a new person was entering. It was the first time we met June, our maternal grandmother; she was fresh out of prison.

■ ■ ■

*Up here. To the right. Higher.
That's it!
Do you see me now?*

■ ■ ■

Michael stood in line at the Heathrow Airport security checkpoint. What's taking so long? He glanced at his watch again and sighed. A sense of loss weighed him down; he missed how she felt in his hands—her sleek form and smooth exterior. As the line shuffled forward, he caught sight of what he longed for; what completed him.

A weapon.

■ ■ ■

Foreword

I can't believe I've been in litigation over my own child ever since he was born, and now he's just about four years old. What is wrong with this picture? Greedy lawyers, a prejudiced judge. Why is it so hard for a brother to catch a break?

■■■

Sonny sensed tension in the hot, humid air that blanketed Detroit. It was a little over a month since Robert Kennedy had been assassinated… and Martin Luther King just two months earlier. Traffic on Kelly Road was sparse for a summer afternoon. Nearing the intersection at Moross, he heard the distinct roar of a muscle car accelerating hard.

■■■

Thank you for supporting our local writing community.

This is the first in a series of anthologies to be published by Writers' Rendezvous. Visit www.btpl.org/writers-rendezvous for details about our group, upcoming writing seminars, and future publications, as well as for writing tips.

* *This book includes content written for adult audiences and may contain explicit language and scenes.*

Contents

SHORT FICTION
3 | Sleeping Single—PART 1: Summer Frustration |
   Diane VanderBeke Mager
8 | The Filthy Few | *Tim Patrick*
42 | All This Brother Wants—Chapter 1 | *P.L. Middlebrook*
48 | Sunset in Kyiv | *Phil Skiff*
52 | The Trouble with Beautiful Women | *A.J. Norris*
60 | Sleeping Single—PART 2: Autumn Longing |
   Diane VanderBeke Mager

POETRY
71 | Composure | *Peter Banks*
72 | Life is Good | *Anthony Stachurski*
74 | Biography of a Shadow | *Anthony Stachurski*
75 | Holy Vows | *Anthony Stachurski*
76 | The Invisible Man | *Anthony Stachurski*
77 | English Weather | *Anthony Stachurski*
78 | Geodes | *Anthony Stachurski*
79 | Absolute Truth | *Anthony Stachurski*
80 | The Wish | *Anthony Stachurski*
81 | A Summer's Day | *Anthony Stachurski*
82 | Let Me Introduce Myself | *Anthony Stachurski*
84 | Duet for Pen and Shed | *Anthony Stachurski*
85 | Decked as a Bride | *Anthony Stachurski*
86 | Side-View Mirror | *Anthony Stachurski*
87 | Oh, Holy Night | *Anthony Stachurski*
88 | Celebration of Life | *Theresa Shen*

Contents

MEMOIRS & ESSAYS
93 | "Grandpa, that's my sweater." | *Theresa Shen*
97 | The Green Beans | *Theresa Shen*
103 | "When the Moon is in the Seventh House . . . Let's Go Blue!" | *Peter Banks*
105 | Uncle Wou's Time | *Theresa Shen*
108 | The Outsider | *Theresa Shen*
114 | The Story | *Phil Skiff*
118 | The Amethyst Adventure | *Theresa Shen*
126 | The Chairs | *Theresa Shen*
130 | Kitchen Lessons | *D.M. Patton*

POETRY
145 | Radiator Poem | *Anthony Stachurski*
146 | The Basement | *Anthony Stachurski*
147 | Shopping at Ralph Lauren | *Anthony Stachurski*
148 | The Way | *Anthony Stachurski*
149 | Wonder Woman | *Anthony Stachurski*
150 | Flower Girl | *Anthony Stachurski*
152 | Water Lilies | *Theresa Shen*
153 | Dandelion, Dandelion | *Theresa Shen*
154 | Men on the Beach | *Anthony Stachurski*
155 | Desert Queen | *Anthony Stachurski*
156 | The Friars of San Francesco | *Anthony Stachurski*
157 | White Clouds | *Anthony Stachurski*
158 | Maple Leaves | *Anthony Stachurski*
159 | Truth Seekers | *Anthony Stachurski*
160 | Winter Scene | *Anthony Stachurski*
161 | Ursa Major | *Anthony Stachurski*
162 | Morning Walk | *Theresa Shen*
163 | The Great Equalizer | *Theresa Shen*
164 | Small Grass | *Theresa Shen*
165 | Politico | *Peter Banks*

SHORT FICTION
169 | A Lucky Girl | *A.J. Norris*
172 | Sleeping Single—PART 3: Winter Diversions | *Diane VanderBeke Mager*
182 | Saudade | *Phil Skiff*
184 | All This Brother Wants—Chapter 2 | *P.L Middlebrook*
191 | Cold | *Phil Skiff*
195 | Sleeping Single—PART 4: Spring Romance | *Diane VanderBeke Mager*
206 | The Trunk in Grandma's Attic | *Phil Skiff*
214 | Swan Lake | *Peter Banks*
219 | The Declaration | *Phil Skiff*
221 | All This Brother Wants—Chapter 3 | *P.L. Middlebrook*
226 | Saudade (Redux) | *Phil Skiff*
229 | Sleeping Single—PART 5: Summer Slayings | *Diane VanderBeke Mager*

CONTRIBUTING AUTHORS
232 | Peter Banks
234 | Diane VanderBeke Mager
236 | P.L. Middlebrook
238 | A.J. Norris
240 | Tim Patrick
242 | D.M. Patton
244 | Theresa Shen
246 | Phil Skiff
248 | Anthony Stachurski
250 | Awards & Works Previously Published
251 | Also by
253 | Acknowledgements

SHORT FICTION

Sleeping Single—PART 1: Summer Frustration

Diane VanderBeke Mager

Shit, it's even louder upstairs.

Raucous laughter penetrates my bedroom windows, traveling west to east as if propelled by a megaphone. Put a few drinks into CeCe, and her cackling is enough to make me want to strangle her.

Why the hell do she and Bob feel compelled to throw outdoor dinner parties past 1 AM? It's not even the weekend! With temperatures in the nineties, there is no way I am closing the windows.

Desperate for a cross breeze, I leave my door open, strip off my nighty, and climb into bed. Sweat gathers beneath my breasts despite the ceiling fan whirring overhead. I roll onto my stomach, careful to arrange the sheet across my bare hips on the off chance that Dean, home from college for the summer, decides to go down to the kitchen in the middle of the night.

Always best to start the fantasy immediately. Otherwise, I get caught up in my to-do list; or worse yet, memories rush in and I'm awake all night. I close my eyes, settling in . . . my personal story of romance concocted to lull myself to sleep—

Clink . . . glasses connect as something hilarious sets CeCe off again. I swear she sounds like a manic goose during mating season.

Enough is enough. I don't care how friendly she is, or how honorable Bob's military service might be; someone has got to set them straight on how to be respectful neighbors. I jump up, grab my nighty, and stomp to the window, preparing my speech in my head. Pulling back the edge of the curtain, I hesitate.

Eight people are seated at the long table, candlelight reflected in empty wine bottles. I watch in fascination as a tangle of arms reaches with wild abandon, feasting upon the fruit and chocolate fondue placed at the center of the table. A striking redhead tosses back her hair.

Her partner pauses, leaning in to kiss her sweetened lips. Opposite, a gentleman wearing a fitted polo shirt nods to a pale blond. With his permission, she takes another decadent bite.

Bob raises his glass to make a toast—

Aaaa-achoo. CeCe's damn incense sticks always set me off.

A man with dark glasses and a sexy scruff looks up at the sound. Shit, I think he sees me. I drop the curtain and race back to bed, torn between utter embarrassment and a burning desire to meet him.

I force myself to close my eyes, restarting my earlier tale of romance in my head; but it no longer appeals. My thoughts wander. I imagine myself joining the party outside . . . escaping responsibility . . . relinquishing control. Senses heightened, a new bedtime story takes shape in my mind. . . .

Lacy checked her reflection in the mirror and waited for the valet to open her car door.

"Welcome. Please follow the lanterns to the rear garden. Enjoy your evening."

"Thanks, you too."

She faltered, her new heels seeking balance on the uneven path. Dulcet strings and lilting voices lured her around the corner of the imposing stone house. She approached the patio, but hesitated. A mahogany dining table gleamed beneath two massive silver candelabras. Four of the eight high-backed chairs were already filled, alternating men and women in adherence to social protocol. Lacy searched in vain for a familiar face.

A waiter appeared, dressed in classic black and white. "Good evening, madam. Please follow me." *He seated her in the position of honor to the right of the vacant host's chair, facing the gardens, a trio of arched glass doors at her back.* "Can I get you something to drink?"

"Water is fine, thank you."

"Stuart Cleeves, Texas oil," *said the tuxedoed gentleman to Lacy's right.* "And my wife, Eleanor," *he added, gesturing to the woman seated across the table, her green silk gown a perfect complement to her auburn hair.*

"Stunning necklace," drawled Eleanor, "it reminds me of an octopus tentacle . . . yum."

Lacy forced a smile. "A pleasure to meet you, I'm—"

"We are the von Eberts," said the man in the power position opposite the yet-to-arrive host. His impeccably tailored black suit and perfectly knotted matching tie punctuated his clipped German accent. "I am Erik, and this"—he aligned his salad fork into proper formation before glancing at the woman unconventionally seated to his immediate right—"is my wife, Evangeline."

Evangeline nodded her greeting, keeping her eyes lowered. Her hair and dress were as pale as her demeanor.

"Nice to meet you," Lacy replied. "My name is—oh!"

A stream of ice water flooded the sleeve of her sheer white blouse. Lacy pushed back her chair as the liquid trailed over the edge of the table, threatening the golden skirt billowing at her feet.

"My apologies, madam. Please let me assist you," said the waiter.

Stemming the tide with her napkin, she masked her annoyance. "That's okay, is there a powder room I could use?"

"Certainly, right this way."

She excused herself and followed the waiter; spine straight, her flowing skirt shimmered with each step. He led her through the glass door on the far right and into the main hall, directing her past an enormous dark wooden staircase, toward a small alcove.

Lacy locked the bathroom door, leaned back against it, and exhaled. What the hell had she gotten herself into? When she'd received the invitation in response to her donation check, she'd been intrigued by the possibility of meeting someone new. Now she found herself surrounded by a bunch of couples and wearing a soaking wet outfit to boot.

Checking the mirror, she ensured the damp fabrics weren't inappropriately clinging to her toned curves and then adjusted the weight of her choker. She'd chosen it because it reminded her of the fabulous jewel-box lighting fixtures at Lincoln Center. But invariably others saw octopi, causing her to shiver at the thought of tentacles wrapped around her throat, entangling and immobilizing her limbs.

She smoothed back her hair and freshened her muted lipstick before returning to the patio. All of the chairs were now filled, with the exception of her own. She took her place as the uniformed gentleman at the head of the table raised his glass.

"Welcome. I am Major Windemere, your host this evening. My wife, Cecelia, and I"—he motioned to the shapely woman in blue seated to Erik von Ebert's left—"are pleased to have the opportunity to thank you for your generous donations to the arts council. We are thrilled to be joined tonight by the von Eberts, the Cleeves, our newest member"—he gestured to a man with dark glasses and facial scruff and then turned to Lacy—"and our guest of honor; we especially look forward to welcoming you into our circle."

The man with the dark glasses and scruff eyed her up and down. Everyone drank.

Cecelia Windemere steered the conversation toward the arts for the rest of the meal, making one final toast at the end of the dessert course. "Thank you again for your contributions. Shall we adjourn to the library for coffee and this evening's entertainment?" she asked, placing her napkin on the table.

She led them through the glass door and down a dimly lit corridor, to a room lined with books. Incense burned, masking the musty odor. They took their seats on burgundy leather sofas and deep club chairs surrounding a wide, tufted ottoman.

Aaaa-achoo.

"Take the ottoman, my dear," said Cecelia.

Lacy rested on the edge and crossed her legs.

"Uncross your legs," said Erik von Ebert.

"Pardon me?"

"I said, uncross your legs."

"Maybe we should wait a few more minutes till it kicks in," drawled Eleanor.

"If I wanted your suggestions, I'd ask for them," snapped von Ebert.

"Eleanor's right," said Major Windemere. "No need to rush. I'm sure Ms.—"

"As lead benefactor, it's my night and my rules Windemere," said von Ebert. "Uncross your legs."

Lacy looked around the circle. Her eyes rested on Evangeline, again seated subserviently, within easy reach of her husband. Lacy did as she was told.

"Now, come stand in front of me."

Lacy rose to unsteady feet. "I really think I should be going"—her voice sounded slurred to her own ears—"I have an early morning—"

"Stand in front of me and hike up your skirt," commanded von Ebert.

"She looks just like a golden statue standing there, doesn't she?" asked Eleanor.

"Well, I do like to play with pretty dolls without names," murmured Evangeline to herself.

Lacy, made a move toward the door, but lost her balance and fell into the lap of Stuart Cleeves.

"Let's get you settled, little lady." He carried her back to the ottoman.

She felt a rush of hands unbuttoning her blouse, sliding her skirt down her hips, and rolling her on to her stomach. The whir of the ceiling fan created a breeze across her bare skin. Like the tentacles of an octopus, they wrapped her wrists, ankles, and throat. Lacy shivered.

"Yum," said Eleanor.

"I think you're going to like this," whispered the man with the dark glasses and scruff, gazing directly into her eyes.

Cecelia cackled loudly. . . .

The Filthy Few

Tim Patrick

Sonny sensed the tension in the hot, humid air that blanketed Detroit. It was a little over a month since Robert Kennedy had been assassinated . . . and Martin Luther King just two months earlier. Traffic on Kelly Road was sparse for a summer afternoon. Nearing the intersection at Moross, he heard the distinct roar of a muscle car accelerating hard. Sonny glanced in the rearview mirror and saw a black Corvette swing out to pass a slower vehicle.

The Vette sped toward him. Sonny eased off the gas as the road widened into a four-lane boulevard, separated by a narrow grass island. He knew from experience that GM frequently loaned out Corvettes to the local police to use as patrol cars.

A moment later, the rumble of exhaust split the air as the Vette blew past. The driver downshifted and slowed as they approached the traffic light at Elkhart. Sonny hung back for a closer look. The chrome exhaust side pipes and Tiger Paw red line tires were common on Vettes. The bright red racing stripe down the center of the hood and the 427 emblem on the hood scope were not. It was a '67, one of the fastest production cars built.

Sonny felt a surge of adrenaline at the thought of a race. He had never lost to a Vette. Another victory here would be sweet. To his relief, there were no discreet police emblems on the vehicle.

Muscle cars fell into two categories: the ones purchased off the showroom floor with the latest performance hardware; and sleepers—unadorned, low-end models with quiet exhausts and cheap hubcaps, but tucked out of site were high performance engines and suspensions. Then there was Sonny's 1963 tan Ford Falcon. It was dressed up with a hood scoop, mag wheels, traction bars, and exhaust headers that made it look and sound intimidating. But under the hood was a puny 170 cubic inch in-line six . . . not the large V-8 engine standard in most muscle cars.

To make up for the shortfall, Sonny had added every high-performance part he could find or fabricate to make the Falcon faster. The combination worked to his advantage on the street, where races seldom lasted for the full quarter mile. At the drag strip, things were different. He owned the bottom end of the track, but at the back half, engine size eventually won out.

Some said the Falcon under full acceleration sounded more like a sewing machine than a muscle car. Regardless, wherever Sonny went, the car drew a crowd. Right now, a crowd was the last thing Sonny wanted. He had gotten plenty of unwanted attention that morning when he'd reported to Fort Wayne for another pre-induction draft board physical. Now all he wanted to do was meld back into the hubbub of the day.

He eased to a stop alongside the Corvette as the driver revved up the engine. Sonny didn't respond. He just looked straight ahead. This portion of the road was lined with retail stores, three parochial high schools, and Eastland Mall. The East Detroit police beefed up patrols at the end of the school day to catch speeders, particularly drag racers. As the light turned green, the Corvette squealed its tires and sped away. Sonny followed slowly, trying to remain inconspicuous.

At Eastwood Drive, the light was red. Cars from Notre Dame High School poured out onto Kelly like rainwater from a downspout. The Vette was in the left lane, next to the Corvair in front of Sonny. The driver of the Vette revved his engine, popped the clutch—lurching forward a few feet, and stopped.

When the light turned green, the Vette waited for Sonny's Falcon to catch up. Side-by-side, they drove toward Eight Mile Road. At the intersection, Sonny didn't flip on his turn signal. Instead, he made a sudden sharp right turn and headed toward the loop around to go west on Eight Mile to the Chatham Supermarket on Gratiot. The move caught the Vette by surprise, causing it to miss the turn.

Cruising along, Sonny rested his elbow on the open windowsill and tried to relax. But his thoughts drifted back to the military draft board physical. Every male had to take one once they turned eighteen, and this morning was his fourth.

Instead of letting me leave as I had in the past, they made me wait at the last station, on a bench in main hallway. I sat there; the paperwork from my previous physicals weighed on my legs. A door opened to my right and a sergeant emerged followed by a line of recruits. He ordered them to line up with their backs against the opposite wall. The recruits looked as puzzled as I was. I felt the heat of their stares and began shuffling through my paperwork to avoid looking at them.

The sergeant went down the line shouting commands. Satisfied, he moved back to the head of the line and ordered them to start counting off in groups of four. And so it went down the line till the end.

Then he announced that the recruits would be shipping out to basic training that evening and were not allowed to leave Fort Wayne. They would have to call friends or relatives to come pick up their cars. All those who called out one were headed to the Army, the twos to the Navy, threes to the Marines, and fours to the Air Force.

As much as I wanted to be in the military and go to Vietnam, the realization that it might actually happen this very day wrenched my stomach into a knot. Terror and guilt struck simultaneously. The only sound I heard was the beating of my heart. No more going home after the physical and waiting for the induction notice to arrive, which in most cases meant a combat tour in Vietnam.

I sat staring at the wall that was now empty and wondered what would become of the Falcon. My only link to the past since Dave and Ed were killed on Christmas morning during a street race. I never heard the corporal coming. "You're free to leave," a voice boomed as a stack of papers fell onto the bench next to me. "Looks like you dodged the bullet again. But don't get too comfortable; we want you back here in six months."

All I remember about him are the yellow corporal strips on his uniform and the sound of his heels on the tile floor as he walked away.

Sonny slammed the shifter into third gear when the light at Shakespeare turned red. *Son-of-a-bitch corporal thinks I'm a draft dodger.* From behind, he heard the Vette heading his way. A moment later, the car slid to a stop next to him.

Sonny looked to his left, at the driver. Their eyes met. The guy behind the wheel smiled. He gunned his engine, raised a gloved right hand, and gave Sonny the thumbs down sign. Sonny turned and looked at the empty road ahead of them. The black driving gloves pissed him off. *Probably some punk from Grosse Pointe out for spin in daddy's car.*

Sonny toyed with the idea of racing the Vette. A moment later, the light turned green and the Vette took off leaving two long dark trails of rubber in its wake. Sonny had a reputation to uphold. If word got out that he'd backed down from a race, it wouldn't be good. He stomped down on the gas pedal and took off in pursuit.

The gap between the two cars closed quickly, and they wound up side by side at the next light. Sonny scanned the area for police cars and found none, but he knew that could change in an instant. The driver in the Vette kept revving his engine desiring a race.

Enough. . . . Sonny brought the engine rpm up to 2,000, held down the clutch pedal, and waited. The light changed. Sonny slid his left foot off the clutch and slammed the gas pedal to the floor. The Falcon leapt forward. The cheater slicks grabbed the concrete, leaving only two small piles of rubber behind and no billowing smoke.

Sonny checked the rearview mirror and shifted into second gear. Four car lengths behind, the Vette fishtailed, desperately seeking traction. He chuckled and checked the Falcon's tachometer as the needle raced toward 6,800 rpm. He was closing fast on Gratiot Avenue.

Sonny glanced at the mirror and saw the Corvette closing the gap. He sidestepped the clutch and threw the shifter into third gear, but it jammed. The engine rpm shot past the red line on the tach. Sonny heard a loud pop and pulled his foot of the gas pedal. The Vette streaked past him. Sonny checked the instrument gauges. The engine temp was rising fast. *Shit.* Leaving the transmission in neutral, Sonny coasted into the Chatham parking lot. He turned off the engine and went into the store.

■■■

Early the next morning, Sonny pulled the Falcon into the number two bay at Morang Standard, where he worked part-time as the morning manager. He popped open the hood and removed the radiator cap. The antifreeze was a milkish white color instead of green. "Oil," Sonny mumbled. He grabbed a wrench and the compression tester and started removing the spark plugs to figure out what had happened the previous day.

"Morning," said Doug Olsen, the station owner, startling Sonny from his thoughts.

"Oh, hi. I didn't hear you come in."

"Whatcha up to?" Doug asked, walking over and standing next to him.

"Trying to figure out what I did to the engine yesterday."

"Let me guess, you were racing again." Doug shook his head.

"Yep," Sonny said sheepishly.

"You win?"

"Nope. Shifter stuck in the gate between second and third and the engine over revved."

"That's not good," Doug said as they stood staring at the engine. "Have you figured out what happened?"

"I think I blew a head gasket," Sonny said with a sigh.

"How do you know that?" Doug asked as he reached under the hood and picked up the compression tester attached to the number four cylinder.

"To start, there's oil mixed in with the anti-freeze. I remembered what we did when I helped you with Kavan's Galaxie 500 a couple of months ago. So, I started by eliminating the possible problems and decided to test the compression levels. Things were going fine until I got to number three—where the compression dropped from the mid-ten to the low twos. Number four is the same. The others are fine."

"Hopefully, you didn't warp the cylinder head."

"God, I hope not," Sonny said, turning toward Doug. "How do I figure that out?"

"Pull the head and bench test it."

"What if it's warped?"

"Since you had it milled three hundredths of an inch, there's probably not going to be much left to work with. My guess is you'll have to replace it."

"Fuck, that's the last thing I need right now." Sonny leaned his head against the edge of the open hood, feeling his stomach muscles tighten. "I've spent the past two years sinking every dime of my salary from the station into the Falcon. The thought of starting over again is depressing."

"You should have thought about that before you decided to drag race." Doug reached into his pocket and pulled out a pack of Pall Malls. He removed one and handed the pack to Sonny, who did the same. Sonny took out his Zippo lighter, lit his cigarette, and offered the lighter to Doug.

"You're right."

"Look," Doug said as he started unscrewing the compression tester. "If you're going to race, things are going to break. And it's going to get expensive. You just have to plan accordingly."

"I know. It's just I give my mom half of my Chatham salary for household expenses. Another chunk goes to pay off the loan on the Falcon. That doesn't leave much extra."

"That's part of life and it's never going to change," Doug said, placing a hand on Sonny shoulders. "You just have to learn to prioritize. And as far as racing goes—that's fine, as long as it's at the drag strip and not on the street. Understood?"

"Yes, sir," Sonny said, looking down at the garage floor.

"I'll help you where I can—but under one condition."

"What's that?" Sonny replied raising his head.

"You have to promise me you'll stop drag racing on the street."

Sonny let out a long breath. "Shit. Do you realize what you're asking me to do? Cars and street racing are the only things I'm good at."

"You don't need street racing," Doug snapped. "You're a darn good mechanic, smart, and a quick learner. Why do you think I give you the complicated jobs?"

Sonny felt his face flush.

"What is it you want to do with your life?" Doug asked, dropping the butt of his cigarette to the floor and crushing it with his foot.

"To work at the GM Tech Center for Chevrolet engineering, but there's no way that's going to happen," Sonny replied.

"Why's that?"

"I'm horrible at math."

"Exactly how is street racing going to solve that problem?"

"It's not." Sonny looked Doug in the eyes. "To stop racing would ruin my reputation. I'd be labeled a chicken, sissy, you name it."

"You're right. It won't be easy, but you don't have to stop racing. Focus your energies on the track and build a reputation there." Doug paused a moment. "This is Detroit. Engineers from the Big Three are constantly hanging out at the track testing new ideas and equipment. You never know who you might meet or impress."

"I never thought of it that way. But that'd be expensive, and I don't have the money," Sonny said, kicking the front tire.

"I'll help you out when and where I can." Doug extended his hand toward Sonny. "Deal?"

"Um, yeah, sure, thanks!" Sonny wiped his hand on the shop towel before shaking.

"Good. But right now, we need to get Mrs. DiPonio's Tempest in here for a brake job and tune-up."

"Okay." Sonny closed the hood of the Falcon.

"Come on, I'll help you push the Falcon outside. For now, you can park it on the east side of the station," said Doug.

■■■

The station bells rang as a car pulled up to the pumps. Sonny set down the timing light and walked toward the pumps.

"I got it," Ken Miller said running out of the station office and past Sonny. A few minutes later, Ken walked back in and over to Sonny. "What's up man?"

"You're late, again." Sonny frowned as he switched on the Sun engine oscilloscope.

"Sorry."

"What's up with the sunglasses?"

"Fucking old man came home drunk last night and started beating on my mom. I stepped in to break it up and got this for interfering," Ken said, taking off the glasses.

"Holy crap," Sonny gasped as he stared at Ken's swollen and bloodshot eye. "Then what happened?"

"Blocked a left hook and caught him under the jaw with an upper cut. Knocked him out. Mom and the kids packed a few things and went to my aunt's."

"What'd you do?"

"Spent the night at Bone's on the basement sofa." Ken pulled a pack of Kool's from his pocket and lit one. "I can't take much more of this shit," he said, exhaling a stream of smoke. "If I can hang on long enough to graduate, I'm out of there."

"What about your mom and the kids?"

"Don't know, but right now I'd rather not talk about it." Ken reached into his shirt pocket and pulled out a small white card printed in bold green ink. "Here." He handed it to Sonny.

You have just been beaten by a member of
THE FILTHY FEW RACING TEAM

"Whatcha think?" Ken asked, unable to contain his excitement. "I figured we should have something to hand those preppies from Grosse Pointe and Birmingham when we beat them in a race."

"Where'd you come up with the name?"

"It was Bone's idea. Look at us, man." Ken held out his hands. "Grease, grime, cuts, bruises, and blisters."

Sonny looked down at his own hands. "He's got a point. No matter what I use or how often I wash them, I can never get rid of the dirt."

"Exactly. You ever notice how clean our customers' hands are?"

"I've never paid that much attention," Sonny replied.

"They're spotless and in some cases even manicured. You know how many times I've gone up to a pretty girl to ask for a date—then she sees my hands and it's an instant turn off."

Sonny thought back to all the times he was embarrassed by how his hands looked. "It's an occupational hazard."

"To a point," Ken snapped. "It's not just our jobs, they're that way because we work on our cars every spare moment we get. We don't walk into a dealership with a bundle of money dad gave us and buy a brand-new car all souped up from the factory. It's about time we stick it to them."

"What the hell got you all worked up over this?"

"Last Thursday, Bone and I were cruising down Woodward when a white Plymouth Road Runner thundered past us. I hit the accelerator to catch it and get a better look. As we got close, Bone noticed something painted on the trunk lid."

"What?"

"'You beat it, you eat it.' Painted next to it was a bright red cherry. We pulled alongside. The driver was a cute blonde with a hot brunette riding shotgun."

"No shit." Sonny whistled. "So, it's no myth."

"Nope, I'm here to tell you, it's a kick-ass four twenty-six Hemi."

"And you fell for it?" Sonny chuckled.

"Don't start."

"You knew it was a setup, right?"

"I figured it probably was, but what the hell." Ken smiled. "A four-oh-nine versus a four twenty-six Hemi, with the possibility of a sweet pay off. How could I pass that up?"

"What happened?"

"You mean aside from me losing twenty bucks and the race?"

"Yeah, aside from that."

"Had to be a factory car," Ken said with a shrug. "The thing raised up like a Super Stock and was gone before I shifted into third gear. It wasn't even close."

"We'll never have enough money or resources to compete with

factory boys." Sonny attached the timing light and oscilloscope to the Tempest engine.

"True, but it still pisses me off," Ken said, sticking the card in his shirt pocket. "We have the knowhow and skills to build fast cars. And I'm not the only one who is tired of this shit. On the way home, Bone said, 'Not much a filthy few can do against the factory.' Get it?"

"Can you do me a favor and start the Tempest?"

"Sure." Ken reached through the open car window and turned the key. "Look what you've been able to do with the Falcon."

"That era may have come to an end."

"Whatcha mean?" Ken asked as he leaned against the fender and watched Sonny adjust the distributor.

"I may have to trash the engine and start all over." Sonny set the timing light on the fender and grabbed a screwdriver and vacuum gauge off the workbench.

"Shit," Ken said, hitting the Tempest's fender with his fist. "What kind of car?"

"A four twenty-seven Vette."

"How'd you do?

"Had his ass off the line and through second—before the shifter hung up."

"On the bright side, here's your chance to get the V-8 you've always wanted."

"I guess so," said Sonny, pushing the carburetor linkage forward and increasing the engine rpm while he watched the scope.

"Looks fine," Ken said. "Going by the horizontal green line on the screen."

"Not really. Every now and then there's a slight intermittent blip."

Ken leaned forward and squinted at the screen. "You're right."

Sonny took a screwdriver and adjusted the carburetor idle mixture screws. "That's better," he said.

"Damn," Ken whistled, "you've got a knack for this stuff."

■■■

The first rays of the sun crept over the horizon as Sonny pulled his mom's car into Morang Standard after a long night's work at Chatham. Unlocking the station door, he headed to the back room and changed into his uniform—dark blue pants and light blue shirt, with the Standard Oil logo on the left breast pocket and his name embroidered on the right.

He grabbed a bag of Oil Dri and began spreading it on the floor to clean up the grease and other fluids left behind by the evening shift. As he reached for the shop broom, he heard the squeal of tires followed by the roar of an engine under full acceleration. He watched as Ken's aqua and cream 1962 Chevrolet Impala SS vaulted the sidewalk and slid to a stop on the gravel parking area at the west end of station.

Ken got out of the car, slammed the door shut, and kicked it several times before moving to the rear fender where he did the same thing. Before Sonny realized what was happening, Ken opened the trunk, pulled out the tire iron, and continued smashing the car.

Sonny dropped the broom and ran outside. "What the fuck are you doing?" he screamed, grabbing Ken from behind. He pulled him away from the car. "Stop it," Sonny yelled. He locked Ken in a bear hug. "What the hell is wrong with you?"

"That son-of-a-bitch, I'll kill him!" Ken shouted, fighting to break free.

"Who?" Sonny asked as he pulled him toward the station.

"My fucking crazy old man, that's who!"

"Damn it, Ken. Get a grip. I don't know what the hell your father did, but pounding the shit out of your car isn't going to fix anything."

"I don't give a damn. I can't take it anymore."

"What happened?" Sonny asked. He moved Ken away from the car and toward the station. "Let's go inside. I'll buy you a Coke and you can tell me about it."

"Yeah sure, just let me go."

"First give me the tire iron," Sonny said, releasing his grip and holding out his hand. Ken handed it over, turned, and walked into the building.

"I need a joint," Ken said. He slumped into the chair next to Doug's desk.

"Best I can do is this." Sonny handed Ken a Nesbitt Orange Soda.

Ken gulped down half the bottle and wiped his mouth with his shirtsleeve. "I spent the night at my aunt's house with my mom and the kids. In the morning, I got up and went back to the house to shower and get a clean uniform. Can I borrow a smoke?"

"Sure." Sonny pulled a pack out of his pocket and tapped the open end against the pop machine until one slid out part way.

Ken took it, pulled out a Zippo lighter, and tried to open it. "Son-of-a-bitch," he shouted when the lighter fell to the floor. "Damn, hands won't stop shaking."

Sonny reached down, picked up the lighter, and lit the cigarette.

"I was pulling into the driveway when I saw smoke coming from behind our garage. I got out of the car, grabbed the garden hose, and ran around back figuring the garage was on fire. Instead, I found a smoldering pile of stuff in the center of the alley. It was all my clothes."

"What the hell did he do that for?"

"Apparently, he found out I spent the night with mom and the kids—and he was pissed." Ken pulled a piece of balled up paper from his pocket. "This was taped to the side door."

Sonny took the crumpled paper and opened it.

> *I warned you to stay away from that bitch. But no, you sneaked over there figuring I'd never find out. I knew you couldn't be trusted. "Just you and me Dad." What a bunch of crap that was. And to think I believed you. I'll teach you to lie to me. What's left of your shit is in the alley. Take it and get the hell out of here. I don't ever want to see you again. Forget about trying to get inside. I had the locks changed. You can go live with that no-good bitch. If I catch you hanging around here, I'll give you a beating you'll never forget.*

Ken titled his head back and drained the soda bottle. "Guess I'll have to find a place to live." He scuffed the floor with his boots.

Sonny leaned against the pop machine, lit another cigarette, and wondered what type of relationship he would have had with his father, had he lived.

Ring, ring. The bell connected to air hoses at the driveway entrance sounded. Sonny looked up and watched as the station's yellow Scout International Harvester pulled up next to Ken's Impala. Doug was at the wheel. He exited the Scout and walked around the Impala before heading inside.

"Morning," Doug said, stopping in the doorway and looking at Ken slumped in the chair. "What happened to the Impala? Looks like someone beat it with a crowbar."

Ken, forgetting to don his sunglasses, looked up at Doug, then out to the Impala. He put his head into his hands. "What am I going to do for a car?" he choked out between sobs. "It's the only thing that's really mine."

The sharp crack of an open exhaust shattered the silence. A moment later, the driveway bells rang, and a black Corvette rolled to a stop next to the Premium gas pump.

"I'll get it," Ken said, grabbing his sunglasses. He walked past Doug and out the door.

"What in the world's going on?" Doug asked, nodding toward the parking area.

"It's better you hear it from him." Sonny shrugged.

"Dude wants you." Ken motioned over his shoulder with a jerk of his thumb as he walked back inside. Sonny crushed his cigarette in the ashtray and went outside.

"You own that Falcon?" the driver asked as Sonny approached.

"I might," Sonny said.

"Name's Conner." He extended his gloved hand.

Sonny ignored the outstretched hand. "What can I do for you?"

"That's a pretty quick two eighty-nine you've got." Conner nodded toward the Falcon. "Too bad you quit so soon, cuz I had your ass."

"Had nothing to do with quitting. I had an appointment to get to." Sonny balled his hands into fists.

"You got lucky."

"Luck had nothing to do with it." Sonny smiled.

"Sure. Regardless, Pitlock's calling you out."

"What the hell does Pitlock have to do with it?" Sonny asked, feeling his stomach muscles tighten. Gary Pitlock's father owned the Chevrolet dealership on Harper. He had a 1967 Red Nova SS that was, according to the rumor mill, the fastest car on the Eastside of Detroit.

Their paths had never crossed. Sonny often saw the Nova in the neighborhood, but never while he was driving the Falcon. It was difficult to miss the Nova, which sat two feet off the ground with mammoth racing slicks in the rear and much smaller tires in the front.

"You recall racing a sixty-six GTO last weekend on Gratiot around two thirty in the morning?"

"Yeah, there were three guys in the car. After I beat them, they wanted me to pull over so they could take a closer look at my car. I didn't."

"Pitlock was in the car." Conner closed the door and took a step toward Sonny.

"So?" Sonny stood his ground

"Same as the other day on Eight Mile, when you jumped the light." Conner removed his driving gloves. "People are getting tired of you and your friend showboating. It's time to put you in your place. We're calling you out for a race. Meet us at two thirty Sunday morning, on westbound I-94—under the bridge, by the Vernier entrance ramp. There's a mile and a half stretch of three-lane road ideal for street racing."

Sonny looked at the Falcon, then at the station, and finally back at Conner. "Gary's big bad Nova's worried about a puny six and a lead sled four-oh-nine?"

"Not at all." Conner stepped closer to Sonny. "In fact, we've got a hundred bucks a race that says you can't beat us. You versus Gary, and I'll take on your friend."

"I'd love to race Gary at Detroit Dragway, but not on the street." Sonny felt his face starting to flush.

"No way, this is about the street man." Conner looked toward the station.

Sonny followed suit and saw Doug heading in their direction. He turned back to Conner. "You need gas?"

"Yeah, top if off with premium, and make sure not to get any on the paint." Conner set his gloves on the roof of the Vette.

"Good morning," Doug said, stopping on the opposite side of the gas pump. "Something I can help you guys with?"

"No, everything's fine." Sonny removed the hose from the pump.

"Thought I'd check because the two of you have been out here a while."

"We were just swapping stories about cars and the young ladies who cruise Woodward," Conner replied.

"I'll bet there's some good ones." Doug smiled and nodded at Sonny. "We need to finish up the Tempest."

Sonny squeezed the handle on the pump as Doug walk away.

"Stop at five," Conner said, pulling a crisp bill from his wallet. "Did you say a six cylinder?"

"I did, that's what's in the Falcon." Sonny placed a shop rag under the pump nozzle to prevent gas from dripping onto the paint.

"Here you go," Conner said, handing Sonny the five-dollar bill.

Sonny reached for the bill, but paused and looked at Conner's hands. There wasn't a speck of dirt or a callus on them.

"No shit, a six." Conner laughed. "What—your grandparents give you the car?"

"The hell difference does it make where I got the car?" Sonny jerked the bill out of Conner's hand.

"You're frigging crazy. There's no way we're going to lose to a scrawny six. Do you have any idea who you're dealing with?"

"I do, his family owns the Chevy dealership on Harper."

"I'll talk to Gary, and we'll get back to you," Conner said as he pulled the gloves onto his hands.

Sonny watched Gary pull away and walked back into the station.

"What was that about?" Doug and Ken asked in unison.

"Pitlock and the boys want to race us on Sunday morning on I-94."

"What the hell we do to piss them off?" Ken blurted out.

"That was the Vette I raced on Eight Mile when I trashed the engine. And Pitlock was in the GTO I raced and beat last weekend on Gratiot. Apparently, they don't like losing." Sonny smiled.

"What'd you tell them?" Ken asked.

"I said yes, as long it was at Detroit Dragway next Saturday. Oh, and it's for a hundred dollars a piece."

"You're fucking crazy," Ken snapped. "First, we've got to fix the cars, which will cost money. And then on top of it, we've got to come up with an extra C-note?"

"Look, I created this mess. I'll go it alone."

"Like hell you will. There's no way I'm missing out on this. I'll figure something out."

"Have you made a decision on the engine?" Doug asked closing the hood of Mrs. DiPonio's Tempest.

"Nope, I really want to drop in a two eighty-nine V-8, but then it's just another muscle car. I like being different. In this case, I might not have a choice. Realistically, my best chance of beating him is with a two eighty-nine. Aside from that, there aren't many other options," Sonny replied as he opened the door and slid onto the driver's seat.

"Gives you something to think about while you test-drive the Tempest," Doug said.

"There is another option," Ken yelled. "Go big with a four twenty-seven," he added with a grin.

"Now who's crazy? I'll be back in a few." Sonny pulled the Tempest out of the garage bay and headed to I-94. As he turned onto the entrance ramp, Pitlock's Nova crested over the bridge heading in the direction of the station. *What the hell did I get myself into?*

He watched in the rearview mirror until the Nova disappeared at the bend in the road. Deep down inside, he knew Conner was right; it was a fluke. Even if he put a 289 into the Falcon, there was no way they could beat Gary and the resources of his father's dealership and GM connections.

■■■

"Thanks for helping me out," Ken said as Sonny merged into the light morning traffic on Hoover Road. "I hope the car is in as good a shape as they say."

"That'd be nice." Sonny wrestled the shifter into third gear.

"You don't seem too excited about getting the two eighty-nine," Ken said, taking a cigarette from his pocket. "Want one?"

"No thanks." Sonny crossed over Eight Mile and onto Groesbeck

Highway. "It's weird—like this thing." He tapped the dashboard of the Scout. "It's butt-ugly yellow, not fast, but fun to drive . . . and different—like the Falcon is with the six cylinder. That all goes away with the two eighty-nine."

"If anyone can make it standout it's you," Ken said, giving Sonny a playful punch on the arm.

"Thanks, I hope so," Sonny replied. He turned left into Highway Auto Parts.

Ken swung open the passenger door and bounded out as the truck rolled to a stop. Sonny shook his head, turned off the engine, and stepped onto the gravel drive. The blare of a truck horn startled him. He stepped back and watched the junkyard tow truck drive toward Groesbeck with a grimy, blue six-cylinder engine on the back deck. He followed Ken into the office.

"Car's like new," the guy behind the counter was already explaining to Ken. "Someone stole it. Stripped out the drivetrain and interior. The insurance company just scrapped it."

"No, shit," Ken said, turning toward Sonny. "You hear that?"

"Yep." Sonny approached the counter. "Are you Hank?"

"Sure am. You must be Sonny."

"Yes sir."

Doug told me you'd be coming with Ken here.

"He did?"

"Called me about twenty minutes ago." Hank extended his hand. "Pleasure. Said he forgot to tell you that if Ken takes the sixty-three Impala, you'll have to come back for the engine because of the Scout's payload capacity. Last thing he needs is the truck down for repairs."

"Bummer. Come on let's go see the car." Ken headed out into the yard.

"Oh well." Sonny shrugged and followed Ken and Hank out the door. They weaved their way through stacks of cars to a shiny black 1963 Impala Super Sport. Ken started examining the condition of the car as if he were choosing a diamond ring. Sonny stopped next to Hank. "It's like showroom new."

"Yep, not a flaw on it," Hank said.

"And all you want is two hundred dollars?"

"Not worth much without an interior and drivetrain," Hank said, turning to see where Ken was. Then he leaned in toward Sonny. "Doug explained what happened, so I cut the kid a break. But that's between the two of us, understood?" Hank squeezed Sonny by the arm.

"Thanks, that's nice of you."

Hank and Ken went back inside to take care of the paperwork and cash while Sonny pulled the Scout into the yard and up to the '63. Sonny grabbed the tow bar from the Scout's truck bed. He was kneeling on the ground by the Impala's front bumper when Ken returned.

"Do you believe this?"

"No, I don't. You lucked out," Sonny said, shaking his head. "Just remember to control your temper next time. Don't trash this car too."

"Come on, let's get this thing back to the station so I can start transferring everything from the sixty-two."

"Okay, but make sure the lug nuts are tightened down. The last thing we need is for a wheel to come off while we're towing it." Sonny handed the four-way lug wrench to Ken and went back to securing the tow bar to the Impala. It took longer than expected because he was constantly swatting away flies. "Ken, anything smell odd to you?"

"Yeah, like rotting food or something. It's starting to get to me." Ken set the wrench back in the Scout. "Take a look over there." Ken pointed to a Ford Fairlane a few feet from the Impala. "What the heck is all over the windows?"

"Beats me, but there are thousands of flies swarming around that car." Sonny walked forward but stopped. "Not sure what it is, but there's something thick and grayish red splattered on the windows. He leaned in. "There're two small holes in the back passenger window. Let's get out of here," he said, backing away from the car.

They got into the Scout and headed to the exit, but stopped as Hank came out of the office door.

"You boys all set?"

"Yes, sir."

"Appreciate the business. Let me know if there's anything else I can help you with."

"Thanks. I'll come back for the engine tomorrow." Sonny started letting out the clutch.

"Oh, right." Hank smiled.

"There is one other thing," Ken blurted out. "What's up with that black Ford Fairlane parked near the Impala?"

"Oh that," Hank said, removing his hat and wiping sweat from his brow. "Some guy got popped in the back parking lot of St. John's Hospital. Cops said it was a drug deal gone bad." Sonny fought back a sudden pang of nausea. He turned toward Ken, who looked pale.

"Dickie June," Ken said in a whisper. Sonny nodded in agreement.

"We better get going," Sonny said, turning his attention back to Hank. He let out the clutch and turned right onto Groesbeck.

They drove in silence for a while before Ken broke in, "I met him a couple of nights ago to get a lid of grass. Shit, I could have been with him when it happened. . . ."

"You need to shake that habit—before it kills you."

"Can't, it's the only thing that keeps me sane."

■■■

Sonny and Ken pushed the black Impala onto the gravel parking area alongside Ken's other car. Sonny walked into the station while Ken got started on the swap.

"I better head home and get some sleep. Tonight's our biggest stock night at Chatham. Fifty-eight hundred cases of product to stock in eight hours," Sonny said to Doug as he put the Scout keys on the hook by the write-up desk.

"Wow, but there's something I want to show you before you leave," Doug said, nodding in the direction of the station service bays. Sonny followed him. In the back, near the air compressor, a green canvas tarp lay atop of a large object on the floor. Doug stopped alongside of it. "I have a proposition for you."

He pulled back the tarp to reveal the grimy, blue engine that Sonny had seen on the back of the tow truck pulling out of Highway Auto Parts. "This is a 300 cubic inch six from a Ford F-150 pickup truck."

"Three hundred? I didn't know Ford made one that size."

"Doesn't surprise me. We seldom work on trucks, and your

generation is fixated on V-8s," Doug said with a chuckle. "What few people know about this engine is that it has the same bore as a two eighty-nine."

"Whew," Sonny said with a whistle, a flicker of excitement coursing through his body. "That opens up a world of opportunities."

"Exactly. So, here's the deal. The engine's on me." Doug turned and looked Sonny in the eyes. "Consider this your apprentice training project. The challenge, if you're interested, is to rebuild this engine so it produces four hundred horsepower."

Sonny rocked back on his heels, his mind racing through the possibilities.

Doug continued, "I'll split the cost of parts with you. You can work here on your off hours . . . when things are slow and in the evening when we're closed. And take the Scout whenever you need it."

"But the race with Pitlock is less than two weeks away," Sonny bemoaned

"It is. Which means you've got a lot of work to do. That is if . . ."

"If, what?" Sonny asked with apprehension.

"If you're up to the task. It's the type of project that separates the good mechanics from the backyard hacks."

"It's not much time," Sonny said, feeling a cool trickle of sweat roll down his chest.

"I guess it depends on how bad you want this. Professional race teams turn cars around in a day. You have thirteen." Doug let the tarp fall to the floor. "It's in your hands."

Sonny stared at the engine as Doug walked away. His mind drifted back to the image of the V-8 at Highway Auto Parts. The engine he thought he'd always wanted was within his grasp. All that was separating them was $150, but that would only be the beginning. He'd need to buy or fabricate parts to install the engine and get it running, plus an entirely new exhaust system. And that didn't include the performance parts he'd need to stand any chance of beating Pitlock.

Sonny set the tarp back on the engine and walked outside to the Falcon. He opened the hood and leaned against the wall. The Falcon was unique. Officials at the dragstrip had a difficult time figuring out what category it should race in.

Staring at the engine, a thought flashed in his mind. Sonny ran into the station and grabbed a tape measure from the toolbox. Back outside, he leaned over the Falcon's fender and measured the width of the exhaust ports and bolt pattern. He wrote down the information and repeated the process on the truck motor. They were the same.

Sonny grabbed the 1964 Motor manual from the shelf and flipped through the pages until he found the engine spec sheet for Ford F-150 pickups. He pulled the 1965 manual, opened it, and began comparing the specs for the two engines.

"Whatcha doing?" Ken asked, sliding to a stop by Sonny.

"Man, you're never going to believe this."

"Believe what?"

"I think I've just found my new engine. I'm ditching the two eighty-nine and going with this. Doug found it at Highway Auto Parts." Sonny pulled the tarp off the engine.

"You can't be serious. There's no way you're going to beat Pitlock with that engine." Ken shook his head.

"Don't be so sure about that. This is a 300 cubic inch six with the same bore as a two eighty-nine. And . . . the exhaust headers from the current engine will fit!"

"No shit, but there's still a matter of horsepower. Pitlock is probably around four hundred."

"True. Doug's challenged me to rebuild it to produce four hundred-plus horsepower. And if I do, the engine's on him." Sonny nudged Ken with an elbow. "And—I have a plan."

"You damn well better have."

"I'll tell you more later. How's the car parts swap going?"

"Not so great. We've been swamped with customers. I haven't had time to do much of anything. Lucky you're off the clock."

"Right. And I get to find out how many days I can go without sleep. Remember, I have to work at Chatham again tonight."

"See you later," Ken said. The station bells signaled another customer.

■■■

"Sonny, your friend's here."

"Okay mom, I'll be right there," Sonny replied, rubbing the sleep from his eyes. The nightstand clock read 9:07 p.m. He had to be at work by 10:00 p.m.

He washed his hands and face at the sink, pulled on a shirt and pants, and bounded down the stairs two at a time. Ken and his mother were sitting at the kitchen table. Sonny kissed his mother on the cheek.

"Hey man." Ken extended his hand as he stood.

Sonny pushed the hand aside and hugged Ken instead.

"Welcome. Let's go down to the basement, and I'll give you a quick tour of your new digs." Sonny pushed past Ken and down the stairs. "This is the bedroom. I picked out some clothes that should fit until you can get some new ones. Over here's the bathroom. Over here's the fruit cellar and the fridge in case you get hungry."

"Help yourself to whatever you want," Sonny's mom said, entering the basement.

"Thanks for letting me stay here for a couple of days while I figure things out, Mrs. Vaughn."

"Glad we could help."

"Gotta go," Sonny said, giving his mom a quick hug. He turned to Ken. "And I'll see you in the morning."

"On time," Ken said.

"I hope so. My mom is going to drop you off."

"I think I'm going to like this arrangement," said Ken.

Sonny smiled.

■■■

Thursday morning, Sonny punched out on the time clock at Chatham and walked to the Scout. He slid behind the wheel, picked up the notebook, and traced his fingers down the Falcon to-do-list for Saturday's grudge race. Doubt was starting to creep in. He laid his head on the steering wheel, closed his eyes, and took a deep breath. Exhaling slowly, he started the truck. There was no margin for error.

When Sonny arrived at the station, the first order of business after unlocking the pumps was to push the Falcon out of the garage bay and park it alongside the building. By the time Ken strolled in, Sonny was flipping through the Gratiot Auto Supply catalogue.

"Trailers for sale or rent, rooms to let, fifty cents . . . I'm a man of means by no means, King of the Road," Ken sang as he walked over to the pop machine, slid two dimes in the slot, and pulled out a Nesbitt Orange and a Coke. "Top of the morning to you," he said, handing a Coke to Sonny.

"Take it you slept well."

"Yep, thanks to you," Ken said tapping the lip of the bottle to Sonny's.

"Good. I'm starving. Want anything from the greasy spoon?" Sonny asked as he pushed away from the desk.

"Nope, your mom made scrambled eggs and bacon for breakfast."

"Guess I'll have to make due with a couple of greasy cheeseburgers and a chocolate shake." Sonny snatched the keys for the Scout. "After that, I'm heading to pick up the block and the rest of the parts for the Falcon."

"When are you going to start assembling and installing the engine?" Ken asked.

"Tonight, starting around eight."

"What about Chatham?"

"I'm taking a sick day."

Doubt and fear began creeping into Sonny's mind. The delicate work of assembling the engine would take all night—if everything went right. Then there was Doug's brilliant idea of equipping the car with dual-quads, which meant he'd have to weld together the intake manifold. He'd spent the past ten days working a few hours each afternoon at Cheetah Racing, in exchange for Bud Wyllie teaching him how to weld, along with a few engine airflow tricks.

■■■

Sonny rolled up to the station at 9:35 p.m., an hour and a half behind schedule. Except for the office clock and a small desk lamp, the station was dark. He unlocked the door and fumbled for the light switch.

He opened the overhead doors and began unloading the parts, spreading them out on the workbench like a five hundred-piece puzzle on a dining room table. Unlike a puzzle, he knew where everything went. But the sequence and tolerances in how the pieces fit together would determine the outcome of the project.

One mistake could spell disaster. And he wouldn't have that answer until the engine was in the car and running. He stifled a yawn, crushed out his cigarette, turned the radio dial to CKLW-AM, and began installing the rings on the pistons.

∎∎∎

Doug lay in bed staring at the ceiling and listening as a gentle breeze rustled the leaves on the pear tree outside the window. Mildred, his wife, slept beside him. He couldn't stop thinking about Sonny and Kenny and wondering if he had made the right decision when he encouraged them to accept Pitlock's challenge. The odds were long, but not impossible.

The two kids had talent, but lacked direction. Ken was too unpredictable with a quick temper. Sonny was different. Doug marveled at how quickly he learned complicated tasks. He was constantly asking questions. However, as much as they were outwardly confident, Doug knew that inside they lacked self-confidence and self-esteem. He could see the doubt in their eyes and in the expression on their faces when he talked to them.

In many respects, they were a lot like he was at their age, which is probably why he liked them. Growing up, his father had been absent from his life, immersed in his work and whiskey. Doug had planned to do better. To be the father he never had.

But after the third miscarriage, he and Mildred had given up all hope of having a family. She'd immersed herself in teaching elementary school—where her students became her surrogate children—while he'd focused on Morang Standard, especially after Jack, his business partner, had died suddenly from a heart attack.

Desperate for help, Doug had started hiring neighborhood kids to pump gas and do odd jobs so he could concentrate on car repairs—the heart of the business and income. Most, like Sonny, Kenny, and Bone, were decent, hardworking kids who were fun to have around.

Mildred rolled to her side, facing the open window. Doug watched her chest slowly rise and fall with each breath.

He checked his watch; it was 2:30 in the morning. Easing himself out of bed, he walked into the kitchen, lit a cigarette, and continued out to the picnic table in the backyard.

The screen door squeaked on its hinges, and he saw Mildred coming toward him. The porch light streamed through her sheer nightgown, framing her slender figure. She approached him and put her hands on his shoulders. "Something bothering you?"

"I keep thinking about Sonny and Kenny. They're running out of time. . . . I feel responsible for them," he said, exhaling a stream of smoke.

"If you're that worried, why don't you help them?" she asked, massaging the tension from his shoulders.

"Believe me I want to, but this is something they need to do on their own. Besides, I don't want them to think I'm spying on them . . . or don't trust them."

"Whether you realize it or not, those young men look up to you. You're their role model. Sonny's father is dead, Bone's deserted his family, and Kenny is better off without his."

"The other day, Sonny asked me to get a notebook from his glove compartment. On top was a photo of his mother holding his baby brother, Bobby. His dad—standing with his arm draped around Sonny, who had a big smile on his face. Sonny was all of maybe eight years old. It's probably the last family photo taken before his father died. Sonny, the Falcon, and that photo are inseparable."

"That's a tough age to lose a parent."

Doug sat quietly for a while, then turned, drew Mildred close to him, and embraced her. "Thanks. I think I'll drive over there. Not sure when I'll be back."

■■■

Sonny saw headlights from a car sweep across the front of the station. "We've got company," he shouted over the music.

"Shit, I hope it's not the cops," Ken said, turning around to look.

"It's Doug." Sonny walked over to the door and unlocked it.

"Thought I'd swing by and see how you were doing. Have any problems?"

"Some, but nothing a few minutes reading the Motor Manual

couldn't solve," replied Sonny.

"It looks good," Doug remarked with a smile as he checked over the engine. "Have you started fabricating the intake manifold?"

"Nope, figured getting the engine assembled and installed was the most important part. The flanges have been fitted and welded, so all that's left are the runners and plates."

"Sounds like a good plan," Doug said, resting his hand on Sonny's shoulder.

"Thanks." Sonny smiled.

"How's the install going? Doug asked, turning toward Ken.

"The interior's in and we're getting ready to install the engine and transmission on both cars," said Ken. "Figure we'd do that together."

"Guess, I came at the right time then," Doug said, grabbing a clean towel from the bench. "Always nice to have a third set of hands for a project like that."

Sonny and Ken looked at each other, shrugged, and smiled. "That'd be great," they replied in unison.

■■■

Early the next morning, Ken started the Impala and pulled out of the station for a test drive. Sonny heard the car go down the road sounding smooth as ever. He donned the welder's mask and went back to assembling the intake manifold. The work was exacting. Luckily, Bud had helped him measure, cut, and number each section of tubing before carting it out of Cheetah Engineering. All Sonny had to do was put it together so the carburetors sat level and the flange was flush against the block.

Ken returned as Sonny finished the last weld. "Here," he said handing Sonny a bag. "Two doubles with cheese, sautéed onions, mustard, ketchup, and pickles, along with a chocolate shake, right?"

"You're a savior." Sonny grabbed the bag and unwrapped the burger. "How's it running?"

"Great! Now we can focus on the Falcon."

"We've done as much as we can for now. Let's get this place cleaned up."

"Think Doug will be on time?"

"I'm sure of it." Sonny replied, tossing the wrapper from a burger into the trash can.

"I don't know. He stayed here pretty late."

"Yeah, thank goodness he did. Not sure we'd be this far along without him."

"You think he'll come to the track on Saturday?"

"I don't know. It's his night to close."

Ken paused. "Be great to have him there. . . ."

■■■

On Saturday afternoon, Sonny drove a rented Ford pickup truck and car trailer onto the side street next to the station. He walked inside where Bone was beating out a riff on a display tire with his drumsticks.

"Going to kick some ass today?" Bone asked.

"Yeah, Bone, something's going to get kicked today."

"Come on man, ya gotta be more upbeat."

"I will be, but right now I've got to get the car loaded and head out."

Doug was already waiting beside the Falcon. "Where's the truck and trailer?"

"On the side street," Sonny replied sheepishly. "I haven't been able to figure how to back the thing up straight."

"Fair enough," Doug chuckled.

Sonny got into the Falcon. His hand shook as he inserted the key in the ignition. The engine burst to life, the open exhaust shattering the quiet air. A chill swept over him—causing goosebumps. He sat for a moment, feeling the car rock side-to-side to the rhythmic beat of the idling engine. *The Falcon no longer had to pretend to be fast. It was. . . . But exactly how fast?*

Doug guided Sonny onto the trailer and helped secure the Falcon. Ken and Bone joined them.

"Damn, this is nerve wracking. I feel like I'm plugged into an electrical outlet," Sonny said, shaking his arms by his side.

"You'll be fine once the action starts. Right now, it's the pre-event jitters. I went through the same thing prior to every dustup during the war. Now, let's go race."

Doug climbed into the passenger seat of the Ford F-150. Sonny turned onto Morang, followed by Ken and Bone in the Impala. Fresh air poured in through the open windows as they merged onto westbound I-94.

"Well, you did it," Doug said, breaking the silence.

"Yeah, we did, in large part thanks to you."

"Not really. I helped, but you did all the heavy lifting." Doug reached into his pocket for a cigarette. "Why is this race so important?"

"I guess the last draft board physical really shook me up. If I'd passed, I would have had to ship out. I'd have lost the Falcon and suffered another setback. I can't shake the look of fear in those recruits' eyes when they learned they'd been drafted. I often find myself wondering how many of them will die in Nam."

"I understand. I lost a lot of friends during the war. It changed me forever," Doug admitted.

"Most of my friends are either dead, or in the military. My dad, grandfather, and uncle are dead. You, Ken, Bone, and a couple of guys at Chatham are all I have left."

The sound of the air surging into the cabin from the open windows drowned out their silence.

"You have any long-term plans?"

"I can't plan anything. Not as long as I have to keep going back every six months to the draft board for another physical. For now, I'm going to focus on the Falcon. It's the one thing I can control—or at least it seems like it." Sonny chuckled. "But I guess that all depends on what happens tonight."

∎∎∎

Sonny pulled off Sibley road and into the lane for pit row at Detroit Dragway. They paid the entrance fee and waited in line for their class designation and number before moving on to the safety inspection. Afterward, Sonny drove along pit row and pulled into a spot near the staging area. Ken parked alongside, and they unloaded the Falcon.

"We need to run as many time trials as possible so we can get the cars dialed into track conditions," Sonny said to the others.

"Remember to check the rear tire pressure. I'm thinking fifteen to eighteen psi should hook us up to track pretty good." Ken tilted his head skyward and inhaled. "Ah, the sweet smell of hundred and ten octane racing fuel."

Leaving Doug and Bone at the pits, Sonny and Ken drove toward the staging area. Sonny saw Pitlock's Nova pull into the left lane across from him a couple of cars up. He had a hard time keeping his foot on the clutch because his legs were trembling so badly. He took a couple of deep breaths and exhaled. Wiping his hands on his jeans, he turned off the engine to keep it cool. The smell of burnt rubber from the starting line filled the air.

The two lines of cars inched forward, little by little, until Pitlock was at the head of the line. Sonny got out of his car and watched as Pitlock did a burnout to warm up his rear tires for better traction. A thick dense cloud of smoke billowed out from under the Nova's rear fenders, temporarily obscuring it from view.

The track official motioned Pitlock forward toward the pre-stage area. The first and second row of orange lights illuminated. Once the GTO in the opposite lane staged, the official scurried backward away from the cars. He activated the Drag Strip Christmas tree with its series of lights for each car. In quick succession, three yellow lights flickered down to green. Sonny watched the front wheels of Pitlock's Nova come up off the ground as the car launched from the starting line. The sweet sound of racing engines at peak performance filled the air.

About twenty feet later, the Nova's front wheels settled onto the asphalt and the car faded from view. The next thing Sonny saw was the Nova's brake lights followed a short time later by the GTO's. Sonny watched the scoreboard at the end of the racetrack. The lights flashed off then back on. The time on Pitlock's side read 12:27 seconds at 98 mph. A wave of despair swept over Sonny. The best he had managed with the old engine was 14.00 seconds at 78 mph.

Sonny followed the starter's hand signals when it was his turn. He stopped with his rear tires in the pool of water in the burnout area. In the left lane was a '65 Chevrolet Impala, its rear side windows plastered with performance parts brand stickers. The two rows of pre-stage lights flashed on. Sonny revved his engine to 2,500 rpm and popped the clutch. The Falcon hesitated for a moment as the rear tires spun for a couple of seconds before the car sprang forward, tires squealing. Sonny checked the rearview mirror. There was a little smoke, but nothing like Pitlock's.

He turned back just in time to see the first yellow light flash on. At the third yellow, Sonny floored the accelerator pedal. The G-forces temporarily pinned him back in the seat. He hung on to the steering wheel and watched the tachometer rocket toward 6,500 rpm. Sonny threw the shifter into second gear and glanced to his left, but he didn't see the Chevy. *Don't think about it; just push the shifter through the gate.*

When the tachometer hit 6,600 rpm, Sonny pushed up and to the right with all his might. The shifter moved about an inch but stopped with a jolt halfway to third. *Damn it, son-of-a-bitch, not again.* Instantly, he lifted his foot off the gas pedal, pulled the gearshift into fourth gear, and watched the Chevy fly past him.

Sonny stopped at the time slip booth and grabbed his from the attendant's outstretched hand. He pulled off to the side of the return road and read it. 13.92 seconds; 84 mph. It was an improvement, but still not good enough to beat Pitlock. He flipped it onto the seat and drove back to the pits where Bone and Doug were waiting for them.

Ken pulled up, jumped out of his car, and ran to Sonny. "Fourteen point two seconds at ninety-eight miles per hour," he said, waving his time slip in the air.

Sonny smiled. "That's good, but I'm not sure it's going to be enough"

"We'll see," Ken replied. "How'd you do?"

Sonny handed him the time slip. "Damn, you beat me." Ken hissed.

"True, but Pitlock's still one and a half seconds faster. But there's a bigger problem."

"What?"

"Damn shifter hung in the gate again," Sonny said with a frown.

"Again? Shit that's not good. Whuddaya think is wrong?"

"Damn if I know . . ." Sonny spotted Pitlock and Conner heading in their direction. "Here comes trouble," Sonny added with a nod in the direction of their archrivals.

Ken turned. "This ought to be fun."

"We'll if it ain't the Filthy Few," Pitlock sneered. "Thought we'd come over and take a look at the Falcon with the mighty six."

"Nice run. Twelve point two seven is fast," Sonny said.

"It's better than nice," Pitlock scoffed. "We're already planning on how we're going to spend your money."

"Cocky aren't we?" Ken said, taking a step toward Pitlock. Bone grabbed him by the arm, holding him back.

"Nah, not at all. We watched your runs. Ken's was good. But you should switch to an automatic because your power shifting sucks."

"That so?" Sonny replied, fighting back his anger. "Time will tell, won't it?"

"Sure will. But I have to give you your due. The car ran better than I thought it would. Mind if we take a look?" Pitlock asked, walking toward the Falcon."

Sonny looked in Doug's direction; Doug nodded his head.

"Not at all," Sonny responded. He walked over to the Falcon and pulled the two pins from the hood lock. Ken did the same on the passenger's side. They lifted the fiberglass hood and set it on the roof of the car. "What you think?" Sonny asked.

Sonny, Ken, Bone, and Doug watched as Pitlock and Conner looked at the engine and then at each other. Their smiles faded.

"Dual quads on a six?" Pitlock sputtered. "You gotta be shitting."

"Nope. What you see is what you get," Sonny replied.

"You need some serious engine parts to support that much fuel and air," Pitlock said.

"That's what they say. . . . And for all you know Gary, we were just sandbagging," Sonny said, suppressing a smile.

"Guess we'll find out, won't we?" Pitlock replied.

Sonny watched as Pitlock and Conner turned and walked away.

"Why did you tip your hand?" Ken asked.

"They're just a little too cocky. I figured it's time we messed with their heads. It's a trick I learned racing the Falcon on the streets."

"What's that?"

"People judge most things based on what they see. If you can create some doubt, it can throw your opponent off balance. Just like when

Mickey Lolich throws a curveball instead of a fastball—it might look the same, but it's not." Sonny winked.

"Forget about the Tigers, we need to fix the shifter. Bone, can you get the toolbox?" Doug said, shaking his head.

Sonny drove the Falcon halfway up the trailer ramps so they had room to work under the car on the transmission and shifter linkage. Ken got into the driver's seat while Doug and Sonny crawled under the Falcon with the toolbox.

"Ken, shift it slowly from second to third a couple of times. Did you bring a can of grease with you?" Doug asked.

"As a matter of fact, I brought the small grease gun."

"Smart. Pull the cotter pins out of the linkage and grease the rod along with the linkage. Then the clutch swing arm. Make sure you see the grease oozing out of the fittings on both ends. The frame and engine block."

"Got it." Sonny backed out from under the car.

"Wait. Where is the contact point on the clutch?" Doug asked.

"At the top of the throw, so all I have to do is sidestep it when I'm shifting," Sonny replied.

"I'm going to move it down closer to the floor. You can still sidestep it, but it will give you more control. And with your leg extended—better leverage." Doug rolled out from under the car. "Done. Let's get this thing off the trailer and back on the track."

Sonny slid into the driver's seat and headed for the staging area. In the burnout area, he revved the engine and popped the clutch. The rear wheels spun for a few seconds before the tires grabbed and the car lurched forward. Sonny smiled. Hole shots were his trademark. *Or as Pitlock and Conner would say, "You got lucky."* He smiled.

Next to him was a 426 Hemi-powered Dodge Charger. It was so loud, Sonny had to check to make sure his engine was running. *Remember to bring earplugs the next time.*

The Christmas tree went live, and Sonny launched first. He hit second gear with ease and kept his foot on the clutch pedal. Doubt started creeping in as he watched the tach climb to the next shift point. At 6,800 rpm, he pushed the shifter through the gate but not as fast as he normally would. He felt the car go into third gear. *Phew.* The Dodge had gained a few feet and was now near the back of his front door. He hit fourth gear and watched as the Falcon approached the end of the quarter mile. He crossed over the line neck and neck with the Charger.

Sonny grabbed his time slip as he headed back to the pits.

"What's it say?" Bone asked, drumsticks in hand.

"Don't know." Sonny handed the paper to Doug.

Doug smiled and handed the slip to Ken, who stared at it and let out a long whistle.

"So what's it say?" Sonny asked, annoyed with himself for not looking.

"How's twelve flat sound?" Ken crooned.

"No shit . . . twelve point oh?"

"Looks like we have us a race. You up to the task?" Doug asked.

Sonny looked at Doug and then down at the ground. "I think so."

"Look at me son," Doug said in a stern voice. Sonny raised his head. "You've got what it takes to win. If you go out there looking for excuses, you'll find 'em. You can beat Pitlock if you want." Doug paused. "It's in your hands. We believe in you. Do you believe in yourself?"

The loud speakers crackled to life, "Attention racers . . . cars sixty-three, sixty-four, one nineteen, and one twenty . . . please report to the staging area."

"It's show time," Ken said and gripped Sonny by the sleeve.

Sonny resisted. Taking a deep breath, he looked at Doug. "See you after the race." He grabbed his helmet off the hood and got behind the wheel.

The track official staged Ken and Conner first. Sonny and Pitlock would go second. Sonny flashed Ken a thumbs up sign and watched the two cars line up. A few seconds later, the cars took off . . . the edge going to Ken. There was no time to see the outcome as the official signaled Pitlock and Sonny into the staging area.

This is it. Sonny looked over the gauges to make sure everything was in order. Both rows of pre-stage lights snapped on. An instant later, the lights walked down the ladder in quick succession. At the last yellow light, Sonny popped the clutch and hit the gas. His head jerked backward as the car accelerated off the line ahead of Pitlock by half a fender.

Sonny shifted into second and picked up a couple extra feet, which Pitlock regained when he shifted. The tach needle soared toward the next shift point. *How bad do you want this?* He sidestepped the clutch and threw the shifter across the gate and into third with every ounce of strength he had. The transmission slid into third.

Sonny exhaled and glanced out the side window. Pitlock's front bumper was just off the rear of the Falcon's front door. There were another couple of hundred feet to go before the finish line. The Nova edged forward, slowly closing the gap. Sonny pushed hard on the gas pedal willing the Falcon to go faster. There was little more than a fender's length separating the two cars as they crossed the finish line—the Falcon in the lead.

The cars drove in unison back to the pit area. Sonny turned off the engine and sat in the car, his body shaking from the flood of adrenaline. He unfolded the timing slip and stared in disbelief. ***11:14 seconds; 109 mph.***

Ken yanked open the door and pulled Sonny out of the car. "You did it, son-of-a-bitch, you did it," he yelled as he wrapped his arms around Sonny.

Doug leaned up against Ken's car and watched.

Sonny broke away from Ken as Pitlock approached.

"Gotta hand it to you, that's one fast car . . . but that's only one race. Trust me, this thing is far from over," Pitlock said as he handed Sonny two crisp hundred dollar bills. "I wouldn't rush out and spend it if I were you."

Sonny smiled as he reached for the bills. Gary Pitlock's hand was dirty, just like his.

All This Brother Wants—Chapter 1

P.L. Middlebrook

My name is Darnell, last name Wilson. I'm sitting here in this courtroom in a cold sweat and all this brother wants is to be a father to my little boy. I love him, and he loves me.

I can't believe I've been in litigation over my own child ever since he was born, and now he's just about four years old. What is wrong with this picture? Greedy lawyers, a prejudiced judge. Why is it so hard for a brother to catch a break?

Sweat is pouring down my armpits. My shirt is wet. My head is sweating too, and I can feel little rivers of sweat dripping down my neck and the side of my face.

I've been sitting in this courtroom seat with a serious butt ache waiting my turn, but the next case up is a Chi Town gang banger. I just watch and listen to this drama go down. My ears perk up when I hear the judge giving this dude some slack. It sounds like dude's baby mama has been slappin' his little girl around and not allowing him to see his daughter. She's eight. I can't help but notice none of these Negroes have lawyers. The grandma is called to the bench, along with the baby mama and young blood gang banger.

Based on what I'm hearing, here's the deal. Grandma and gang banger dude get their little girl every weekend. Dude lives with his mom. Judge Bullshit tells them to deliver and pick up the child at the police station. When Dude's baby mama hears this, she starts hollering about how Dude ain't right and the grandma is lying. Of course, Judge Bull Shidety Shit announces she needs to shut her mouth, or she would be handcuffed and held in contempt. She literally stomps out of the courtroom kicking the courtroom door open. At this point, I'm in shock. Those daytime courtroom TV shows couldn't televise this kind of crazy.

All the while, Judge Bullshit doesn't even look my direction and I am sitting up front. My mom is out in the hall. You have to be formally part of a case to sit in the courtroom. Mom told me later she saw and heard the whole drama go down. They had some kind of Friend of the Court official or appointed lawyer try and talk some sense into Dude's baby mamma's head. Then Dude and the grandma join baby mama crazy girl in the hall and you better believe there was some verbal ruckus going on. Bottom line, crazy girl would have to comply or risk losing her child altogether. Mom said she was all hollering and claiming she could not get off work in time to comply like that every week. After all, she has other kids too.

A few minutes later, crazy girl comes back into the courtroom with the biggest attitude I could never get away with. Bottom line, I think she will comply. I'm sitting here thinking the judge has got to know Dude with all the tattoos and saggy pants has got to at least have some weed around his mama's house. I get the distinct impression Dude does not have to take a million drug tests.

I've had so many drug tests I've lost count, six, seven, eight. My boy isn't even four years old yet. OK. That first test, I flunked. I was young and stupid. I had no lawyer. The judge and the guardian ad litem demanded I take a drug test same day, that day. I figured I had no choice. The guardian ad litem is my boy's lawyer, by no choice of mine. Over my objections that I couldn't pay, the judge appointed her anyway.

Well, I had forgotten about a joint I had smoked. I'm no pothead. I smoked a little weed before that first test, but all the rest of the tests, I was cleaner than clean. The most I ever did was smoke a little weed here and there, and ever since that one test, I don't do that shit no more. Between rent, food, my iPhone, Wi-Fi, cable, ad infinitum, I wish I could spend some money on weed. It ain't that serious. Even my friends know I'm caught up and nobody smokes around me anymore. Damn. They have marijuana stores for sick folks and fake sick folks. What's the big deal? Especially since all my other tests have been clean. I don't get it. Duh!!! My baby mama has lawyers.

My baby mama, let me give her a name. We will just call her Eva as in Eva Langoria, Eva Mendes. Please, she is nowhere near gorgeous Hollywood as them. If I was honest with myself, I did think she was hot when we first met or we'd never gotten together in the first place. I guess you could say she's Latina. She speaks Spanish and her mother is Hispanic. Whatever.

As it turns out, her mother is loaded, lots of money. Her mother hired a high-profile law firm, the ones that represented a big-time NBA player who wanted a divorce. He took his children from his wife and kept it moving. The spin was something was off about his ex-wife, but I'm not so sure about that.

Damn, Little Eva and I aren't even married. I did the honorable thing and offered my hand in marriage when we hashed out the pregnancy. Little Eva wanted the baby, but she sure as hell did not want me. I had a nice ring to give her and everything. After all this crap, I thank God that we didn't marry.

I have to pay a supervisor just about every time I see my child and it is very expensive. Little Eva doesn't care because her mother pays for everything. It's all about putting obstacles in my way, but so far, I've been like that big blowup clown. You punch him, stomp him, he falls, and he comes right back up. The harder you knock the crap out of him, the faster he comes right back.

I'm hopeful today though. This is supposed to be the "Final Judgment." Hope rings eternal. I've had to represent myself in a lot of this litigation because money is so tight. I guess I'm luckier than most because my brother is a lawyer in Michigan and he has helped us a lot, but he's married with three kids and his time and money can only go so far.

I love my family. We pooled our resources and found Jessica Larson. She has been the best lawyer we have had. We had what we thought were going to be good lawyers with a TV Fathers' Rights law firm. All they did was take our money and never filed one motion. Their bills were outrageous and I was worse off than when I was representing myself. Little Eva stopped visitation altogether when I had the TV lawyers. We had to get rid of those greedy crooks.

My brother helped me get rid of them. Now I have Jessica. Talk about a fighter. She speaks up. She files motions. She runs interference when the judge, the guardian ad litem, and Little Eva try to f-bomb all over me. We brought her in for this so called "Final Judgment." Jessica's fees are fair. I have to shake my head in disbelief. Here I am trying to be a good dad and do the right thing and in Chicago, and the theme is may the best lawyers win. They don't care about my child.

When this court crap first started, I told the judge and anyone else who would listen that I could not afford a guardian ad litem who charges $400 to $500 an hour. Really? I make seventeen bucks an hour. The judge ordered that my baby have a lawyer too. For what? And how am I supposed to pay an outrageously expensive GAL on money like that, but that's the strategy. Smoke him out. Bankrupt him. He'll go away.

I love my boy. He's my family. I can't imagine him growing up thinking that I didn't care enough about him to fight for us to be a part of each other's lives. How many boys grow up fatherless? Not my son, I refuse to allow it. But at the rate this crap is going on, Little Eva's lawyers and the GAL will have this shiggety stretched out until my kid is good and grown. It's so stupid and so unfair.

I can't believe how naïve I was when I first got to court. I thought all I had to do was prove my paternity, ask to be a part of the baby's life, pay my child support, and that would be it. I talk to people around the Daley Center. I've heard some pitiful stories about men being shut out of their shorties' lives.

Jessica leans over to me and whispers, "We'll be up in a few minutes, let's go out in the hall and talk before we have to approach the bench."

"OK." It's a relief to go out in the hall. The courtroom gets suffocating. I see my mom talking to gang banger's mother. They seem deep in conversation, but smiling. Mom looks up and joins us.

Jessica speaks first, "Darnell, when we go back in there, I want you to look sad not mad. You are a sad father who just wants to see his child. And Mrs. Wilson, I will probably call you up to the bench."

"Great," Mom says. "I want to offer to supervise so they don't have to pay all that money to supervisors. Did Darnell tell you I taught school for years?"

"That's real good. I'll make sure the judge knows. Just wait out here until I come and get you."

Little Eva is around. Her lawyers are around. The GAL is around. And nobody acknowledges anyone. We've been going through this court crap for years. Even though it is July, there is a serious wind chill around that courtroom, and Eva and her lawyers just suck the air out of the place. They are like energy vampires. After the pause, we head back into the courtroom.

Why can't we just get along? I'm sitting in the courtroom looking sad, which believe me ain't hard to do. Little Eva's lawyer speaks first. I couldn't tell you exactly what he said, but I do hear him say my mom put her hands on Little Eva and called her a bitch.

Now that is the last straw. My mom doesn't even talk like that. She's not about to call someone a bitch. That's too simple minded for her, and she damn sure wouldn't put her hands on anyone. If she did all that, Little Eva would have said she felt threatened and, believe me, called the police. Where's the police record? How do they get away with telling bald-faced lies like that in court and on my mother?

I snap and speak out loud, "That's a lie. This is racist." Jessica quickly shushes me.

The judge speaks quickly, "One more outburst and you will be held in contempt." I don't think he could have said it nastier.

My God, this is a new low. Jessica and the other lawyers are at the bench, and I can hear Jessica object to more than a few outrageous assertions. Jessica goes out to get my mom. Now it's me, Mom, and Jessica at the bench. We thought Mom would get to offer her help with supervision, after all she is the grandmother and loves and adores our boy. But that judge goes all the way HAM on my mom, saying what seems like a lot of poison and crap, but all we actually hear him finally say is, "No, you will not supervise. There is no way."

Mom is red faced. "I don't understand," she says to the judge. She turns to Jessica, "I don't understand." Jessica quickly gathers us and we head to the hall. She leads us into a small conference room so we can talk privately.

"Mrs. Wilson, I am so sorry you had to be subjected to that. I had no idea the judge would say those kinds of things to you. I apologize. I am so sorry."

"That was so uncalled for. Here I am, a professional, a retired schoolteacher, bona fide, certified, excellent reputation, excellent citizen, and I get spoken to like that? It's not your fault, Jessica. This is so ugly." Mom just shakes her head. "What's wrong with that judge?"

We're all shaken by this, me, Jessica, and my mom. "Aren't there some rules of decorum in a courthouse? Damn, I thought people had to at least act civil. Where does he get off talking to my mother like that? I smell a rat. I smell a bunch of rats."

"Strategically, I had to agree for you to take five more random drug tests within eight months' time."

"Five more! What for? How many drug tests can one person who is not on any drugs take? Who is going to pay for all these tests? If they haven't found any drugs yet, why are they making me take so many drug tests? Little Eva needs to take the damn drug tests. Why won't the judge make her take some drug tests? It's not right, and it's not fair."

When it comes to the courthouse, here's my pronouncement, an axiom . . . lawyers ruin relationships.

Sunset in Kyiv

Phil Skiff

Vadim had never experienced pain like this before in his life. When he was thirteen, one of his uncle Dzhey's plow horses had kicked him right in the chest when he'd gotten too close. He'd rolled around on the ground unable to draw a breath, terrified he was going to die. The pain from two cracked ribs had been excruciating. But even that paled in comparison to this.

Vadim lifted the blood-soaked tablecloth. The sight of the metal rod protruding from his chest made vomit rise into his throat. He dropped the cloth and laid his head back on the pile of shattered concrete, his vision going dark, his head spinning.

Three days ago, Putin's Russian-backed insurgents, along with hundreds of what everyone knew were regular Russian army troops, had surged across the border near Basivka. Using the H07 motorway, they'd cut through eastern Ukraine like soft cheese. Pushing over a hundred fifty kilometers in one day, they took Romny without meeting any serious resistance from the heavily outgunned Ukrainian military.

The sound of weeping mingled with tinkling glass roused Vadim. Marina was in the tiny kitchen ransacking the cupboards. She insisted on finding something to disinfect Vadim's wounds—a useless gesture. All he wanted was for her to sit by him and hold his hand. But she was unable to, trapped in convulsive motion.

A ghostly gray figure appeared in the kitchen doorway. Marina—covered head to toe in the concrete dust that still choked the air—tears cutting streaks down her face. She clutched a half dozen plastic and glass bottles to her chest, her whole body trembling. Her beautiful brown hair hung in gray ropes around her face.

"Vadim," she choked. He could hear in her voice she was on the verge of hysteria.

"Moye sertse," *my heart*. "Show me what you've found."

They'd been spending the weekend with Marina's cousin Lena and her husband in Makiivka, making wedding plans, when the first reports of the invasion came over the radio. Vadim's first instinct had been to return to their flat in Kyiv where the Ukrainian defenses were concentrated. They'd rushed down to the H07, joining a torrent of people fleeing towards Kyiv.

Vadim and Marina had almost made it to Kyiv. Riding on Vadim's aging Dnepr motorcycle, they'd cut through the crowds and around roadblocks caused by collisions and broken-down vehicles. Abandoned cars, busses, trucks, and even tractors had littered the sides of the highway, pushed there by the thousands fleeing west.

Marina knelt beside Vadim. Her body jerked with gasping sobs as she showed him the items she'd found, placing each one carefully in a line on the dust-covered floor. Vadim named the fluids, Marina unable to speak over gasping sobs.

"Floor cleaner, probably too harsh my heart. Ah, bleach, that's good." She held out a glass bottle with amber liquid. Vadim squinted to read the faded label. "Vinegar, Sertse?" Marina blinked, sending a cascade of fresh tears cascading down her cheeks. Vadim's heart nearly stopped, the pain so sharp in Marina's eyes.

They'd been just outside Kyiv, on Kutuzova street, cutting through a section of Kyivs'ka oblast, when artillery shells began falling around them. The Russians, under Putin's direct orders, had been indiscriminately shelling Kyiv—provoking panic, choking the roads with people, hampering the movement of the Ukrainian military.

A shell had exploded in the street less than a hundred yards in front of them, throwing bodies and concrete in all directions. Shrapnel had whistled past Vadim and Marina as the motorcycle toppled, their bodies crashing to the pavement. The world had gone silent for Vadim as he struggled onto his hands and knees. Unable to hear them, he'd felt more shells exploding, making the ground move like an earthquake.

Frantic, he'd scanned the bodies piled around him. Seeing a flash of red fabric, he'd crawled to find Marina lying on her stomach, dazed, but alive. Throwing an arm around her waist, he'd lifted her from the street and carried her through a door that stood open just a few meters away.

Inside, had been the living room of a small flat. He'd paused for a moment, scanning for shelter, then started for the door to a tiny kitchen. Marina had begun struggling in his crushing grip.

It hadn't been so much a sound—still hearing nothing other than ringing in his ears—perhaps a pressure change. Flinging Marina through the kitchen doorway, he'd wrapped his arms instinctively around his head as the earth moved beneath his feet.

When he awoke sometime later, he was laying on his back on a pile of jagged concrete that used to be part of the second floor. He couldn't move. His legs were pinned under a huge slab. He couldn't feel them. What he could feel was a sharp stabbing pain in his chest with every breath he took. The air was filled with choking clouds of gray cement dust and he immediately began coughing—then screaming with blinding pain.

"Vinegar will be good," he said, taking the bottle from her shaking hand. He set it on the floor beside the others. Vadim coughed, choking on liquid pooling in his lungs. The movement caused sheets of fiery agony in his chest, and the room darkened around him.

"Vadim!" Marina screamed, taking his head in her hands. Vadim struggled back.

"I believe I was a good carpenter," he said, realizing he was making no sense. He must have been dreaming. He'd apprenticed as a carpenter, but that was years ago. An age ago.

"Mishka," *little bear*, "you are an excellent carpenter." Marina spoke quietly, her face close to his, her hands still holding his head.

Vadim realized he must have passed out for a short time. "You will certainly be the finest carpenter in all of Kyiv, Vadim."

"Nothing is certain moye sertse." The pat phrase sounded foolish on his lips, and he regretted it instantly as Marina's face fell. "Ty taka krasyva!" *You are so beautiful.*

The building shook as more shells fell nearby. Cement chips and grit rained down on them. Marina covered Vadim with her body. He felt her heaving chest against his, and a whiff of her Shalimar perfume, his gift for her birthday, mingled with her sweat, filling his senses.

The Trouble with Beautiful Women

A.J. Norris

Michael stood in line at the Heathrow Airport security checkpoint. *What's taking so long?* He glanced at his watch again and sighed. A sense of loss weighed him down; he missed how she felt in his hands—her sleek form and smooth exterior. As the line shuffled forward, he caught sight of what he longed for; what completed him.

A weapon.

The fact that this particular gun came attached to an Air Marshal was only a minor problem. He preferred a Sig Sauer, but any 9mm could fill the void, for now anyway.

He ducked into a bathroom behind the guy he'd followed since spotting him in the security line. The non-descript man had been given a pass around the metal detectors and shared a laugh with one of the guards. An Air Marshal for sure. Although the sky cop was probably well trained in hand-to-hand combat, the U.S. government made sure Michael was more skilled.

Three minutes later, Michael peered around the door. One quick over-the-shoulder glance, to ensure the man was still out cold, and he emerged from the bathroom with a small duffle in hand and a set of bruised knuckles. He pulled his baseball cap down over his eyes and blended in with the masses.

Oh, man, he couldn't wait to get back to the States.

Michael stretched his long legs under the seat in front of him. After his failed mission to Russia, all he wanted to do was relax on the connecting flight across the pond. ". . . Ladies and gentlemen, please fasten your seatbelts, we may encounter light to moderate turbulence as we fly around a storm cell. . . ."

The plane jostled its passengers and rattled the overhead compartments. The woman seated next to him at the window gasped and white-knuckled the armrests. He yawned. Turbulence put him to sleep. Familiarity shone in her expression. He rolled his eyes. Guess that last gold medal immortalized him forever.

"Aren't you that Olympic—"

"Nope. I get that a lot." He angled his face away from her scrutinizing gaze. *Leave me alone lady.* He sighed and glanced at the ceiling.

Nothing about this assignment had been routine. He was just supposed to make contact with the undercover and steal a cell phone from someone named Katja. The phone was known to hold bank account information used to fund a terrorist organization.

Timmons had promised that everything would go as planned. What a load of crap; he couldn't even find Nikoli. The whole operation was a shit show from start to finish. He ran his hand down the front of his leather jacket. The carbon fiber gun he'd taken from that Air Marshal back in the airport bathroom was snuggly inside his breast pocket.

He rose from his seat for a sweep of the cabin. A thick-bearded man eyed him with a dark expression that crept over his skin like fire ants. Michael cocked his head side-to-side, covering up a shiver; he recognized the man. God, he really wished the silencer wasn't stashed away in his carry-on.

"Excusez-moi."

Michael turned and found a breathtaking, red-haired woman behind him. *Ahhh . . .* "Um, yeah. Sorry." He swallowed and moved toward the front of the plane, parking between the lavatories. His tennis shoes squeaked on the grey rubber floor.

The redhead sat next to the bearded, dark-expression man. Who, without taking his eyes off Michael, kissed the woman's temple. She turned into him. He whispered something in her ear that brought a half-smile to her face. Michael's eyes traveled down her slender legs. *Jesus.* Even in skinny jeans, she looked fantastic, and the platform pumps didn't hurt either. The gold from her anklet glinted in the overhead lighting. He exhaled slowly and imagined running his hands over her curves. *Quit it.*

After pretending to use the bathroom, Michael wandered back to his aisle seat. He grabbed his bag from the overhead bin, sat down, and placed it between his feet. His hand met with the cool silencer inside the luggage. Concealing it in his grasp, he waited thirty minutes. "I shouldn't've had that last drink," he said to his anxious row mate and headed to the back of the aircraft for another fake piss break.

An Air Marshal nodded to him. These guys were easy to spot. Always wearing a lightweight, khaki coat and sporting a mustache. This one was also too relaxed on an international flight, suggesting he flew all the time. However, the cheesy haircut and cheap pants said that under normal circumstances, he couldn't afford to fly overseas.

Michael reached the cramped toilet closet. *Occupied.* He knocked on the folding door; the person inside rambled a few words in Russian. Michael raised his hand to knock again and the door snapped open. An obese man shook his head and squeezed past him. The aftermath of what had just transpired invaded his olfactory receptors. "Oh—" He held his breath, his eyes watering. Whatever, he didn't have time for this.

The ambient hum of the airplane rung in his ears. The plane pitched sideways. His hand landed in the sink and the silencer in the toilet. *Shit.* He face-palmed and dragged his hand downward. Blowing out a breath, he retrieved the silencer.

His phone vibrated in his jeans pocket. *What now?* He rolled his eyes and answered. There could be only one reason his handler, Timmons, called. "Job's not over, is it?" asked Michael.

"Cardinals fly west in the winter."

"I thought all birds flew south for the colder months."

"Well, this species doesn't; what can I tell you."

"I don't suppose they prefer British Airways."

"Nope."

"Lufthansa, maybe?"

Timmons snorted. "Get real." *Great.* A long exhale escaped Michael's lips. "You know what you have to do, right?"

He sighed. ". . . Yeah." Why did cardinals have to be so damn beautiful? He tapped "End" and pocketed the cell. The timing had to be perfect—just before touching down on U.S. soil. He'd need to escape undetected. Timmons would be waiting.

A downdraft slammed into the aircraft and Michael was weightless for a moment. He banged his head on the mirror above the sink; the glass spider-webbed. Blood dribbled down his forehead. Grabbing some tissue, he dabbed at the wound. *Ow.* Several women and one man screamed as the plane plummeted. *What the hell?* His lunch perched at the back of his throat. He forced his hands out to steady himself and waited for the plane to stabilize before he wrenched open the door. A flight attendant greeted him with a scowl.

"Take your seat, sir," she told him.

He recoiled. "Don't you know who I—"

"On this plane, you're just another passenger. Now, take your seat."

Yes, ma'am. He thought about saluting her.

Michael used the headrests for support and made his way back to his seat. All around him babies cried and passengers whimpered, some chanted prayers. The Air Marshal was missing. The woman who sat next to him had tucked her head between her knees. *Not going to help lady.* The metal tube with wings dropped ten or fifteen feet at a time. Michael's stomach bottomed out. His eyes darted to the window. Lights twinkled below. They were over land. The sense of relief that should've washed over him was replaced with dread. A watery crash didn't always mean death, he could swim well, but one over land. . . .

The plane shuddered as it made a steep, banked turn to the North. *Jesus, who's flying this thing?* Purses, laptops, and other loose bags slid from one side of the cabin to the other. Michael gripped the armrests. The seat next to the hot girl was empty. Now was the time to finish his mission; he jumped out of his seat. She was slumped down and he would've missed her, except some of her fire-truck red hair stuck out into the aisle.

He closed the distance between them in two strides. Her eyes went wide as he yanked her up. With the Glock pressed into her back and an arm around her neck, he marched her toward the back of the 767. He hauled her into the space behind the bathroom, next to the galley.

"Hey, you can't be back—" a flight attendant warned. He flashed the gun. She put her hands up and backed away.

Michael frisked the woman in his clutches. "Where is it?"

"Where's what . . . hmmm, Katja likes that . . .," she purred.

I bet you do. "Knock it off. You know what I'm talking about."

"Search my body more if you'd like."

He took a deep breath. "I've got no problem killing you. Where's the phone?"

"Nikoli is keeping it safe." He clicked the safety off. "Okay, okay—" The Boeing made another steep banked turn to the left. Michael took the brunt of the force as he and Katja fell against the side of the plane. His finger curled around the trigger. Her body went lax. When the plane leveled out, he realized they were headed back out to sea.

"Ladies and gentlemen, we are being temporarily diverted—" The passengers on the overcrowded plane erupted.

"Let her go," the missing Air Marshal said with the barrel of a gun pressed to Michael's head. Michael released Katja and she dropped to the floor. He handed the gun over. "That's it, nice and easy."

"I'm CIA."

"No kidding." The Air Marshal cuffed him. Before planting him in a retractable seat reserved for the flight attendants, he handed Michael a key. The Glock was also shoved into his chest pocket.

"Who are you?" Michael muttered.

The man smirked and walked away. He flung the dead woman over his shoulder, stuffed her inside the kitchen elevator, and lowered her down. When he turned around, several flight attendants swarmed him with questions. They ushered him away.

Michael worked the lock on one of the cuffs loose. The bearded man came barreling down the aisle toward him, shouting in Russian. "What did you do?"

Just as the Russian reached the back, the plane banked hard to the left and headed south. The roar of the engines briefly grew louder. The passengers behind the man screamed in justifiable terror. Stress from the abrupt maneuver shook the plane and caused both of them to hold onto something. Once they leveled out again, Michael charged the bearded man. White rings surrounded his irises. "Katja!"

Michael used his shoulder like a battering ram into his opponent's gut. He thrust his arms around his waist, taking him to the rubber flooring. Straddling his hips, he pummeled his face. Katja's lover rolled up and head-butted Michael. Blood spewed from his nose; he jumped up and staggered into a refreshment cart. The man pounced on his back, grabbing him from behind. They swung around. At six four, Michael easily took control. He threw his weight backward and crushed the man against the wall of the plane until he went limp. Michael pulled his weapon out and shot the guy twice in the back of the head. "Jeez, any more surprises?" he said aloud.

He turned to find more than a few passengers looking on him with horror. The Air Marshal parted the small crowd and winked at him. "Everything's under control here . . . flight attendants, please clear the area. Give the champion some room."

What? Why did he say that? Now they worshiped him like some kind of hero, some even clapped. One took video. Awesome, just what he wanted to see headlining TMZ tomorrow: Former Olympian Saves the Day. *Yay.* The passengers began to take their seats but continued to gape at him.

A corner of Michael's mouth perked up. "All right, who are you?"

"Bob."

"That's it," Michael pursed his lips, "just Bob. Not Air Marshal Bob or something I dunno, more *creative*?"

Bob rolled his eyes. "We need to get you off this plane before it lands. Ever done a HALO jump before?"

Oh, boy. "Once."

"Good, then I don't have to explain it to you." The Air Marshal removed the carts from under the galley counter and revealed an access panel just wide enough for Michael to fit through. "Here, this leads to the animal cargo. It's empty but pressurized. Beyond that is another access panel that leads to the tail. There's a control-box that will lower the cargo-bay door. Everything you need is down there."

"Why are you helping me?"

"Just get going. But don't jump until we're closer to land. Even you couldn't swim far in this ocean." Bob opened the panel and Michael lowered himself into the hole. A cell phone got tossed down before the metal panel was sealed.

"Who are you?" he said to himself.

Michael used the flashlight on his iPhone to navigate the low ceiling and uneven metal grating. Inside the animal compartment, he found a small oxygen tank, helmet, suit, and a parachute. Biting his nails, he studied the equipment. *Christ. Oh . . . this sucks.* He dialed Timmons.

"Michael?"

"Who else would it be—listen, ah, I'm going to text you some new rendezvous coordinates."

"What for?"

"You don't wanna know."

"I don't like the sound of that." Timmons sounded edgy.

"That makes two of us. Do the words, 'fallen angel' mean anything to you?"

"Uh uh, no way, not again," he sighed, "just don't puke again—"

Michael hung up and texted the coordinates. After donning his new outfit, and maybe his last, he entered the non-pressurized area. He pressed the button to lower the cargo door, said a prayer, and jumped out of the plane—grateful that HALO chutes were equipped with an FF2. Blacking out at 33,000 feet was almost always a given.

Michael didn't exactly land where he'd wanted and had to walk five miles up the coastline on shaky legs. He cussed Timmons out along the way, blaming him for a faulty jumpsuit pocket and his phone dropping sometime during the 20,000-foot free fall. Katja's phone wouldn't hold a signal. Luckily, he'd stuffed the Nokia inside the suit.

The Lincoln MKX idled next to a warehouse. Ashes from a lit cigar littered the asphalt next to the vehicle. Michael breathed in the stale smoke and salty air. A rotten fish smell clogged his sinuses. If it hadn't been twenty-four hours since he'd eaten anything substantial, he would've puked. The driver's side blackout window lowered. "About time you showed up . . . get in, this place reeks."

"And your cologne isn't much better. Damn. Do you bathe in that shit? I smell it out here."

"Cute," he sighed, "anyway, where's the package? Nikoli said he gave it to you. Knew he'd get searched and didn't want it to fall into some dirty agent's hands."

"I never made contact with *Nikoli*." Michael opened the door to the backseat, needing to lie down after his long walk. His eyes went wide. *Huh?*

"Sure you did. I'm Bob Nikoli. Oh, and thank you, I could never bring myself to kill Katja. Damn beautiful woman."

Sleeping Single—PART 2: Autumn Longing

Diane VanderBeke Mager

I retreat deeper into the folds of my comforter . . . but it refuses to live up to its name.

My bedroom windows are open a crack, and CeCe and Bob's wind chimes mournfully call out each time the cool breeze caresses my wet cheeks. I want to take solace in another bedtime story, but I'm loath to free my imagination.

I reach for a tissue and blow my nose, stuffy with allergies and sorrow. Raindrops strike the metal gutters, releasing a torrent of nature's emotions to mirror my own.

Everyone is moving on with their life except me. Dean is back at college. All of my friends are working full-time or busy with their husbands. And just today, Bob announced he and CeCe are heading down to Florida for the holidays before embarking on a six-month, cross-country motorcycle trip to celebrate his Army retirement. He wanted to let me know their friend Jake will be house-sitting for them come January.

So, when am I finally going to meet *my* travel partner? I like to tell myself, and others, I stayed single for the past twenty years because I was busy launching Dean into independence . . . or I wanted to safeguard him from the disappointment of being abandoned by another man. But it is becoming increasingly clear; it is really me I have been protecting.

Closing my eyes, I count on one hand the number of times I have fallen asleep beside a man in the past two decades. On my other hand, I count the number of times I have been betrayed. Just when I think I can't take anymore, I picture it . . . the memory of the little old couple sitting beside each other, holding hands on a bench in some quaint European village. That was supposed to be us one day. . . .

A sob escapes, and I curl into a ball, clutching my pillow. Out of habit, I gently stroke the back of my neck, recalling the tenderness of a lover's touch. But my loneliness and self-pity only intensify.

What am I so afraid of? Personal bedtime stories have never failed me before. I got hooked as a child, when I discovered I held the power to take down playground bullies with the perfect comeback, if only in my head. In my twenties, I plotted action-packed adventures to faraway places I later visited. By thirty, I was turning out tragedies, more often than not, ending in some variation of me falling to my knees crying out in despair, "But we have a one-year-old child!" This in response to my ex-husband's classic and indelible line, "It's too late, I love someone else," proclaimed as he walked out, leaving me to raise Dean on my own.

I'm over that now . . . well mostly . . . able to fill the bedtime void with elaborate tales of controlled bravado, mysterious strangers, and undying romance, reconfiguring a cast of familiar characters to fit each storyline. Until like clockwork, this dual onslaught of autumn allergies and seasonal depression sweeps me into a vortex of mangled memories and unfulfilled desires.

On nights like tonight, it's best to wallow. Only a story of disappointment, humiliation, and bitter yearning will provide the catharsis I seek. I inhale deeply and unleash my imagination. . . .

Laney exhaled. Crisp autumn leaves blanketed the empty gravel driveway. She was the first one to arrive.

When Stuart Cleeves had invited her to his annual Halloween party, she was both excited and anxious. She told herself she could use a bit of fun. But did it have to be hosted by an ex?

The two of them were never serious. "Booty-call Stuart," she had called him. Although . . . his voice did still make her swoon.

She hadn't seen him in ages. Maybe this invitation was his way of signaling he was finally ready to settle down after sowing his wild oats for the past decade. . . .

Laney smoothed her red dress, tiptoed her way up the drive, and rang the front doorbell. A Sexy Nurse greeted her. The skimpy costume exposed overly enlarged breasts and barely covered a taut ass.

"Hi! I'm Eleanor," chirped the cliché.

"Laney. Nice to meet you."

"Stuart will be back in a minute; he forgot the lemons. You can lay your coat upstairs in our room. It's the first door on the left," she drawled with a level of self-confidence reserved for the young and oblivious.

Laney bit her tongue, wanting to respond, "Yeah, I know the way," or "Been there, done that." Instead, she traipsed up the steps and deposited her coat on the bed, wistfully recalling the time Stuart had thrown her down across the silk comforter. . . .

She plastered a smile on her face and descended the stairs. Erik and Evangeline von Ebert had arrived, dressed as JFK and Jackie—still attempting to mask their failed Camelot it would appear. Erik was Stuart's business partner, one of those types that didn't wear a wedding ring and regularly cheated on his wife, somehow managing to convince her it was her own fault.

Laney could never understand what Stuart saw in Erik or why he turned to him for advice. She'd met Erik first, serving together on an arts committee. When she discovered he was married, she'd rebuked his advances. In response, he'd set her up with Stuart. She had thought it a conciliatory gesture at the time. Later, she discovered it was his way of staying in control, playing the puppet-master over both her and his best friend.

She avoided the von Eberts and made a beeline for the bar, helping herself to a club soda.

Guests continued to arrive, and Eleanor jiggled her way through the prescribed welcome and outerwear drop-off instructions until Stuart finally showed up with a bag of lemons and some extra ice. Laney watched in fascination as Stuart wrapped a possessive arm around Eleanor's tiny waist. Of all the sophisticated, highly educated, and *stunning women Stuart had juggled over the years, who would have thought he would go for the obvious—though her long, red hair* was *rather striking. . . .*

In walked two more familiar faces.

"*Howz tings over by you?*" *asked the Major in his best Chicago tough-guy accent.*

Dressing like a '20s mobster suited him. The loudness of his pinstriped suit, wide tie, and two-toned shoes was offset only by the severity of his fedora pulled low across one eye. His wife, Cecelia, was dressed as his moll. Her blue dress clung to her voluptuous curves.

"*Hey, nice tie,*" *joked Stuart.* "*Trading in your army camo for pinstripes . . . not bad.*" *They clasped hands and did the bro hug.* "*Cecelia . . . lovely as always.*" *Stuart kissed her warmly on the cheek.*

Drink in hand, Laney parked herself in a corner, near the pool table temporarily serving as the buffet. She surveyed the scene. Stuart had gone all out with the decorations this year, transforming his man cave into a "Forest of No Return" straight out of Disney's Babes in Toyland, *complete with "No trespassing" signs, recorded night sounds, and a fog machine.*

A group of five women approached the table and started filling their plates.

"*Get a load of the redhead on Stuart's arm,*" *sniped the one in the Sultry Kitten costume.*

"*I hear they met on Fourth-of-July, at the casino. Cocktail waitress,*" *said the one in the Hot Stewardess outfit.*

"*I got the inside scoop from his friend Major Windemere, the guy over there dressed as a Gangster. She's twenty-four, with a toddler in tow. They moved in last month, and Stuart watches the kid while she works nights,*" *chimed in Foxy Milk Maid.*

Racy Secretary squinted, adjusting her glasses. "*Who would have th—*"

"*How many women here do you think Stuart has slept with?*" *asked Sultry Kitten.*

"I count eleven from where I'm standing," quipped Hot Stewardess.

"He nailed half the office before he and Erik branched out on their own," responded Naughty Dominatrix.

Laney hiccupped but refrained from adding her own name to the list. The ladies gave her a wary look and moved on.

Stuart, dressed as the Surgeon to Eleanor's Nurse, worked the crowd, making his way toward her. Laney met his eyes as he approached, confident in the way her sleeveless red dress hugged her hourglass figure. They embraced, brushing cheeks. She felt a pang of regret that due to her four-inch heels, he hadn't had to adopt his usual wide stance before bending down to sweep her into his arms. She'd always found that move rather irresistible.

As he released her, she nearly stumbled, quickly rearranging the length of cord fastened into a noose dangling from her wrist, a leather-bound volume clutched in her hand.

"Let me guess . . . Miss Scarlet did it in the Library with the Rope!"

Laney chuckled. "You always were quick on the uptake. So good to see you. Thanks for inviting me."

"Can't have you missing out on all the fun again."

"I met Eleanor. Striking hair color."

"Yeah, it suits her. Have you met any of the guys?"

"Guys? What guys? All I see is a long line of half-dressed former conquests hoping to win you back."

"Come on, what about the guys from the office over there?"

"You mean the ones dressed in full-out hunting gear? Ooooh, animal assassins . . . every vegetarian's deepest desire."

"Okay, how about Stan? The one in the lab coat by the fog machine. He's an engineer and collects GTOs—"

"I've been set up with enough straight-laced engineers to satisfy any unresolved Daddy issues, thank you very much. Not to mention, you know I hate muscle cars."

"Yeah, but I thought you'd had enough of us slick-suited jerks in our German imports, talking business on our cell phones and ignoring your intellect."

"True. Maybe I need to appeal to my softer side this time around . . . someone in touch with nature and mind/body/spirit."

"Don't forget, you're allergic to nature and you get fed up with weed smokers."

"Way to rub it in, Stuart. Alas, you are the only man for me. Ditch Sexy Nurse and we'll run away together!" She fake swooned, but he caught her in a dip to the beat of the '80s dance music Cecelia had turned on.

"Gotta run, babe. Eleanor can be the jealous type after a few drinks," he said, kissing her on the cheek. Laney watched him walk away and then glanced from side to side to make sure no one had noticed the look of longing on her face.

Why hadn't they been able to make it work? He'd once told her they were combustible . . . all anyone had to do was throw a match down on the table and they would ignite. The sex had been stellar, and they'd never had a bad date; but somewhere along the way her independence and penchant for debate had conflicted with his need to be needed and desire to avoid confrontation.

Alone, Laney wandered from room to room, catching snippets of office gossip and collecting "essential" bow-hunting tips until she landed in the back den, surrounded by Stuart's collection of finance manuals and Disney DVDs. His man/boy duality did have its element of charm, but best to leave him to the ministrations of Sexy Nurse. *We'll see how long that lasts.*

Stuart was smart, attractive, and ambitious. He was also generous to a fault, footing the bill for friends and family alike. Let him get a taste of what it's like to parent a young child 24/7. Unlike Eleanor, she'd hidden that side of her life when they'd been together, maintaining strict rules . . . no overnights and no meaningful child interaction unless dating exclusively for six months—not that they'd made it that far.

She heard Cecelia's distinctive laugh out on the back patio. Drinks were flowing, and the Sexy quintuplets and he-man hunters were climbing into the hot tub. Time to exit gracefully. She'd put in an appearance and successfully masked her emotions concerning Stuart.

As Laney maneuvered toward the front door with coat in hand, Erik von Ebert stepped forward, wife in tow.

"You never stood a chance," he said, blocking Laney's path.

"Excuse me?"

"You never stood a chance with Stuart." His eyes pierced her like an arrow. Evangeline von Ebert stood silently next to her husband, staring at the floor as he went in for the kill. "I asked him once . . . what he saw in you . . . and do you know what he said? He said he was attracted to you because of your financial independence, your availability, and your nipples. I told him no harm keeping you in the stable, as long as he didn't get the urge to ride you home."

Laney's heart pounded; a hollow pit formed in her gut. She yearned to accuse him of manipulating her entire relationship with Stuart out of petty jealousy, but she held back in Evangeline's presence. The poor woman had suffered enough indignities at her husband's hand.

"Thanks Erik, I'll consider the source," Laney replied, chin held high.

She fled the house, struggling to keep her balance as her heels skidded on the gravel drive. The forecast had called for showers, and it didn't disappoint.

She slid into the driver's seat, tossed the soggy book and rope onto the passenger side, and slammed the car door shut, ignoring the urge to stomp back in there and tighten the noose around Erik's neck. With friends like that, no wonder Stuart wound up with Eleanor. It wouldn't surprise her if Erik had introduced them so he could bang Eleanor on the side while Stuart stayed home with the kid.

Laney pulled forward out of the circle drive, unaware of the man with the sexy scruff, dressed all in black, watching her intently from behind his Zorro mask.

She drove the back roads, her latest sob-song on repeat, belting out the lyrics as tears streamed down her face. Raindrops pelted the car; the windshield wipers kept bitter time. What had her therapist called it? . . . "Getting cute for nothing."

She headed upstairs with an empty heart to an empty bed, longing to be ridden home.

POETRY

Composure

Peter Banks

The back of napkins kept
tears gently wept

and though moistened by tears
she journalized fears

wrung from life, as it were,
between the folds, pen sputtering.

The pale panes inherit
the black weight of her spill

and though content with
far less than their fill

blank slates of the barfly set
prove less efficient when wet

with tears and remembered pain,
grasping weakly the words they stain

the place of her nightly confession.

Life is Good

Anthony Stachurski

Life is good
if you don't weaken.

But someone up on Sunshine Lane
hasn't opened the drapes today.

And someone's drunk the bourbon
hidden underneath the bed.

Come on! Pull those shoulders back
and stand up straight!

Life is good
if you don't weaken.

But someone's thrown a plate against the wall.
A Cadillac has just turned off the road
onto a corn field.

Who could it be?

Look just eat your carrots and shut up!
Remember to have your prostate checked
this year.

Life is good
if you don't weaken.

But someone's just misspelled another word
and can't remember where he placed his hat;
it's just a hairline crack.

I won't mention any names.

And who could tell?
He's only sitting in the park, alone.
She's just returning a shopping cart.

Life is good
if you don't weaken.

Maybe some people are stronger than others,
like being born with good teeth.
Or is it that they're still untested?

Or is it needing one more cigarette?
Sex, one more time.
Maybe they haven't been to Disneyland yet
or want to bring the new year in.

Maybe it's the children.

Life is good
if you don't weaken.

Besides, it's spring and seventy degrees.
The leaves are budding on the trees.
People are planting flowers and bicycling.
Someone's sweeping out the garage.
An old woman is putting lipstick on her mouth.

Life is good
if you don't weaken.

Biography of a Shadow

Anthony Stachurski

Every man casts a shadow: that dark part
of himself who played with matches, fought, stole,
grew up a drifter, chef, bouncer, fork lifter.
Almost killed a man once, over a woman.
Lived in a trailer by himself, and drank.
Played rugby and raised white doves.
Who knows what else. Never owned a car.
Married once, for six months, until she kicked him out.
Never talked much. Like a lot of other men, never
gave a damn about religion.

Word was he lost the trailer and became a bum.
No one's seen him in years, or even knows if he's still around,
though didn't you say you thought you saw him once
passing under a streetlight, turning down an alley
on the wrong side of town.

Holy Vows

Anthony Stachurski

We vow upon this moor today,
to love one another,
You, in cloudy gown, hem trimmed
with heather.
Behind Your veil of drizzling rain,
a bluebell, I suspect, or distant star,
for me to kiss.
I, in jeans, perhaps too old for this.
No altar but the simple rise of sky
and earthen rug beneath my feet
worn and lichened black.
Faint shadow, my best man, stands
silent at my side as my old selves like stones
lie weeping in the grass at this betrayal.
Nonetheless, I've thought it through.
And so, respectfully, the sea comes to a hush
as the sun beams through a leaded pane
of sky-stained blue.
The wind pipes up as quail and brook
begin to sing.
And on this cold November hill,
We *do*.

The Invisible Man

Anthony Stachurski

Red Dogwood stains the snow
where he staggers bleeding into the woods,
shot up, confused, forgetting the words,
the way to be whole.
He knows that knowledge will not bring him back—
the experiment—a successful failure, the notes
and calculations, the books, fallen behind the shelves
for naught.
He sees a log—like a leg, a rock—like a head,
the trees gaping like goons that could never understand
his predicament.
God knows he tried to save himself.
Here and there, loose strips of Shagbark Hickory
litter the snow like ragged bandages,
the cry of a Blue Jay forever lost
in the impenetrable fog.

English Weather

Anthony Stachurski

The wind sobs against my window,
wailing like a torn bagpipe, beating
its wrinkled fists against the house.
Outside it could have been St. Margaret's Hope,
the sky paved gray with flagstones.
Come home. Come home, it shouts howling
its words, weaving among the chollas
and the prickly pears, slurring my name
over and over like a lush in the rain.

Geodes

Anthony Stachurski

In pretty skirts
and ribbons in their hair,
women forage in the hills
where men reside, to pick
their hearts from rough outcroppings
of the earth, and with a kiss,
split them.

O crystal paradise!

Only in the light of women's love
do men shine like this.

Absolute Truth

Anthony Stachurski

I'm walking around town
seeking truth, Real Truth,
when I find a Spiegel catalog
someone left on the seat at Taco Bell.
Someone's written on the cover page:
For the absolute truth turn to page 19.
I get excited. This is definitely a sign.
So, I do.

But I don't get it. *Men's Shoes!*
Now turn to page 34. I'm wary now,
and being a trusting person, I do.

But I'm confused: what do all these *Bras*
have to do with the truth?

Now turn to page 58. No way!
I'm no sucker.
But I do. *Home furnishings?*
And written at the top: *You are a gullible,*
naïve idiot. And your mother knows it too.
That's the absolute truth. For more truths
turn to page 72.

And I do!

The Wish

Anthony Stachurski

*Fall asleep with a wish
on your lips,* she said.
So he wished, for a year.

The vision then revealed:

suspended in mid-air, high
centered in a sky-blue, old cathedral dome—
a glowing crown of red-white blossoms
and leaves a shining green, a trunk pure white,
and roots of gold.

He woke and ran about the house
in his underwear shouting:

*God! God is a tree!
God is a tree!*

All the lights came on.
Everyone started yelling:
*What's the matter with Dad?
John, what's wrong with you?*

The dog barking wildly
at the top of the stairs.

A Summer's Day

Anthony Stachurski

I'm almost done! my Bride calls out
from the fitting room stall at *Forever 21*.
And even though She's been trying dresses on
for forty days and nights, it's alright.
I brought a bag of Snicker's bars to eat,
plus *Cien Sonetos de Amor.**

Well worth the wait when She steps forth
onto the runway of my heart, showing off
Her sky-blue summer dress, bare shoulders
soft as clouds, and lips and hips in bloom.
She spins around—such sexy knees—
Her skirt hem swaying pleated fields of daffodils
and jewelweed.

She poses in the tri-fold mirror, flirting with Herself,
then snaps a shoulder strap and blows a kiss.
What a tease! What vanity! But that's OK.
In fact, I love it!

Do you like it? She asks.
Of course! my eyes like flashing camera bulbs.
But how much will this cost?
Oh, silly boy! She chides. *Everything's on sale today.*
Besides, it's free, because I'm so pretty.
And if you love me like you say you do, then you
won't mind if I try on another day or two.

* *One hundred Love Sonnets,* by Pablo Neruda

Let Me Introduce Myself

Anthony Stachurski

Up here. To the right. Higher.
That's it!
Do you see me now?

You look surprised.
You've never heard of sylphs?
Well, I'm one.
A sylph! you say.

Yes, an elemental being, a ruler of the air.
In Latin, sylph means *forest. Butterfly* in Greek.
When you see the sky in all of its variety,
you're seeing me, my personality.
And if you love my work, nod or smile,
or thank me directly.

I'm wind and cloud.
See my broad white wings outspread.
Now a dragon, swan, a unicorn—
anything that loves to fly.
I am the sheer transparency of sky.
Sometimes I'm red. Sometimes I'm blue.
It all depends.
When you see swaying trees, or feel a breeze
across your face, that's me.
I'm at my best up high, wispy, cirrus-like,
wind-blown snow upon a mountaintop.

I am the Northern Lights.
If you'd like to look me up, I have my own web site.
I never sleep. It's such a waste of time.

Do you like storms? I do.
I love to bang around up there and ride the lightning
to the ground.

I'm full of moods and whims, wild and free.
I have a base speed of infinity.
I can be anywhere I want, immediately.
And I can talk with birds and see into eternity.
It's fun to be me.
I'm magic and mystery.

Well, I've got to go.
I'm putting on a show tonight.

Come see.

Duet for Pen and Shed

Anthony Stachurski

I was writing a God poem
in the shed today, when a wind
picked up, and the limb

of a blooming Oleander tree
began drawing across the edge
of the open door like a bow,

playing the shed like a cello,
accompanying me, adagio.

How sweet is that!

Decked as a Bride

Anthony Stachurski

Queen of the May,
who wouldn't fall in love
with You, today,
a million pink-white blossoms
in your hair?

And such perfume!

And now with clouds arranged
like angels in the air,
the apple trees like bridesmaids
at each curve.
the pines, my best men
dressed in green,
I run that country mile
up to the altar of the sky and cry
I do! I do! before the sun
has even asked.

Author's note: Queen of the May is the title of a hand-colored photograph by Wallace Nutting.

Side-View Mirror

Anthony Stachurski

Down the road at sixty-five, you never
think you're going to die, pushing

everything aside like roadside clover
that parts and bows behind you, so full

of what's ahead you hardly ever check
the side-view mirror (except to pass)

to see the birds sucked into the glass,
the towns knocked flat, the clouds

dragged down the corner of its eye,
the way one thing after another falls

into that crystal ball.

Oh, Holy Night

Anthony Stachurski

So maybe the clouds weren't angels,
and the stars weren't vigil lights,
or the air vent *dervishes that whirled in ecstasy*
throughout the night.
And I admit that in that moonlight pure and tender
I saw fish floating belly up in the river
and packs of rats in the trash bins,
that it was poetry to write, a bridge at prayer,
its rosary of lights upraised in decades to the shore,
an outright lie to say, I knelt before the altar
of the sky and took the moon into my mouth,
that, for all I know, before
bright lightning bolts shut heaven's door.
I'd only wished it so.

Celebration of Life

Theresa Shen

Wind singing through the meadow.
Birds chirping, bees humming, and butterflies fluttering
as spring arrives.
Hummingbirds sipping nectar from red geraniums in summer.
Autumn trees, gleaming in the yellow moonlight, suggesting
a coming harvest.
Snowflakes veiling the world with dazzling whiteness.

Devoted friends bow their heads to receive Holy Communion.
Siblings laugh out their differences after a harsh argument.
Mothers whisper secrets to their grownup daughters.
Friends, far and near, sending love and prayers share their
tears and laughter.
My beloved and I walk through the neighborhood after sunset.

A kettle steaming on the stove.
Aroma of fresh baked French pastry wafting in the air.
Peaches, berries, pears, apples creating a yummy fruit salad.
Chatting and joking voices along with grilled scents rising from
the backyard porch.
We enjoy a delicious Sunday Brunch.

The tinkling of piano keys, the rustling of violin strings resonate
sweet melodies.
The stroking of a paint brush, the smudging of a charcoal stick
release stress.
Flowing words across a page calm the worried heart.
Carefree traveling, on land or water, brings joy and memories.
Each day, full of wonders, creates anew the celebration of life.

MEMOIRS & ESSAYS

"Grandpa, that's my sweater."

Theresa Shen

My father and I were strangers. When I was a child and busy with fairytales, my father was actively involved with the politics of the Republic of China. He never had any time to converse with me and my other siblings.

One day when I was about eight years old, he was taking a nap. On that day, I was very excited about practicing jump rope, a sport that I had learned the day before from a child in the neighborhood. I jumped vigorously in our family room while I counted aloud, "One, Two, Three . . ." I jumped well and was excited, so I counted louder and louder.

All of a sudden, Dad walked into the family room and shouted at me, "Mei, what're you doing, making so much noise? Don't you know I'm taking a nap?"

I stopped jumping and stared at him.

"Go outside if you want to jump," he walked toward me and patted my head.

"Yes, Dad." I walked out to the yard, turning to see if he was still watching me. He was, with a smile, standing in front of the window.

Father was an active and a loyal member in the government. When the Communist uprising started on Mainland China, he knew that the country was in big turmoil. Father decided to move our family to Taiwan. At that time, I was in the middle of fourth grade. But luckily, I could continue my schooling in Taiwan.

Our life in Taiwan was harsh. We had to give up all the luxuries we enjoyed on Mainland China, but we adjusted well. Once again, father was actively involved in politics, but sometimes he wrote poetry or recited poems from the Tang Dynasty to his children. I learned to love poetry during that time.

Father didn't have time to check on my schooling, but he seemed to believe that I was doing okay. When I was ready to graduate from college, I asked him if he would like to attend the commencement.

"You are graduating from the college? Boy, how time flies!"

He did not attend the commencement, but I forgave him. I knew he trusted that I did graduate.

A year later, I decided to study abroad in the U.S. or Europe. At that time, the government required all students who wished to study abroad to pass a scholastic exam to make sure that they were qualified. The exam was known to be difficult.

On the day of the test, I waited outside to enter the examination hall and talked to my friends Jean and Virginia. I saw my dad walk toward me, carrying a small brown bag in his right hand.

"My dad is here," I said to my friends, wondering why he had come.

"Hi, Dad," I greeted him.

"I'm glad I've found you," he said.

He handed me the brown bag and said, "I thought you might be hungry after the exam. I got these dumplings from Silver Wings. They are delicious . . . and they are vegetable dumplings." He knew that I was always weight conscious.

"Thanks, Dad." I was moved.

"I've got to go. Good luck on your exam." He smiled, patting my hands. I watched him walk away, disappearing in the fresh morning sun.

I took the test with great confidence. After I was done, I felt a bit hungry and ate the two dumplings.

A month later, I received my test score and learned that I had passed it. Even now, I still think my father's blessings and the two veggie dumplings did the trick for the exam.

Years later when my daughter Janis was four years old, my father visited me and stayed with me for a few months. At that time, I was working at a college in downtown Detroit, and I had to leave home early in the morning. So, I asked my father if he would walk Janis to the nearby nursery school. He agreed and took her to the nursery school every day.

"Grandpa, that's my sweater."

One crisp morning when the forsythias were blooming, Dad and Janis held hands, walking toward the nursery school. Dad saw a red sweater on the sidewalk a few steps ahead. Holding Janis's hand, he tried to pass the sweater without stepping on it.

"Grandpa, that's my sweater," Janis alerted my dad, trying to pick it up from the sidewalk.

"No, no, don't pick it up. Some kid might have lost the sweater!" He held Janis's hand tightly and walked straight to the nursery school. Neither Janis nor my dad said a word about the sweater when they came home.

Dad walked Janis to the nursery school again the next day. They always followed the same route. When they were walking, they again saw the red sweater on the sidewalk, untouched.

"Grandpa, that's my sweater," Janis again reminded my dad.

"Well, I have an idea! The sweater is small, perhaps no one can see it. Why don't I hang it on the tree? That way when people are walking by, they will see it easily." He picked up the sweater and hung it on one of the branches.

Still I knew nothing about the sweater.

On the third day, when my dad walked Janis to nursery school, he saw the sweater still hanging on the tree, waving in the fresh spring air.

"How come no one claims this sweater?" Dad asked.

"Grandpa, that's my sweater." Janis raised her head and pointed to the red sweater waving on the branch.

"OK, Janis, why don't we take it home and show your mom? She will know if it's yours." Dad figured if no one had claimed the sweater, it might be Janis's.

After checking with me, Dad smiled and patted Janis on the head. "Sweetheart, you were right. It's your sweater!"

When the semester ended, Father left for California to visit my sisters, Min and Debbie, and their families. He had left fond memories with my children, especially Janis.

"Mom, when is Grandpa coming back?" Janis asked me one day.

"He'll be back soon," I said.

But he never returned. After staying with my younger sister Min for a few months, he decided to go back to Taiwan because he missed his old friends and his care-free lifestyle—dining, drinking, and playing Ma Jiang—killing time and enjoying his retirement.

Father died in 1983 of liver cancer. I went to Taiwan for his funeral. In the midst of the funeral, when the hall was jammed with friends and relatives, I cried my heart out. But then I looked out of the window and saw my father sitting above a cloud, smiling at me. I dried my tears and smiled too. Even today when I think of him, I can still feel him patting me on my head. I smell the two delicious dumplings and remember the story of Janis's red sweater.

The Green Beans

Theresa Shen

"Kids, do you know what we'll be doing this semester?" asked Mr. Chang, our Home Economics teacher, on the first day of school as he walked into the classroom and pointed to us. He was in his late twenties, medium height, and wore silver-rimmed glasses.

The room was quiet.

He then continued, "You're going to plant green beans. Each one of you will be assigned a parcel of land; you'll plant the seeds after digging and plowing the soil, then you'll water it frequently. By the end of the semester, the plant will have grown taller than you, and it'll be loaded with green beans. When that happens, I'll give you good grades and you will take the green beans home for supper."

His lecture was so exciting that the kids nodded and smiled knowingly, but I didn't have a clue.

"Don't worry, I'll help you," whispered the little girl sitting next to me when she saw muscles wrinkle my face.

I looked at her. She was my age, a 4th grader, with jet-black hair, dark brown eyes, and long eyelashes. She was very pretty, but wore the ugliest overalls I had ever seen. When I looked around the room, I noticed that my other classmates were wearing similar outfits.

I smiled back and said, "I'm Lan, what's your name?"

"Cui Xia."

Lessons in math, reading, and calligraphy followed the Home Economics class. By 3:00 p.m., the school day had ended. When I went home, my mom greeted me at the door, "How was school?"

"It was okay, except Home Economics class. Our teacher, Mr. Chang, talked about planting green beans, digging soil, and something, but I couldn't grasp what he meant."

"Well, you'll know later," said Mom, a woman in her thirties, with a beautiful complexion, straight white teeth, and soft hands because she never had to worry about cooking and housekeeping. My dad was able to provide her with a fairly comfortable life before the Communists took over Mainland China.

My dad, who had a prominent position in the Chinese government, sensed that something bad was going to happen, so he said to my mom one day after dinner, "You'd better go stay with your sister, Ching, for a while. When the situation gets better, I'll send for you."

"What about you?"

"I'll stay here for a while; if the situation gets worse, I'll leave Nanking."

So, my mom, my siblings, and I left our home with a couple of servants and headed for Babu, a small town located east of Guiling in Quanxi province. We were all to stay with Auntie Ching and her husband, a high-ranking government official for the whole region. My mom knew that the local citizens would treat us with great respect, so life wouldn't be too harsh for us even though we had to change our lifestyle.

When we first arrived in Babu, we felt as if we were lost in the wildness. The citizens of Babu were very provincial. They spoke a different dialect and dressed differently; boys and girls all wore shirts, pants, or overalls. Looking around the neighborhood, I didn't see one girl wearing a dress or skirt.

One day, I was playing ball with our maid in the plaza near our house. It was a beautiful spring day. The wind blew gently. The birds warbled in the branches; some butterflies flew back and forth. We were having a great time. All of a sudden, about ten girls burst into the plaza and surrounded me. Several of them pulled up my shirt, trying to find out what was underneath it. I was scared to death.

Fortunately, my maid, who was in her teens, rescued me.

"Get out of here, you rascals!" she yelled at them as she chased them away.

A few days later when I went to school, I discovered that some of these rascals were my classmates. That made me apprehensive about

The Green Beans

further attacks, and I felt uncomfortable about my clothes, too.

I was worried about planting green beans because I was raised in big cities, and my only interactions with green beans happened at the dinner table. Our servants from time to time would serve a dish of green beans for supper.

That night before going to bed, I asked Mom, "Mom, what does it mean to plant green beans? Mr. Chang, our Home Economics teacher, said this morning that's his assignment."

"Don't worry, that's the silly stuff the country kids normally do; I'm sure you'll pick it up quickly."

I felt relieved and slept well that night.

The next day in our class, as soon as Mr. Chang walked in, he told us to follow him to the field where the assigned plots were. My classmates were excited about working in the field because most of their parents were farmers, and they were familiar with that sort of work. Besides, they loved fresh air and enjoyed working outdoors. As soon as we got there, I saw some farming tools and a bag of seeds lying on the ground.

"Kids, each one of you pick a hoe and go till the land. After the soil is loose, you'll plant the green bean seeds. Remember you must water and fertilize the soil frequently; otherwise, the green beans will die," said Mr. Chang.

My classmates nodded, seemingly grasping every word of Mr. Chang's comments. Only I was dumfounded. Mr. Chang left soon after he finished his speech.

"Let's go. . . ." My classmates rushed to pick up the hoes one after another. I followed them and picked the last one on the ground. I had never seen a hoe in my life, and I certainly did not know how to use one.

While my classmates were busy plowing the ground, I was standing on the side, watching them. Following Mr. Chang's instructions, they were doing the assignment with great energy and enthusiasm. Laughing and talking to each other, they were having a ball. Suddenly, my impression of those country kids went away; their knowledge and interest in farming were beyond my comprehension.

I thought, Mother Nature has taught them so many things! Looking back, I saw myself standing among them, wearing a beautiful flowery dress and a pair of patent leather shoes with the heels sinking in the mud. I felt embarrassed and out of place.

"Lan, do you need any help?" asked Cui Xia.

"Oh, yes." I was so grateful that Cui Xia came to my rescue.

Cui Xia grabbed my hoe and walked straight to the plot that Mr. Chang had assigned to me. She started digging. I stood aside and watched her with great admiration. After a while, another classmate called to her from a few feet away, asking her about something in the local dialect. I had no idea what it was about. She raised the hoe without looking, and at the same time I walked in front of her to get stuff from the classroom. Accidently, the hoe landed on my right hand between the thumb and index finger. It was bleeding heavily. Cui Xia was scared, and my other classmates rushed to see what had happened.

"Don't worry, it's an accident," I said, though it was very painful. I knew what would happen if the accident were reported to Mr. Chang or my mom. I didn't want Cui Xia to get into trouble because of me. The kids were also very helpful. They managed to wash off the mud with a pail of water that was supposed to be used for watering the green bean seeds. Then they bandaged my hand with a handkerchief to stop the bleeding.

"Oh, my God! What have I done? Lan, it must hurt badly," Cui Xia said.

"It hurts, but not much." I tried to comfort her.

The incident was never reported to Mr. Chang or my mom. When I went home after school, Mom asked me what had happened to my hand.

"I accidently tripped and scratched my hand."

"Does it hurt?" asked my mom.

"Yes, but not much." I replied.

That was the end of our conversation. After a few days, the wound healed, but it had left a permanent scar on my hand.

School went well. I got along well with my classmates. The teachers

The Green Beans

adored me, thinking I was a genius who read and wrote so well. My Mom no longer insisted on my wearing city-girl's dresses to school; instead, she had the seamstress make me two overalls that were similar to my classmates'. I was happy that I could experience something new. I loved school and my classmates, especially Cui Xia, who became my best friend. I helped her do math and reading; she managed my green bean plot and did the watering, fertilizing, and spreading of pesticides. I did small jobs, such as picking the undesirable leaves and trimming the side of my plot so it would look good.

Cui Xia and I often walked to school together. Being raised in the country, she was an early riser. Many times, she came to my house, waiting outside until I was ready, then we went to school together. Being a country school, classes started early, around 6:30 a.m. On our way to school, I often heard dogs barking in the distance or the heavy footsteps of the farmers on the unpaved streets.

It was a bit scary to me, but Cui Xia always said to me, "Don't be afraid. They are our guardian angels . . . the dogs and the farmers who have made Babu a safe haven for its citizens."

Cui Xia had a small family: mom, dad, an elder brother, and her. Her father was a farmer who grew vegetables and fruit; her mother kept the house, but sometimes also helped her husband work in the fields. Her brother, sixteen, studied at a nearby high school. He also helped his dad in the fields whenever he could. When Cui Xia came to my house to play or wait for me to get ready for school, she often brought me a bag of sweet potato chips for a snack. I always looked forward to her visits since my other siblings were occupied with their own business and seldom had time to be my companions.

Growing green beans was fascinating to me. After class, I went every day, alone or with Cui Xia, to check on my plant's growth.

One day I said to Cui Xia, "How come it grows so slowly?"

"When it's ready, the green beans will come. It just can't be pushed," said Cui Xia.

"When will it be ready?" I asked.

"I don't know. Mother Nature will take care of it," Cui Xia added.

I was totally lost; I couldn't grasp what she was referring to.

Time slipped by fast, a few weeks later, the green beans started growing. When the green bean stem grew too tall, we had to put sticks around it, so the plant would climb on the sticks. I didn't know how to do this sort of thing. Of course, I relied on Cui Xia's help. Soon, my green bean plant had grown as beautifully as my classmates'. Of course, that was Cui Xia's accomplishment.

Near the end of the semester, when the pods were laden with beans, my father came to Babu unexpectedly. He was able to escape Nanking just before the Communists invaded the city. We were overjoyed to see him. To our surprise, he told us that for our safety we must leave Babu as soon as possible. He felt that the Communists would soon take over Mainland China. My dad knew that he would not survive under the Communist regime. So, we rushed to prepare for leaving.

That night, I snuck to my mom's room and asked her, "Mom, what about my green bean plant? It has just started to grow green beans."

"Don't worry, Lan, you'll have plenty of green beans to eat later," said my mom.

"What about Cui Xia and her family?" I added.

"Don't worry about them. The Communists won't hurt country people as much as they would us," said Mom.

We left Babu in a hurry; I never had a chance to taste my green beans and to say goodbye to Cui Xia.

After we left for Taiwan, the Communists eventually took over Mainland China and I lost touch with Cui Xia. As years went by, I often wondered what had become of her, my other classmates, Mr. Chang, our teacher, and my green beans. My short stay in Babu inspired me to love nature and green beans.

"When the Moon is in the Seventh House . . . Let's Go Blue!"

Peter Banks

"When the Moon is in the Seventh House, and Jupiter . . ." an all-time classic, and even if you don't immediately recognize the lyrics you get the feeling, "This is the dawning of the Age of Aquarius" funky, groovy, heavenly, I get that feeling anytime the opening lines of Fifth Dimension's biggest hit begins. Even without the lyrics—that music, that melody, groovy is groovy man, I know it's not just me.

The New Year's Eve announcement of Jim Harbaugh as the new Head Coach of the University of Michigan football team though it's only been a few days and no official actions have been taken, (aside from the ultra-rare, jaw-dropping* sight of a Harbaugh smiling at a press conference), a heady, warm-fuzzy glow has taken over. That butterfly fluttery feeling you get deep down in the pit of your stomach, from the soles of your feet up to the hair on top of your head. Exhilaration, man. Exciting as puppy-love, or your first new car or . . . I don't know . . . Spring Break! That's the atmosphere around Arbor town right now, the sky is yellow (maize), the moon is blue, hell, Wolverines everywhere are inspired. Each and all, connected. And that excitement, that hopefulness is not misplaced.

Fifty Million Dollars!?!

Try $100 million, try a thousand million, oh wait, but what's the ROI, what's that really worth? Where's the value? What intangibles will this hiring affect? Recruitment, of course. Renewed national notoriety, yeah but those are givens, immediately impacted by his presence.

Let's go deeper, let's be economists, or at least think like they do. You remember, way back in college, freshman Econ 101, I was always impressed when the professor connected obscure and non-obvious dots between pork belly production and knee-sock sales in China, and somehow it all made sense. Okay full disclosure, the exact point of that analogy eludes me right now but the general lesson enters my mind on most days—there are always far-reaching consequences to every action. Big or small, every . . . always. The thing is that most repercussions remain hidden until they blow up in your face or knock you over the head, especially the non-obvious ones. Like that infamous butterfly flapping its wings in Tokyo somehow eventually affecting the weather in Detroit.

Seeing Jim Harbaugh, Michigan Man, step up to that podium on Wednesday brought me to the immediate thought that the most non-obviously gleeful segment of society right now must be the writers of the world. Journalists, advertisers, copyrighters. You can't make this stuff up, write it, or even think it. Certain stories just tell themselves. "This is the dawning of the . . ."

*pun, of course, fully intended

#HarbaughSongs (alternate takes)
Blue Bo You
Great Bo's Ghost
Everything Old is Blue Again

Uncle Wou's Time

Theresa Shen

"Let's go to see Uncle Wou," I said to Marianne, my best friend. We always ran to Uncle Wou's apartment after school since L'Université de Fribourg was a few blocks away from his home.

Snowflakes were falling gently on the ground outside Uncle Wou's apartment. A melody could be heard playing softly, Debussy's L'Apres-Midi d'un faune.

"Come in and have some tea, Marianne and Theresa," Uncle Wou greeted us when he opened the door. "Tea time" was always relaxing and enjoyable after a long day of classes.

A small breakfast table stood in the middle of the kitchen, covered with a creamy-peach lace tablecloth. Three sets of white china teacups and a dish of Swiss chocolate cookies rested on the table. The teakettle was whistling.

The afternoon sunlight streamed through the glass of the narrow window, warming the kitchen. A bowl of birdseed sat on the windowsill, ready to feed the unexpected visitors, winter birds.

We sat at the table to have our tea.

"How was your day? How is school?" Uncle Wou asked.

"It was okay," said Marianne.

Sometimes we talked about other things, such as our homesickness, our worries about exams, and our financial problems. He always listened to us attentively and encouraged us to go on fighting our hardships until we reached our goals in life. He always had faith in people and things. He was a great storyteller with a good sense of humor, and we loved to hear him tell jokes.

■■■

One day, Uncle Wou decided to tell us the story of his life. We sat in the living room. Painted in light beige, the same neutral color was prescribed for the curtains and sofas. The doors and bookshelves were in light brown teak.

The room took its elegance from a combination of Uncle Wou's favorite things—an oriental rug, two Chinese calligraphy scrolls, a seventeenth-century Swiss still life, and a set of drawings by Oudry of *Les Fables de La Fontaine* hung over the fireplace. The bookshelves were full of language books . . . Chinese, English, French, Russian . . . and books about horology. A clock in the shape of a woman's head was on the mantel, while a blue and white Chinese vase stood in the corner. A small candy dish, an ashtray, and a half-opened book were on the coffee table.

Winter light filled the space, changing the colors of the room throughout the course of our visit. Pippo, Uncle Wou's canary, sang in his cage, adding to the peaceful beauty of the room.

Uncle Wou explained. He was a linguist, an ex-diplomat, and a horologist. In the 1930s, he was an overseas Chinese student studying European languages at the University of Paris in France. He received his PhD in linguistics, specializing in Slavic languages. After graduation, he worked as a diplomat at the Chinese Embassy in Yugoslavia. In 1949, when the Communist party overthrew the Chiang regime, he was forced to leave Yugoslavia immediately.

"You know something, my best friend, Zhi-Hong, betrayed me. He wanted to turn me in the day after the Embassy changed color," said Uncle Wou. "But I believed in peace and freedom, so I left for Switzerland in a hurry. I started looking for a job when I arrived in Switzerland, but there weren't any available. After looking at my résumé, people would say to me, 'Monsieur Wou, you are overqualified for this job.'"

Uncle Wou's story continued. Disappointed and desperate from job-hunting, he soon realized that he must pick something else for a living. With strong determination, he locked his diploma in a suitcase and went to apply for a job in a watch factory. After several years of apprenticeship, he became a horologist. He designed clocks and watches and was honored as a member of the Swiss National Horologist Association—the only foreign-born member.

"When I lived in Switzerland, I became awfully sick and was hospitalized. Unfortunately, I suffered from a severe skin disease because I had accidentally eaten some contaminated food during the War," he said. "Luckily, I met Marie. She was my nurse and took great care of me. When I was well, we began dating. We fell in love and got married."

Uncle Wou always smiled when he talked about his love for Tante Marie, a kind, gracious lady, who was so good-natured that she never got mad even when he joked about her "half-cooked Swiss rice."

∎∎∎

Uncle Wou lived in Switzerland for the rest of his life, but his nostalgia never diminished. He would often say, "I wish I could go back to China and do something for the country, but when I think of Marie, I give up. You know, she would be miserable living in China; she doesn't understand the language, the culture, or the customs!"

∎∎∎

In 1983, twenty years later, on a snowy day, I received a letter from Tante Marie, saying that Uncle Wou had passed away—of heart failure. I had the fondest memories of him. I cried and cried.

"Mommy, would you like to drink some tea?" My seven-year-old son tried to comfort me with a cup of my favorite beverage. I stopped crying, hearing the teakettle whistling, the canary singing, and Uncle Wou's jokes. . . .

The Outsider

Theresa Shen

It was beautiful when I came in this morning. There was no trace of winter on earth. It was warm and comfortable; the air was pure and fresh. Yellow forsythias were in full bloom. Golden daffodils swayed with red pink tulips in gentle breezes. Robins chirped among the fresh green leaves, and squirrels played on the dewy grass in my backyard. I should have called in sick.

Sitting in front of a dumb computer in a stuffy, windowless basement, I dreamt of the world outside my metal-framed, box-shaped high-rise building. *My life has been going down the drain for the past ten years. Computers tell me what to do. I feel great distress when I make a careless mistake.*

Raising my head, I saw the heavy, dusty loose-leaf folders leaning against the bare wall, which blocked my mind as those tall, stern evergreens blocked the noise from Woodward Avenue in my neighbor's yard. *I can't stand reading those manuals, which as dry as roasted peanuts put me to sleep.*

I got up from the shabby, faded brown chair and walked towards the spot where I hid whenever I felt frustrated. The phone rang; Janet was on the other end of the line.

"Hi, Faith. It's gorgeous outside. I wonder if you'd like to have lunch with me."

"Sure, I'm so sick of the computer. I need to get out and breathe some fresh air." *Janet had rescued me from disaster. I was just thinking of getting a rock and crushing the computer into pieces when she called.*

"Where do you want to go?"

"Anywhere."

"Well, how about Hamtramck? You've been talking about going there for ages."

"That sounds great, but do you know how to get there?"

"Sure. I'll show you."

Janet was Polish. She had lived on the east side of town since childhood and was familiar with the stores and restaurants in Hamtramck. *I'm sure she won't have any problem finding a good restaurant.* Janet couldn't drive. I could drive but was terrible with directions. My husband always teased me that if I drove to L.A., I would end up in New York.

"I'll meet you at the guard station upstairs at eleven o'clock," she suggested. We tried to beat the luncheon crowd.

Janet and I were very close. We shared the same interest in art and music. She loved to travel and often brought me souvenirs from her trips. She also collected objects of art. Her chess and stamp collections were exquisite. During holidays, she sent me greeting cards or small presents. One Easter, she brought me a basketful of hand-painted colorful Easter eggs. My family liked them very much. Once I had an operation. She visited me in the hospital and brought me a handful of pink baby orchids. My roommate predicted that those delicate orchids would speed up my recovery. I left the hospital in two days.

After hanging up the phone, I checked my watch, which read 10:45. I fussed with items on my desk and tried to find something to do for fifteen minutes. But my mind was disorientated. I just could not do anything.

Going to Hamtramck was really exciting. I always liked Polish food and music very much. Polka, Chopin, and stuffed cabbages were my favorite. I even fixed stuffed cabbages at home but never succeeded. My children described them as gluey spaghetti sauce spread over leftover cabbages. I suppose I should learn some trade secrets before cooking ethnic food.

At 10:55, I put on my pumps, grabbed my purse and windbreaker, and rushed upstairs. Janet was already waiting at the guard station. She wore a red brass-buttoned suit paired with a white silk blouse and was chattering with the security guard when I walked in.

"You're on time." She smiled at me.

"I tried." I was always late.

Joe had the *Free Press* spread over his desk; a TV monitor stood on a stand next to his chair. He peeked at the monitor every few seconds.

"It's a nice day, isn't it?" he greeted me.
"Yes, it's gorgeous. I'm going out to lunch," I said, smiling.
"I wish I could go with you," he joked.
"Come and join us."
"No, I can't. Thanks anyway."

Janet and I left for the parking lot. When we passed the courtyard between Downtown Campus and my building, I noticed that the leaves had grown fuller and greener. Two or three sparrows hid in the branches, greeting each other with enchanting notes.

We reached my car. I first opened the door for Janet and then got in the car.

"I've got directions from my father," Janet said to me just before I turned on the ignition. "He said to take the Lodge to I-75, get off at Holbrook exit, drive straight on Holbrook for about two blocks, turn east, and then we'll see Zosia."

"It's so simple. I'm sure I'll find it."

We drove on the Lodge and then to I-75. The traffic was not as heavy as we expected. The sun was glistening in the blue sky, brushed with loose, thin, drifting clouds. I opened the window. A soothing breeze whistled with the passing cars, making me feel cool and relaxed.

I thought of a girl I met in San Francisco. She was from Battle Creek. She told me she missed the four seasons in Michigan. I thought she was stupid for thinking that way. I admired the warm climate and the greens throughout four seasons in California. I even tried to move there. The long, cold winter bothered me for years, but each spring I would forget all the headaches of shoveling snow on the driveway and my car skidding on sheets of ice. So, I remained in Michigan for good.

We got to the Holbrook exit quickly and then drove straight on Holbrook. After passing two traffic lights and an overpass, I saw the road in front becoming sloppy. I thought I was heading to another expressway and became nervous. My foot stepped on the brake. *I don't want to get back onto the expressway.* I immediately pulled my car to a small side street. No sooner had I made a right turn than I discovered that I had driven into a dead-end street.

"What am I going to do?" I asked Janet.

"Just make a U-turn and drive back to the street we just came from," Janet suggested.

I did what she said. We drove back to the same street. There were two big trucks speeding toward us. I quickly changed to the right lane to avoid a head-on collision. After driving about two hundred feet, I realized I was driving on a one-way street.

"Janet, what am I going to do now?" My voice trembled.

"Just go straight. Maybe you can turn at the next traffic light."

Janet had a calm temperament. She never got upset about anything. I followed her advice. All of a sudden, I saw a car with two blinking lights driving toward us. The driver signaled me to stop, but I was focused on the traffic light a hundred feet away. I didn't pay attention to him. I kept on driving.

"Stop the car!" He shouted.

The police officer got out of his car and walked toward me. He had eyes like a dead fish and lobster cheeks.

"Do you know you are driving on a one-way street?" he yelled as loud as a thunderstorm.

"Yes, sir." My voice was tight and trembling.

"Are you trying to get killed?"

"No, sir."

"Let me see your license!" he bellowed.

I handed him my license. My hands were shaking. His appearance frightened me. He grabbed my license and walked back to his car. I felt as if I had been attacked by an alien from outer space. His vehicle looked like a UFO.

Despite my protests, Janet opened the car door and ran to the officer's car while I sat in the car, waiting for her to return.

A few minutes later, Janet came back, looking optimistic.

"What did you say to him?" I asked.

"I just told him this is our first time in Hamtramck. We didn't know the street well. That's all."

"What did he say?"

"Nothing."

We waited there anxiously. After a few minutes, the officer came back. He looked humane and his tone of voice became softer.

"Where are you going?"

"Zosia, for lunch," Janet answered.

"Do you know how to get there?"

"No, sir," Janet replied.

"Follow me, I'll take you to the parking lot left of Zosia. Next time, just don't drive on a one-way street, okay?" He winked at me and handed me my license.

"Thank you, Sir."

We followed his car. After a couple of turns, we were right at the entrance of Zosia's parking lot. He beeped his horn as he drove away, smiling. Janet and I waved him good-bye.

We parked the car and went in. When I saw the faded sign, "Zosia," hanging on an old two-story red brick building, I was a little disappointed.

As I opened the door, Janet explained, "Zosia is in the basement."

"Oh, my God, I didn't know I was running from one basement to another." I laughed.

We walked down the stairs. The waitress seated us at a small table in the corner. The restaurant was dark even though the windows were open. There was no tablecloth, only paper placemats. Salt and pepper shakers rested on the table. The waitress wore a Polish costume with a red-checkered skirt, a white lace-trimmed apron, and a small cap.

"What would you like to order?" she asked us with a strong Polish accent.

"I would like a combination plate of kielbasa, pierogi . . ." I pointed to the menu.

"I prefer the pork chop with green beans," Janet ordered.

When we were waiting for our lunch, we talked about our experience with the police officer. We laughed wholeheartedly.

"I thought he was going to give you a ticket," said Janet.

"I thought so too. I was surprised he didn't. You know he scared me to death when he yelled at me. I have never seen anyone as angry as he was. By the way, if it were in Birmingham, the police officer would have spoken to me politely, but handed me a gigantic ticket," I said to her.

"I don't know why he changed his mind. Maybe that's the Polish courtesy to outsiders," Janet joked.

When we were eating lunch, Janet told me about Victor Hugo's *Les Misérables,* which would be performed at the Fisher Theater soon. She had seen the play in London. The acting was splendid; the music passionate. She suggested I see it at the Fisher.

After a while, the waitress brought our orders to the table. The combination plate was delicious, especially the stuffed cabbages. Janet told me the pork chop was very tasty. After tipping the waitress, we left Zosia in a hurry.

"We'd better hurry. I have to get that out." I thought of the printouts piled on my desk.

"Faith, what are you talking about?"

"Oh, Janet, I'm sorry. I didn't mean to rush you."

"Well, Faith what do you think about—"

"The lunch was scrumptious; the adventure was unforgettable. I enjoyed Hamtramck very much," I interrupted her before she finished.

We drove back safely. After saying goodbye to Janet, I buried myself in the windowless basement and started digging data from the computer.

The Story

Phil Skiff

    I have often wanted to describe the experience of writing. To offer some explanation for why writers think and act the way they do.

    But, I've found this pretty much impossible. Not for lack of words or eloquence, it's more because there is no such thing—an "experience of writing." Writing is not like an event or an activity where you can stand outside of it later, observe it objectively, and describe its outlines.

    I've been unable to separate from myself something that stands alone as the experience of writing. For me, it doesn't exist separately from the rest of my life. It's woven through it—impossible to tell where it begins and ends, and what the rest would consist of without it.

    From the outside, you, looking at the writer—if you've ever spent a little time around them—might be tempted to point to those times when writers attach themselves to a keyboard or notebook and spend minutes, hours, or days, pounding out words and sentences, paragraphs and chapters. You say, "That must be the experience of writing. What's it like?"

    Unfortunately, those manic times hammering thoughts into phrases feel more like reporting. Mechanical, much like digging a ditch. Except, there would have to be someone buried in that ditch—suffocating, screaming, the clock ticking on their life. Also, this buried-alive person would have to be someone you care for. More than that—someone you love. Who loves or hates you in return. Someone whose life is inextricably bound to yours such that their death, if you don't uncover them, might be yours as well.

    What I'm trying to say is this "experience" extends far beyond those mechanical efforts. It's integral to your existence, never absent, whether awake or asleep; when you're doing other things people would call your "life." There it is. You never escape it; you're never apart from it. It never stands alone.

I know this must all sound like exaggeration, mystique, perhaps even petty self-importance. I can assure you it's not. It's much closer to obsession, maybe even disease because often it feels like illness—physical and mental.

The horrible, briefly wonderful cycle includes times where it makes you sick, tormented, and praying for release from it. There are other minds, other lives, with their own unique and separate agendas—dwelling inside you. Sometimes, it can be unsettling.

Melodrama, you say. Yes, it sounds like it. Feels like it too. Even looks like it when the writer gains a brief appalling view of themselves from an outside eye.

People often attach the word "creative" to this process, but that somewhat distorts the truth. "Creating" sounds like you're building or making something that didn't exist before. In writing, the writer is rarely, if ever, conjuring something out of thin air. The writer often feels as if they're unearthing something that already existed. They are "discovering."

Think of painting a picture—applying individual formless colors and lines to a blank canvas resulting in a brand-new image. In contrast, the writer often steps up to a substantially complete picture. But, they can only dimly perceive it—some is visible, the rest hidden, covered. As if someone had dashed a bucket of paint over the top of a masterpiece. You can see vague shapes, bolder outlines. It evokes emotion, but you don't really understand why yet. The writer then takes up a rag and begins laboriously wiping away the barrier between themselves and what is there underneath, yearning to be known.

This is actually a frightening process. You fear losing sight of what is hidden before you can reveal it. And like the earlier metaphor, it's not an inanimate object you're striving for—it's alive. And you're responsible for it. And to it. You fear your skills won't be adequate to reveal a true and clear representation of it. You fear your resolve will falter and it will become yet another accusing, condemning voice in the chorus from the pile of unfinished starts all writers have.

You fear it will despise the final result of your manic labor. You fear you will kill it, or worse yet, disfigure it such that it emerges, not as its true self but a hideous caricature of what it should have been.

Call this thing, this lover, this fiend, this possessing demon, "The Story." It's alive, but you didn't make it so. It's more powerful than you, and you don't control it any more than you own it. Any attempt to force it to go anywhere, do anything, contrary to its predestined path, is to afflict yourself with misery.

As The Story is alive, so are the Characters of The Story. They aren't you, but you share the same body, the same experiences, the same feelings, the same torments. You live their lives and want them to live yours—though they never would. They have no love, no concern for your life. But much as you desperately want to, you can't sever yourself from them. You love them, you desire them, you hate them. They suffer, you suffer, they die, and you die.

So, I understand. If anyone had described it to me like this, before I experienced it myself, I'd have laughed—probably been embarrassed for them.

But, just the same, The Story consumes you. You and your life are its meat, its wine. In the process of this consumption, the supposed "real" world you live in fades to hazy black and white, hollow meaninglessness. All the while, The Story thrives and grows, vivid in Technicolor, rich in texture and emotion, pregnant with possibility.

It can reach a point where you're genuinely at a loss to determine which is real. At the peak, the world you live in seems one-dimensional. Just like a page in a book. You won't even acknowledge the other fear—that in fact The Story is real. And you are not.

This is impossible for me to explain any better. Much less understand. Those that live in close proximity to writers might recognize the symptoms. They deserve your sympathy. They perceive the writer's agony, tolerate their moods, try, without success, to sympathize with their struggle—but it isn't their own. For them it's a burden, a price they pay for whatever benefits they might obtain from a relationship with a madman.

The writer, on the other hand, is tormented by their inability to explain or convey their state, their situation—the "experience" that causes them to be the way they are. All their words, their dictionary minds, their delicate phrasing, their imagination, their passion—all of it is useless, impotent, derelict to even sketch a picture of this space. This "experience of writing."

Yet, The Story remains.

The Amethyst Adventure

Theresa Shen

"How about going to visit an amethyst mine with me since it is nice and warm now?" John asked me when we were sitting at the kitchen table sipping afternoon tea.

"It sounds great!" I knew John was a fanatic about stones. And I adored amethyst, its color and texture. Imagining I could grab a huge piece of amethyst similar to ones displayed in a museum or a jewelry store, I became excited,

"When are we going?"

"I have the whole trip mapped out. We will leave on May thirteenth and return on the nineteenth. On the way, we'll visit some small towns in the Upper Peninsula and Canada. I heard there are several interesting small towns around Lake Superior.

"Oh, that sounds fun. I love small towns." I often meet simple, friendly people in small towns and also enjoy local arts and crafts.

On the first day of our trip, John loaded everything we would need in the car.

"It might be cold in the U.P.; we better bring our winter coats," he said just before starting the engine.

"You think so? It's spring!"

"You never know what could become of us if the temperature drops."

We each grabbed a snow coat. We stuffed them in our car and off we went.

Driving to Mackinac City was smooth with light traffic. We arrived there around 9:00 p.m. and stayed at Hamilton Inn, which was the most popular hotel in town. The next morning after breakfast, we stopped at the park facing Lake Huron. John picked up a few small stones on the beach while I checked the novelties in the gift shop. We then drove across Mackinac Bridge and headed to Sault Ste. Marie. We stopped at the observation deck facing the Canadian side.

"I was in charge of the project when I was with ENGA; my colleagues and I flew here to check the site and flew back the next day," John told me.

"That's great! How come you never mentioned it?"

"I did."

"Oh, really!" I didn't want to admit that I was forgetful.

The observation deck looked aged and depressing, but I still took a few pictures of John standing in front of it before we continued our journey.

John kept driving while I listened to the radio and ate snacks.

Before reaching the Canadian side, John said, "There are a few interesting small towns around Lake Superior and on the Canadian side. We might stop by to visit some."

"Which town do you have in mind?"

"Wawa."

"Oh," I immediately filed that name in my head. *Wawa sounds like a native Indian word. I'm sure I'll see lots of Indians and their arts and crafts.*

We kept driving and passed a few small towns. They didn't have hotels or motels, just one or two gas stations on the dusty roads. The sun was going down soon; I was a bit apprehensive. *Where are we going to stay tonight?* John sensed my concern.

"Don't worry; we are close to Wawa. If you want, we'll stay there tonight."

So, he kept driving until we reached there. As soon as we got in town, we saw a sculpture—a big black and white bird stood on a big stone, facing the road with its mouth wide open. I could almost hear the bird shout, "Wa-wa." *Oh, that's what it means!*

It was getting dark and we were hungry. We decided to stay in Wawa overnight. John looked for a motel, but there wasn't one in town! He had seen a good-looking one outside of town, so we drove there to check.

After one minute, he came out and told me, "We can't stay here; all rooms are smoking permitted."

I'm a lung cancer survivor and certainly wouldn't want to be buried in a smoking room.

The motel owner told John to check on another motel. We did. When the young lady at the desk wanted to show us the room, she couldn't get the door open. She tried a few times, but the door was still locked. A couple of young men who were smoking outside the room came to help, but still, the door refused to open.

"Well, thank you Miss, but we better try another motel," I suggested.

We went to the Bristol Motel, which was next door to the stubborn one and smoke-free. The manager gave us a room on the first floor. It was very tiny. It had one double-bed and a small, crowded bathroom. The towels were old, dark brown and maroon.

"What are we going to do? You either spend a night here or sleep on the street," John said as he observed the expression on my face.

"What a room! I'll stay here tonight for sure!" I said, hoping to ease John's peace of mind.

We were hungry. For dinner, the motel manager suggested the Viking Restaurant across the street. We went there. I had pickerel; John had fish and chips.

"The pickerel is so fresh and delicious. Is it from the lake?" I asked the waitress when she came to serve dessert.

"Oh, yes. The fisherman just got it from the lake this morning." She smiled, pointing to Lake Superior.

We spent the night at Bristol Motel with good humor. The next morning before checking out, I asked the lady manager, "Are there a lot of Indians in town?"

"Not a lot, but a few."

"What do they do to make a living?"

"They do small jobs here and there."

"Does 'Wawa' have anything to do with the Indian language?"

"No. In this town, everyone is a fisherman," she replied pointing to the relic on the upper right side of the wall. "I caught that one. It's a pickerel or walleye. Americans call it walleye," she added.

The Amethyst Adventure

When we walked out of the Bristol, it suddenly dawned on me that women as well as men are all "fishermen" in Wawa.

We were heading to Thunder Bay where the amethyst mine is. Unexpectedly, as soon as John started the engine of the car, "Wa-wa!" Two big Canadian geese flew toward the lake as a gesture of goodbye.

"What an adventure!" I felt good that we stopped in Wawa.

We arrived in Thunder Bay around 7:00 p.m., but the mine had closed at five. So, we spent the night in a hotel and planned to visit the mine the next day. John found a Comfort Inn, much more expensive than the ones in the U.S.

We then drove to downtown to see the city, but there wasn't much to see. The city was still in the developmental stage. We didn't want to get lost in the industrial park, so we drove back to the inn and tried to find a place for dinner. Across the street from the inn, I saw a good-looking, modern building named Mr. Chinese, glittering in the chilly evening air.

"Why don't we try this restaurant?" I suggested. I remembered the Chinese restaurants in Toronto were super.

"OK."

The interior of the restaurant was decorated with images of the soldiers from Emperor Chin Shi Huang's tomb. Wall hangings as well as posters on the wall were filled with terra cotta soldiers.

Since we both were tired and hungry, we ordered the meal as soon as the waitress, a young lady in her twenties wearing heavy make-up and glittering jewelry, came to our table. The menu didn't have many varieties. Most were chop-suey style Chinese food. We quickly picked something edible and washed it down in no time.

When we got out of Mr. Chinese, John said, "How depressing! We were having dinner in Emperor Ching's tomb!"

"That's why the food tasted so good!"

Early the next morning, after checking out, we headed to the amethyst mine, which was about a sixty-mile drive. When we got to Blue Point, we saw the sloppy, unpaved road, which would lead us to the mine. As John drove through, my heart palpitated. *All my excitement and dreams will come true now! I'll dig a big and glittering amethyst from the mine as soon as I get there.*

An old man in his seventies, wearing dusty old clothes, greeted us. While he was talking to us, I noticed a small, old wooden building along with a display table filled with pieces of amethyst. There were many blue plastic buckets scattered in the front yard. He gave us a brief history and his rules for picking amethyst from the mine.

"You can pick as many amethysts as you can, but when the bucket is full, you'll bring it back and give me twenty dollars, and then the amethysts will be yours."

"It sounds terrific." We thanked him for his instructions.

"The mine has a lot of iron, which often mixes with amethyst, so sometimes the crystal looks brownish," he added as we were heading toward the mine.

The mine was about a few acres large. It was an open pit mine, very sloping. The mine opened a whole new world to me. Amethysts, amethysts, big or small. Everywhere, glittering in the scorching sun. Wearing sunglasses and heavy leather working gloves, we both started picking and digging. After two hours of hard labor, our bucket was only half full. The man thought we might have gotten lost in the mine and came to search for us.

"Well, you're still digging? How're you doing?" he smiled and picked a tiny amethyst from the ground. "You should look for amethyst with crystal in it, like this one." He then threw that tiny piece into our bucket. "I'll be waiting for you when you're done."

We continued searching, digging until we were exhausted and not caring about what we found. We just threw a few stones in the bucket. We went back to see the old man and paid him $20.00. Then John loaded those odd-looking amethysts in his trunk and drove off.

"I hope you'll enjoy those amethysts you picked," the man said as he waved good-bye to us.

"We will. Thanks."

After entering the highway, John said, "What do you think of the journey to the amethyst mine?"

"It was fun!"

After the treasure hunt in the amethyst mine, we headed to Duluth, Minnesota. On the way, I noticed the mountains along the highway were made of rocks. I was impressed by their colors, black, reddish brown, or brown. When sunlight hit those rocks, the colors transformed into different shades. *How lucky are the Canadians to have such unique landscapes!* We felt happy and relaxed when we reached the U.S. border.

We then stopped at Teetegouche State Park and spent the night in Two Harbors, where hotels were jammed with Canadian tourists because of the Victoria Day weekend. The next day, we drove to Wisconsin and stopped at a store. We bought some cheeses and Wisconsin beer to take home for friends.

After Wisconsin, we headed to Houghton, Michigan. John kept driving on Highway 2. The driving was pretty smooth until John hit Highway 64. From far away, he saw a sign with "64." Without thinking twice, he immediately turned to "64," which dragged us into the woods.

The road was narrow, bumpy, and muddy. Broken branches were lying on the ground one after another. John kept driving for about twenty minutes; not a soul or car was in sight. When reaching the end of the road, we saw a big sign "The Bridge is broken, do not proceed." John stopped in dismay.

"Now, what are we going to do? Should we go back?" I asked.

"No, we must continue. . . ."

He ignored me and made a turn to another direction. He was pretty sure he would find the right outlet as long as he followed the sun. I didn't want to confuse him, so I kept quiet. The road had become scarier. Tree branches, big and small, were all over the road and in the woods.

John continued the journey for forty-five minutes. The road became wet, softer and muddier. The car splashed through water puddles, small or big, that spread across the road. Luckily, John managed to pass through safely until he hit the swamp. In no time, our car sank in the muddy water and stopped.

"Now, what are you going to do?" I became hysterical and yelled at him.

"I don't know. I have to go straight!"

"No, you can't. Look at the big swamp ahead. If you go there, we'll drown."

We thought of calling 911, but we forgot to charge our cell phones when we were in Canada. I imagined getting lost in the woods and spending a night in a swamp. *What would become of us?* Either wild animals would devour us in no time, or we would be bitten to death by the vicious mosquitoes, which have always been in favor of my blood type.

Thank God, John finally managed to get the engine restarted. He turned the car around and we headed back along the same route. Still, no soul was in sight. After more than half an hour driving, we saw a paved road and a truck coming. John pulled close to the truck and asked the driver for directions.

"Go straight and drive about five minutes, you'll hit Highway 64, but be careful when you're driving. It's dangerous," he said.

We thanked him for his advice. After a few minutes, we hit Highway 64 and John then saw the small print below the big letter "64," which said, "1/4 mile ahead." We realized we had been misdirected by the road sign.

The rest of the trip was safe and pleasant. We went to Houghton, visited Northern Michigan Tech University campus, had a delicious dinner at Ambassador Restaurant, and spent a night in Magnuson Inn. The next day we drove to Mackinac City and stayed there overnight. It was freezing cold in the U.P., no sign of spring. We were lucky that we had brought our snow coats with us.

On our way home, we stopped in Cross Village, Harbor Springs, where we had visited in 1965, and where John had designed *An Artists' Colony* for one of his graduation projects. The scenic drive along Lake Michigan was impressive. Miles and miles of trees, nodding to their quiet neighbor, white trillium, sometimes unconsciously carried us to another world.

After all the hassles, I felt John deserved a treat. We stopped at Bavarian Inn for dinner in Frankenmuth. We had their famous chicken dinner and enjoyed seeing the servers' costumes and the murals in the dining room.

We arrived home safely around 10:00 p.m. After unloading the luggage, John dumped the amethysts in our backyard.

"Why do you leave those amethysts outside?" I asked him curiously.

"I'll take some small ones, but the big ones are just stones, not amethysts."

My fantasy of bringing home a huge, shining amethyst has never become a reality, and I feel sorry for the stones left in our backyard unattended after we spent so much time, money, and effort to find them. But the journey to the amethyst mine was exciting and adventurous. We were lucky we survived after all our adventures. Imagining the hard labor of the miners, I now feel more respect for them than a piece of glittering amethyst in a museum or a jewelry store.

The Chairs

Theresa Shen

"Theresa, the chairs have arrived; I'm going to pick them up now!" John walked into my study while I was checking my email.

"Oh, really? Why can't we wait until tomorrow? It's snowing now; driving might be tough," I said.

"No, I have to get them today. The office closes at five; we need to get there," he added, looking determined.

"How are we going to take them home? Our car is too small for those chairs." I tried to make him change his mind.

"Don't worry, I've rented a truck." He smiled.

"You did? When?" I was always absent-minded about what he was doing.

"An hour ago."

So, I grabbed my heaviest snow coat, got in the truck, and off we went. Trans-Overseas Corporation was in Romulus, close to Metro Airport. Because of the wicked weather, driving was slow and slippery. Since John had never driven a big truck with no rear window, I was petrified the whole time and secretly murmured, "Alleluia, Alleluia . . ."

We arrived at Tans-Overseas Corporation ten minutes before it closed. It was hailing; the parking lot was very slippery and we didn't see a soul but cars. John had to find those chairs, so he went to the office. When he got out of the truck, he almost fell because he wasn't used to high steps. Luckily, his one hand held the doorknob; otherwise, I probably would have had to call EMS to rescue him. "Oh, my prayers worked," I murmured.

I waited in the truck while the engine idled. In about five minutes, John walked out with a tall guy, who loaded the chairs for us. Then off we went.

The return journey was even scarier. It was hailing heavily. And we got caught in a traffic jam. To hasten the windshield wiper and get rid of the ice and rain, John turned the heater on high. I was sweating in my heaviest snow coat, but didn't say anything to distract from his driving.

We were on Telegraph, driving slowly like a snail.

"I'm going to make a turn, would you check the right side for me?" John asked.

"Yes, I will."

The ice had covered the whole mirror; I couldn't see a thing!

After a few tries, John finally made a right turn on Maple. He then continued driving slowly until we got home.

It was dark, cold, and slippery on our driveway. John tried to back up, so unloading the boxes wouldn't be too strenuous. But without the rear window, he couldn't see. The truck skidded on ice and headed toward our garage.

"Stop, stop, you are going to hit our garage wall!" I yelled.

Thank God he heard me and stopped the engine; otherwise, we would have had to rebuild our aged garage!

I helped him unload the boxes one by one. Since there was no light in the truck, he passed the boxes to me. I then tossed them on the driveway without mercy. All I could think of was that my big fat snow coat and New Zealand wool hat had saved me from freezing to death. John then moved the boxes from the driveway to our garage and left them to chill in the cold while we went in the house to have a nice warm dinner.

After dinner, John said to me, "Should I open a box?" He smiled at me as sweet as ever.

"Why not? Haven't you waited for those chairs for three months?"

He rushed to the garage, brought a box into the house, and then opened it.

An elegant round chair popped out of the box.

"Wow, it's so beautiful. John, I didn't know you were such a good designer!"

John nodded and smiled.

He dragged the chair to the dining room and put it at the table.

"Oh, my God, the color is off. It doesn't match our dining table. Damn, they didn't follow my drawings!"

"Really? How come?" I looked and then said, "I thought you had the chairs made in the same color as our dining table."

"Yes, I did, but they ignored my drawing; besides, the legs are too thin compared to the arms."

"Well, what can we do now? Could we hire someone to refurbish them to match our table?"

"You're right. Maybe that's what we'll have to do."

"Would you like to see the cushions? I saw a box labeled cushions," I added to ease his disappointment.

"Sure."

He went to the garage and found that box. He quickly opened it and unraveled the wrapping for the cushion.

"Boy, bluish-grey cushions? Would I ever order that? I told them the color should be beige!" John's face turned red. He was angry!

"Well, you were not there. Maybe they thought that beige is bluish-grey. The cushions are well made, though." I added this little footnote to ease his pain.

He shook his head back and forth.

Looking back, I remember our "chair story." We had a beautiful round Danish dining table with a set of chairs. For some reason, John never liked the chairs. He said the chairs didn't match our dining table. He had searched for round chairs with no success, so he decided to design them. We'd had those chairs for over thirty years.

"The table is old; why not keep the chairs we have," I tried to discourage him each time he brought up the idea of designing new chairs.

"What am I going to do with these chairs if you design the new ones?" I added.

"That's easy. Give them to the kids. Those mid-century chairs are in fashion now and they are costly."

"I'm not sure the kids want them—they might end up in the garbage can or at a garage sale," I cautioned him.

"No, I'm sure they would like those chairs. They're free!"

The Chairs

Being a product of Cranbrook Academy of Art and an artist and designer by heart, he went on designing the set of chairs to match our aged round dining room table. He first thought of building them by himself, but he didn't have the tools and skills. So, he decided to look for a chair-making factory in China. Luckily, he found Shenzhen Ida Furniture Company, which had made chairs for Herman Miller.

John did the drawings and sent them to the company, negotiating back and forth for about three months. Finally, the chairs were made and shipped to us. It was a big joy to see his design become a reality; it was sad to know the tradesmen had not followed his design. We ended up having sixteen imperfect chairs and twenty wrong colored cushions. What a shame!

I asked myself, am I going to have fourteen square mid-century chairs and sixteen modern round chairs? I could hear them chat and fight for space with each other day and night!

"For my peace of mind, John, darling, would you design another big dining table to fit your round chairs?" I whispered to him, smiling.

Kitchen Lessons

D.M. Patton

When I was ten, and my sister, Audrey, was eight, our parents divorced. It was the summer of 1973. Divorce was still considered a shameful event, especially for us Catholics. I was in 5th grade. As my father was leaving my life, a new person was entering. It was the first time we met June, our maternal grandmother; she was fresh out of prison.

No one told us, but quiet children like me were often ignored. Adults would forget I was in the room and would talk freely without regard to what I might hear. I was nine, but I could read at a college level, and I knew a lot more than I allowed them to think I knew. My mother was having difficulty with money. When her mother needed a place to stay, my mother allowed her to live with us—"with strict conditions."

My grandmother never wanted us to call her *Grandma*, *Grandmother*, and certainly not *Nanna*. "Call me June," she said. "That's my name, so use it." I thought June was a pretty name. But my mother wouldn't allow it. In her mind, children were never to address adults by their first names. We were taught to call adults *Mr.*, *Mrs.*, or *Miss*. Close friends of the family could be *Aunt* or *Uncle*. My grandmother and mother fought over this distinction, leaving my sister and I confused. Ultimately, we learned how to appease both. We called her June when we were out of earshot of Momma.

June lived with us for about a year. She and my mother often argued. Audrey and I listened to the details through our closed bedroom door. There was to be no discussion about Asbury Park. No discussion about her being in prison.

"What the hell do you think I am going to do Linda, corrupt my own grandchildren?"

"You tried to corrupt Cathy," my mother would say. Cathy is my mother's younger sister. I called her Kandi. At the time, Kandi didn't seem corrupted to me. "These are my rules. My house, my rules. Remember when you used to say that to me?" my mother would ask. And my grandmother would back down.

I wondered why June didn't cuss my mother out like everyone said she would. June was known to have a sharp wit and a sharp tongue. What puzzled me most about their relationship was how they spoke to each other. I wondered why my mother seemed to oversee June. Audrey and I were never allowed to talk that way. We were never allowed to speak to any adult in anger. It was as if she was not the daughter, but the mother. It would be another three years before I understood.

Soon after June moved in with us, she found a job cooking for a wealthy family in Grosse Pointe. She took us to work with her one day. The lady of the house said we could play in the backyard. But Audrey wanted to play in the front yard. It meant trouble for all of us. The police were called. Grandma shuttled us out of the house and drove home cursing and yelling about us not following directions. By the time we got home, both Audrey and I were in tears. We didn't understand all the fuss.

My mother was furious that June would put us in danger. The year was 1972. Five years after the Detroit Riots. The city was still on edge. June moved out shortly afterward. Audrey and I wondered if we would ever see her again.

Shortly after, my mother lost the house. At the time, I did not understand homelessness. However, I knew enough to know that the constant moving was not normal. Each time we needed to complete forms at school—name, address, emergency contact—I didn't know what to write. I had memorized our old address and could sing it like a song: *Seventeen five eighty-five Roselawn, Detroit, MI 48221*. So that is what I wrote. But I knew that was no longer where I lived.

It made me feel ashamed not to have an address. When the school started to get the "return to sender" mail, they called my grandmother June. I had put her as the emergency contact. June had me memorize her phone number in case I ever needed her. My mother was furious. She made us memorize a new address: *Sixteen Twenty-seven Burlingame* and the phone number *Townsend five oh nine one oh*.

"That is your Aunt Cliffie and Uncle Kenneth. That number has been the same all my life and I don't see it changing anytime soon," she said.

We moved house-to-house. We lived at Aunt Cliffie's home and shortly afterward moved to my great-grandparents' home. It must have been frustrating for my mother. The lovely and fun mother I knew had turned into a dull and lifeless person. She seemed to always be working. When she wasn't working, she was sleeping. For the sixth-grade school year, she sent us to live with our father in Connecticut. We stayed for a year.

When we returned to Detroit, Momma was living with June and June's new husband, Micky. He was two years older than my mother and very proud to be a factory worker at Ford. He didn't say much to us. Clearly, June was in charge.

We stayed for two school years. June believed in three square meals a day. She made us breakfast before school. Scrambled eggs, bacon, toast, omelets. She never asked us what we wanted and I didn't care. She packed us wonderful lunches, and dinner was always ready when we came home from school. June was a wonderful cook. I was so happy to eat, I just said thank you, Jesus, because I wasn't always hungry anymore.

Despite the food, it was horrible living in June's home. No one seemed happy. June and Micky fought. Momma and June fought. Momma and I fought. Audrey and I fought. I escaped into a world of books. June belonged to the "Book of the Month" club. And, I think it saved my life. I read everything. I wasn't allowed to sit on June's white sofas, but I was allowed to read any book I wanted.

So, for two years, that's what I did. I ate delicious food and read captivating books. I read everything and learned about life. I read poems by David Frost, Erich Segal's *Love Story*, Fredrick Forsyth's *The Day of the Jackal*, and Richard Bach's *Jonathan Livingston Seagull*. I read Kurt Vonnegut, Maya Angelou, Anaïs Nin, Wayne Dryer . . . whatever I could get my hands on. I discovered the world through the eyes of Toni Morrison's *The Bluest Eye* and in novels by Donald Goines and Iceberg Slim.

Kitchen Lessons

At the end of eighth grade, my mother, sister, and I moved into our own home again. It was nice, just the three of us. But I felt like I was in a vacuum. All the worlds that were so readily available to me through books were taken away. After reading novels like *Pimp* and *Trick Baby*, the novels assigned by my ninth-grade English teacher, Mrs. Guynan, *Catcher in the Rye* and *Of Mice and Men*, seemed dull and uneventful. But the worst part was the food. I missed my grandmother's cooking.

Audrey and I begged our mother to allow us to visit June. At first, I didn't understand why our mother wanted to keep us apart. After weeks of begging, our mother relented and arranged the visit.

I think my mother allowed us to go that night in the hopes that I would learn to cook June's signature curry dish and then June would not be the only one that knew how to make it. I saw her give June the look. Clearly, they'd discussed this.

But in true form, June did and said exactly what she wanted. Without any regard for the opinions of others. She was a "let the chips fall where they may" type of person. She didn't mince words and she was loud about it. So very different from me. Somehow, I seemed to be her favorite. She never showed me her ugly side. But I knew it was there. I listened to the stories. I was in awe. I wanted so much to be like her. To say what I wanted and to have people listen to me. Fear me. Adore me.

Throughout that evening, I finally understood my mother's concern. It wasn't that June was a physical danger to us. I think my mother was afraid of what June would say. And she had a right to be apprehensive. That night, under the guise of teaching me to make curry, June would tell me all the shocking details of her life.

My mother dropped us off at June's house. It was Christmas time. June would watch us while my mother was shopping for gifts. I knew this wasn't true. My mother never bought us Christmas gifts. We learned that after the divorce. We never expected anything from her. And we had not had a babysitter since I turned eleven. I wasn't sure what was going on, and I didn't care. Someone who thought I was special was going to teach me the secret to love.

Audrey and I held hands as we walked up the porch stairs to June's home. She opened the door. She had been waiting for us. Her home was sparsely furnished and smelled of cinnamon, and onions, and garlic, and chitlins. They smelled so good I almost wanted a taste. Almost.

"Grandma, are you cooking chitlins? I thought we were making cookies!" Audrey said with her arms opened wide for a hug. June scowled at her. Audrey ignored the scowl and hugged June's legs. Audrey never cared if people loved her. She was going to make them love her.

"I thought I told you not to call me that. June. My name is June. And we are not making cookies. We are making chicken curry. The chitlins are already done. I can't tell you all my secrets. They won't invite me to anything else."

Chicken curry, I knew, was the key to making people love you. No matter what June said or did throughout the year, she was always invited to any family event that involved food. The food was the thing that kept our family together. It was the solution to everything. When Uncle Lloyd came home from the Vietnam war, we had curry. When Cousin Suggie came home and said she was marrying her white biker boyfriend, Beard, we had chicken curry. When Great-Grandma Geneva, June's mother, became a Christian after years of being a heathen, we all celebrated with chicken curry. And every holiday, especially Christmas, we ate chicken curry.

We hung our coats, removed our shoes, and went straight to the kitchen. Everyone in the family agreed that June was the best cook. Unlike her daughter, my mother Linda, who could not. Audrey and I suffered through numerous disasters—slimy okra, gray-green spinach, lathery liver, and burnt Rice-A-Roni to name a few. I started cooking for my sister and me as soon as I was tall enough to stand on a step stool to reach the stove. It wasn't good, but in comparison to my mother, it was gourmet.

When I saw June's kitchen, I was amazed. There were huge pots and utensils hanging from the ceiling. She had cutting boards and frying pans, five different kinds of potato mashers, and colanders, etc. All things I had read about and seen pictures of in catalogs, but never up close. Our kitchen at home consisted of three pots, one cast iron skillet,

Kitchen Lessons

a muffin pan, and a rusted cookie sheet. I whispered to Audrey, "This is what makes her the best cook, all this stuff."

"Stuff?" June said. "This is not stuff. These are cooking utensils; these are pots and pans. These are what every good cook needs in her kitchen." She proceeded to name all the items in the room.

"I am hungry," Audrey interrupted.

June scowled at her. "Your mother didn't feed you?" She opened the fridge. It was filled with food—milk, and cheese, and eggs, and containers filled with things I could not name. "You like ham?" she asked. Audrey simply nodded. For once even she was speechless.

June sighed. "No wonder you are both so small. I've told Linda over and over, children need to eat real food to grow." She made us both chicken sandwiches on thick crusty bread, piled high with ham, red onions, lettuce, and tomatoes. I didn't like onions as a rule. But we'd had oatmeal for breakfast and lunch, so we didn't complain. It was the best sandwich I had ever eaten.

"Audrey, you can watch TV in the living room. Take these cookies with you, but don't make a mess on my couch," June said. Audrey was happy to be out of the kitchen. Cooking and cleaning were work, and she wanted nothing to do with it.

June sat down at the kitchen table and poured herself a drink. Scotch on ice. It was the same drink my grandfather liked. I knew they divorced when my mother was a child. But my mother was tight-lipped about anything to do with her family's past. I knew she had something she wanted to say. I had lots of questions too. I relied so heavily on Audrey to speak for me that I had no idea how to break the silence.

June's hair was licorice black and curly, clipped close to her head like a boy. I noticed her hair was the sleek glossy kind like my mother and sister. Not like mine. Mine was embarrassingly red; fine, spiraled coils that needed to be pressed straight with a hot comb.

Her appearance was different from me in every way. She was tall and shapely, while I was small and flat. She was wearing black stirrup pants and a black turtleneck. She had high cheekbones; mine were unremarkable. She was a goddess. For a long time, I thought she and Lena Horne were the same person. Audrey and I had a big fight about it until my mother intervened. June didn't look like anyone's grandmother. She didn't look like my grandmother.

"Your mother warned me not to tell you my story. But you ought to know it. You have a future. I don't want you to be like me."

She was speaking directly to me and not Audrey. I was flattered. Like June, my sister is the beauty of the family. She had chubby cheeks and hair that curled into perfect ringlets with water and a finger twirl. A brown Shirley Temple. She looked like my mother, who looked like her mother. Different shades of brown, perfect noses, straight teeth, and strikingly beautiful. I, on the other hand, was small, with a chipped tooth and short unruly red hair. June was talking to me, and I was fascinated. I wanted to be just like her. Beautiful, and smart, and vocal, and the master of her signature dish, chicken curry.

She pointed to a cupboard instructing me to get a bag of onions and potatoes. "I heard you have a good memory," she said to me in a voice different than the tone she used with my sister. When she talked to Audrey, she was direct, curt, to the point. When she talked to me, her tone was softer. Inviting. But I said nothing. I simply nodded my head.

At fourteen, I knew the power of words, but I was most comfortable with the power of silence. I knew speaking allows people to label you. Audrey was vocal. She was labeled *charming*, *conniving*, and more often than not, *a liar*, and *exaggerator*. She would say anything necessary to get what she wanted. My labels were *strong* and *smart*, and that is how I liked it.

June, however, was never short on words. She barked out orders for me to start prepping the vegetables. "You know how to use a knife?" she asked me as she lit her cigarette. The kitchen table sat under a window. The shade was drawn, but I was sure it looked out over a beautiful backyard. June positioned her chair against the wall and leaned back crossing her legs. Her bright red lipstick left a stain on the glass and her cigarette. I nodded.

"Look. Let's get something straight. If we are going to get along, you have to talk. When I ask you a question, you need to answer in full sentences. You can't go through life nodding and shaking your head. People will think you are an uneducated idiot. That catholic school you attend is expensive. I am sure those nuns have taught you the Kings English. Correct?" She gulped down her drink in one swallow and looked up at me with one brow raised. "That's a question."

"Yes, ma'am. English is my favorite subject. I am going to be a writer one day," I said in a voice so small I wasn't sure she heard me. June snuffed out the first cigarette and poured herself another drink. I heard stories that she was a mean drunk. I didn't know exactly what that meant. My mother and all of the adults I knew never drank around us. The concern must have shown on my face. June scowled again at me and my heart skipped.

"The smoke bother you?" she asked

"No ma'am."

"Don't call me ma'am. It was almost Augusta because I was born in August. But my father didn't like it. He preferred June because that was the month when they met. He was Indian. From Pakistan. He taught me to cook. It was a horrible experience, but I am thankful for it now. They tell me you have a photographic memory. Is this true?"

"I don't think so. Momma says I can't remember from the living room to the kitchen."

June burst into laughter. It was the first time I remember seeing her laugh. It was an honest laugh. She seemed genuinely amused. "That is what I used to say to her."

She instructed me to retrieve a huge, orange-colored pot from the cabinet. I never saw a pot so big and heavy. The lid had a wooden knob on top and the words *Le Creuset*. I asked her what the words meant.

"Le Creuset. It's a Dutch Oven made by the French. It's heavy because it is made of cast iron dipped in enamel. If you promise to take care of it, you can take it home with you. I know Linda is too cheap to buy one."

In the sink lay a whole chicken, headless, but with feet. She handed me a knife. I tried to follow her instructions, but she finally lost patience and cut it into pieces herself. She instructed me to cut the vegetables, green pepper, onion, and garlic. Audrey peered into the kitchen, making sure she didn't miss anything. June ignored Audrey and took several jars of spices from the cupboard. I was in tears from the onion. Audrey scurried back into the living room without saying a word. I knew she was afraid she would have to work. Audrey liked to eat, not cook.

Following my grandmother's instructions, I poured oil into the pot. The spice jars had no labels. I asked her how did she know which spice was which. She raised an eyebrow and pursed her lips tight. She opened one of the bottles and waved it under my nose. I remember it smelled like the woods and sweat. I must have made a face because she smiled at me. Finally.

"This is cumin," she said. "Essential to any good curry mix. I don't need labels because I can smell. And this is clove, cinnamon, coriander, nutmeg, allspice, and turmeric." As she named each spice, she let me smell it and add it to the hot oil. The individual spices soon became one, and the kitchen came alive with their aromas. I felt so important standing on a stepstool next to the stove. I concentrated on carefully stirring the spices in the oil while June talked.

"When I was your age, my father showed me how to make this dish. He said it reminded him of home. It doesn't remind me of home. Home for me was a rundown shack in Virginia. We never had enough food. I was skinny as a rail, like you." She gave me a disapproving up and down look.

"I was smart like you. But I never had any hope of going to school. I wanted to go, but we were poor. My mother could not even conceive of me doing anything but cooking and cleaning. She was a hateful and jealous woman. I was smart. When I was about fourteen, and her man friends started noticing me, she sent me up north to live with her aunt and uncle. That's your Aunt Cliffie and Uncle Kenneth. Kenneth was her brother. He had found a good paying job in the Ford factory. I am sure she was relieved to have one less mouth to feed. It was right after Sweetie died."

"I don't know Sweetie," I said.

"Sweetie, Kathleen. She was my older sister. She died in a car accident. My momma was inconsolable. She kept asking why it was Sweetie and not me that died that day." June's voice trailed to almost a whisper. "Anyway, the next year, here in Detroit, I met your grandfather, Herbert. My first husband."

"You had more than one husband?" I asked. We were Catholics. All the women I knew had one husband. My grandmothers, aunts, even my friends' mothers.

"Of course. And you should too. Don't limit yourself. You live in a different time. You don't have to marry at all. Anyway, at fourteen, I came to Detroit. A year later, I met Herbert. A year after that, I got pregnant, got married, and your mother was born. The year was 1942," she said with almost no emotion. Her face and voice were expressionless. It was like she was reading the newspaper. "When the spices bind together and look like mud, this is good. This is what you want. Smell that? That pungent smell? That's good."

We added the vegetables, onion, bell pepper, garlic. June continued, "By the time he came back from the war, we were no longer the same people. It was 1945, and I had spent the last three years raising Linda all by myself. I found a job at the grocery store. I was the first black cashier in the city. Mostly because they didn't know I was black. Your mother was dark like Herbert. I kept her out of sight. But when Herbert came home, he wouldn't hear of it. He didn't want me to work, and he didn't want me to pass. We broke up. He kept Linda and moved in with his mother. I went to New York."

"Is that why Momma grew up at Grandma Watson's house, not yours?" I asked. I was feeling bold. I was taller now on the stool and June was confiding in me. She trusted me. My grandmother was the first person who spoke to me like I mattered.

"Yes, but that is another story for another time," she said. "Today is about you. I want to make sure you don't make the mistake I made. I was smart enough to be a doctor. But, I found out what men were willing to pay to be alone with me." She gave me the eyebrow again. I was sure I was supposed to understand what she was talking about, but I didn't. I nodded my head anyway. "You read the newspapers?" she asked. I nodded. "Good. You can learn a lot from newspapers," she said.

She took the chicken from the sink and placed the pieces in the pot. The spicy oil sizzled and my stomach grumbled. It smelled wonderful and I was hungry. She smiled at me. "You know why I was in prison?"

she asked. I shook my head. "Solicitation. Do you know what that word means?" she asked. I shook my head again.

"That's the third time you didn't answer the question." Her voice this time was sharp. Was this the June I had heard so many warnings about?

I didn't want to know, so I quickly said, "No."

She instructed me to bring her the dictionary from the bookshelf in the living room. Audrey was wrapped in a blanket on the couch. She had fallen asleep watching Lawrence Welk on TV. I never understood why she liked that show. It always made me sleepy. I found the book and went to the kitchen table to look up the word. *Solicitation.*

June was adding water to the pot. She continued to talk. "Bring the whole thing to a boil, and then you turn the heat down. Put a lid on it and let it simmer till the chicken is done. About an hour. Your mother should be back by then. The pot will still be hot, but I have a box for you to carry it in."

I read to her, "Solicitation: 1: the practice or act or an instance of soliciting; especially: entreaty, importunity. 2: a moving or drawing force: incitement, allurement."

June sat down at the table with me. She looked me in the eyes and spoke in a soft voice. "I made good money. When I was growing up, I wanted to be a doctor. I was smart enough, but I was also born with multiple strikes against me. I was a woman, half black, half Indian—Pakistani, not American. I learned quickly that I did not have the means to go to school. I didn't want to be just a housewife."

She continued, "Looking back, I am not proud of what I did. I should have made better choices. But, I liked to party and drink. I made enough to live in a big home with lots of nice things. I could pay for your mother to attend the most expensive school in the state—enough for them to forget she was black. When any of them were in trouble, they called June to help them pay their way out. No one had a problem with my choices until the money stopped flowing. Only then did they get righteous."

I didn't really know who "they" were, and I wasn't clear on what she was alluding to, but as she continued, I eventually caught on. I had read enough adult novels and romances to figure out the details.

I was glad I finally knew the story my mother did not want us to know. And as a Catholic-educated girl, I knew my grandmother was not the type of woman who would be welcome at the PTA meetings. But I found her story fascinating. I held no judgment. She was my grandmother, and she not only loved me, she liked me. She thought I was smart. She thought I was important enough to save. She warned me to stay in school. Graduate from college. Make something of myself. I gave her my word that I would.

When my mother found out what June had told me, she was furious. She liked the curries I made. But her mother's past was something she did not want to discuss. She swore me to silence. And so, I was silent. Never revealing the truth. Until my children were born. I have told them the stories with more detail than they wanted to hear. But I felt they needed to know.

June was a complicated woman. Throughout my high school and college years, she popped in and out of my life. Mostly holidays and my birthday. She bought me clothes my mother could not afford. When I was in college, she bought me food and cookware. And she continued to show me how to feed myself. How to love me. She gave me advice on men and relationships. To me, she was more mommy-like than my own mother.

She is gone now. But I will always wonder what could have been for her. I find comfort in knowing that despite her shortcomings, she loved me. And she gave me the confidence for me to love me too.

POETRY

Radiator Poem

Anthony Stachurski

Though love is beautiful,
as is *amor,*
in love, any word will do.
I *kettle* you, my dear.
I'm falling in *cement.*
See! It works!
I'm in the mood for *hubcaps,*
the breathless *hub*, the force of *caps,*
the liquid *s* that makes her blush.
Love succeeds with any word
if it's meant.

Imagine this:
full moon on a summer night.
In a garden, jasmine blooms.
You embrace and kiss,
then whisper in her ear
the words she longs to hear:
Oh, my *propeller*, my sweet, sweet,
briefcase.

The Basement

Anthony Stachurski

Going in is frightening, at first.
The dark can make one turn and run,
and be undone.

It's cold and damp down there
with fetid smells of sin and sex.
There may be ghosts expecting you,
to tell their stories and regrets.
There you'll find the root of all despair,
pain and shame, hostilities, the reason
for your fears, your wasted years,
lies, and more lies, cover-ups,
causes and effects.

There will be glints of light
like streaks of silver in a mine.
What you find will humble you
and bring you to your knees.
I could tell you what it is,
but you need to find it for yourself.
Besides, all Truth is intimate: you'll want
to be alone.

All you need to know is down below,
where everything above is understood.
Be afraid or not. But go.
It's what you wanted, right?

Shopping at Ralph Lauren

Anthony Stachurski

They were an old and homely couple.
It seemed strange to find them browsing
in a store like this with funky hip-hop music
in the air.
She was wearing purple nylons and a short skirt
even though her legs were bowed.
He was bald and slightly stooped and wore
a golf shirt and baggy, green pants.
Under the fluorescent light, they seemed so basic
in appearance, unmiraculous, the last
of the human batch, proof almost
that there was no God.

I thought of the experiments of Stanley Miller
and imagined the two of them naked in a flask.
It would be humid inside, a little lightning and thunder
still crackling over their heads,
traces of methane stinging their eyes.
She would walk over and touch the glass repeatedly
to test its reality, then shed the first human tears.
I'm sorry, Margaret. her husband would say.

Here, try on this blouse, sweetheart. You'd look so nice.

The Way

Anthony Stachurski

No one ever did a thing for you, you say.
And now, you'll do the same.

Kung Fu had to deal with a man like you,
who did not love his neighbor as himself.
To a man in need, he would not share his bread.

Kung Fu looked out at the line
separating the earth from the sky.

That must be a hard way to live,
he said.

Wonder Woman

Anthony Stachurski

What does it take John?
A UFO landing in the back yard?
The blonde next door gardening
in the nude?

It's a beautiful day. The birds are singing.
It's spring. The sky is wild and blue, and you,
you're still lying on the couch as if
there were nothing to do.

Did you know that butterflies taste
with their feet, John?
that dolphins sleep with one eye open?

Of course not.
Look, let's do something new!
We'll go up on the roof tonight
and count the shooting stars.

Or go down to the zoo;
the howler monkeys raise all hell at ten.
I'll wear black lipstick and my tightest jeans,
then hurry home and ground ourselves
in wonder once again.

Flower Girl

Anthony Stachurski

Over here! Look at me!
See how pretty I am.
Do you like my dress?
It's just for you.
I've caught your eye, haven't I?
Otherwise, you wouldn't *bee*
buzzing around me.

You think I'm sexy when I sway?
You men are all alike.
By the way, I know your name.
But don't worry, I won't tell your wife
that you're in love with me.

Did you know that I was sent here
just to flirt with you?
To be your flower girl?
And don't you just adore the smell of my perfume?
It's called *Divinity*; it drives men wild.

So, take a guess who sent me here.
You silly goose! Did your parents buy you
at a baby shop?
Look, sweetheart, I come from God.
If *little ol' me* can steal your heart so fast,
just think what She can do.
Anyway, you'd better go;
some friends of mine are dropping by.

Stop by later if you'd like. But come early;
the weatherman's predicting frost tonight.

Water Lilies

Theresa Shen

We buzz to and fro,
not hearing warblers chirping in early spring,
cicadas singing during a summer night,
raindrops dripping from quiet eaves.

Day and night we strive,
hanging onto fragile things,
feeling lonely,
holding our breath,
in fear of being snapped by a toothless mouth.

We seek peace,
softness and gentleness,
like morning dew lingering upon water lily petals,
clinging to our distant mothers' hands,
and embracing their blessings,
we buzz to and fro.

Dandelion, Dandelion

Theresa Shen

Dandelion, Dandelion, you are strong and stubborn,
standing on my lawn and smiling at me as if you were in control.
I want to kill you and dump you in a trash can,
but you refuse to go.

You die today but live tomorrow.
Immortal
Prevailing in wind and rain.

You nod at me like a king after the sun has crowned you in gold.
You order me to surrender and I do.
I lose the battle in despair
but soon you cheer me up.

Starting your day with fresh thoughts and new dreams,
you continue upward.
I try and
become strong and stubborn like you.

Men on the Beach

Anthony Stachurski

Conch shells jut from the beach
like old men's ears

as driftwood twitches in the breeze
lifting the thin, gray strands of seaweed
from their shoulders.

With each receding wave
slips glittering away
the fortunes at their feet.

All day the wrinkled caves suck
at the shore drooling down
the corners of their vowelled mouths

as the dolphins leap
with their curious smiles
out of the blue, insatiable sea.

Desert Queen

Anthony Stachurski

She sleeps outstretched in sheer moonlight
Beneath the dim tiara of the sky, her crown.
Nearby, a dozen motel towns like campfires burn
As shotguns boom across the dunes.

The tall saguaros love her so
And guard her loyally, though old, demented,
Stupefied with gin, too drunk to even flay
The bats away.

Now tire marks scar the land.
Shattered bottles glint like fallen stars
Along the trail.
Coyotes prowl among the gray bouquets
Of prickly pear, and owls,
As if down halls and out of broken doors,
Glide and disappear
Over the rubble of early morning clouds.

The Friars of San Francesco

Anthony Stachurski

Nearby the church Saint Francis built,
the Friars harvest olives on the trees.
Beneath the warm, November sun
they laugh and sing, inspired, as water gushes
from a rock.

Just now, I long to hear somebody shout
Ho, Brother Anthony,
to feel against my skin the poverty of cloth,
to rest my little ladder on a branch and also sing,
a small, brown bird of God.

White Clouds

Anthony Stachurski

The clouds were glorious today,
billowing as if Someone were pouring
vats of paint onto the sky.
What talent! What a show!
And when the sun broke out,
I was blinded with the beauty of it all,
knocked off my donkey-self
and filled with mighty awe.

But others weren't looking, just walking on,
talking, texting, waiting for the traffic light to change.
Not one person fainted and had to be revived.
Not one fell to his knees to pray, or sing,
or weep with joy.
Not one cared! *The clouds—what about them,*
they'd say.

Had they no eyes for the splendor of the sky?
No hands to applaud the greatest Artist of all times.
No desire to go Home.

Maple Leaves

Anthony Stachurski

My father loved Windsor, Ontario, Canada,
especially for the opportunity to lay floors
and work on the assembly line at Fords.
And taking odd jobs because
he enjoyed raking leaves and painting houses
and meeting a wide variety of rich people.
And, to him, the simple, austere life of a carpenter
was noble, almost religious.
He enjoyed worrying because it kept him thin
and mentally occupied.
When on vacation from work, he would read
the want ads to improve his English or stand
at the window to watch the cold October winds
blow the Maple trees bare to the bone.
He especially liked his walks to the unemployment office
down the streets paved with gold.

Truth Seekers

Anthony Stachurski

They've given up—that old couple
in folding chairs having the garage sale,
Truth Sucks printed on their matching t-shirts.
On a card table, all that's left is a crucifix,
The Dialogues of Plato, a faded Rubik's cube.

He's nursing a beer and reading the biography
of Jane Mansfield.
She's smoking e-cigarettes and making faces
out of the clouds.
They're tired and don't look well.

Everything now is a quarter, or best offer.

Winter Scene

Anthony Stachurski

Ponds stare at the sky
like the eyes of dead fish.
Red Dogwood stains the snow
like frozen blood.
The creek is twisted into ice.
The marsh—in ruins again.

Soon the night will shift
its spotted turtle's back.
The Crab will crawl
across the starry-graveled sky.
The ground will stir again
with the tiny plans of ants.
Come spring, the earth
will bear her jelly mass,
scattering leaves and stars overhead
with a tail's wag,
as if that was that.

Frozen silence now.
Only the Ironwoods speak when they sway,
bending and groaning in the North Wind
like the slow grinding of teeth.

Ursa Major

Anthony Stachurski

Night after night, the Bear lopes south across
the frozen tundra of the sky, stalking us.

No screaming, running, back doors slamming shut,
only his face, forming like frost on the windows
of each house.

There's been no blood or threatening displays, as of yet,
nor has he ever growled, but of his reputation and legendary tales,
we know too well.

Still, we lie, as fangs of icicles glisten in the moonlight,
as high winds shoulder the door, and tree branches claw at the house
wanting in.

And the clamor in the kitchen, paws slipping on the tiles,
stars knocked off the shelves, the sky heaving, creaking
under his weight.

Or is it just fear, wild imagination, or the cold, suspicious noises
of a winter house?

Then silence and relief, as he slowly moves on down the street,
the stars softly crunching under his feet.

Morning Walk

Theresa Shen

Enchanting morning sun, peeking through wavering leaves,
foretells the coming of a beautiful fall day.
Gusty wind blows mercilessly,
trying to chase summer leaves off the branches.
Falling maple leaves etch prints on the dew-wetted earth,
heralding the arrival of a new season.
Two robins chat on the lawn, bidding farewell to their last stop.
A black squirrel, proud and jolly, walks across the road,
ignoring those blithe folks.
A lonely old man, walking with his dog,
tips his hat in greeting as he passes along the friendly earth.
Noble, elegant, hardy mums in a neighbor's garden nod their
pearl petals and gold hearts to greet me.
Pink fragrant roses wave in the morning breeze
in the front yard, waiting for my return.

The Great Equalizer

Theresa Shen

Walking on a snowy day.
Snowflakes drifting,
draping the drowsy city with dazzling whiteness,
silently sifting, shrouding streets, sidewalks, and shingles,
evening the uneven.

Pedestrians pass.
Drifting snow tosses lacey flakes
on ladies' fur collars, men's cashmere coats,
and shivering street-wanderers' ragged clothes,
equalizing the unequal.

Small Grass

Theresa Shen

Small grass's tiny steps chase the hideous winter away
Gentle wind shakes budding leaves
Robins, cardinals, blue jays sing and dance
Squirrels hop on the wooden porch
Haughty deer stroll in the backyard

Feeble age hits me like winter's ragged hand
Rough wind shook my youth away
Dreams and ambition crushed long ago
Shall I live and draw sweet dreams
till a new life comes and my sorrow ends?

Politico

Peter Banks

. . . and I,
carving art from premonition
can barely perceive
the difference between
truth and fiction

can they coexist?

Bogus and brilliant
simultaneously.
When what whiffs . . . ?
Does one man make a difference
twisting ignorance,
                into irony?

   . . . when I,

carving art from premonition

                barely exist.

SHORT FICTION

A Lucky Girl

A.J. Norris

I was angry as I boarded the plane then settled back in my first-class seat. Unfortunately, as the plane took off and reached cruising altitude, my fury was *almost* overshadowed with a sweat-inducing mild nausea. I gripped the arm rests like a baby monkey holds onto its mother for dear life. In other words, my hands were going nowhere.

Looking over to my right, I faked a smile at the blue-eyed man next to me. He had a friendly enough face. The knuckles on my "vice grips" had turned white. He glanced down at them. It seemed like he wanted to say something from the look of his furrowed brow, but a flight attendant stopped at our row, interrupting his thought. He raised his chin which caused me to follow the line of his vision.

"Would you care for a refreshment?" she asked, recognizing from years of experience how anxious I was. She returned shortly with a rum and diet coke with a lime twist. "First time flying?"

With the glass up to my mouth, I said, "No." This surprised her, but she simply nodded her head, patted me on the shoulder, and moved on.

The plane made a sudden lurch and I swallowed hard. The flight attendant was forced to grab hold of the back of another passenger's seat. Blue-eyes next to me recoiled a bit. I'd heard myself grunt softly as more turbulence shook the plane but was unaware the sound had been audible. I swallowed again then licked my lips.

"I hate flying," I said, rolling my eyes at myself.

"Can see that." His tone wasn't teasing or even sarcastic, instead there was understanding. My pre-flight wrath slipped and was slowly being replaced with mild irritation. "Would it help if I told you a story?" He paused probably because of the look on my face. "I mean to pass the time."

"Uh huh. What's it about?"

"Hmmm . . . how I met my wife."

I sat up straighter; this I had to hear. He chuckled at how I'd prepared myself for listening—sitting up straighter, pushing my hair behind my ears, and taking a sip of my drink.

"Ready?" He raised his brow.

"Yea," I cocked my head. As he began to tell his tale, I traced the outline of his face with my eyes. He was undeniably handsome, but ruggedly so; not too perfect, just right. His eyes sparkled as he described being in Vegas just a few days before being deployed to Afghanistan. There had been a club he and his buddies had wanted to check out. I rolled my eyes as it turned out to be a strip joint. We laughed as he tried to tell me he didn't know where they were going.

"Sure, you didn't know," I chided him. He didn't deny it because he knew nothing he would've said on the subject could have mattered at that point. I didn't believe him.

"Okay, okay," he said with his palms up in surrender, "I may have had some idea." I pursed my lips and nodded my head with my eyebrows raised. The story was helping to calm my nerves, or maybe it was just the drink.

He paused to smirk then continued, ". . . then this girl walked in and, *oh man*, my heart stopped. I didn't even know what day it was anymore."

I shook my head. "Stop, no way. How's that possible?"

"It's true. Okay, but my world *did* come to a stand-still," he conceded.

"So love at first sight?"

"Definitely," he turned and looked past me out the window—his eyes distant. As he turned to look forward again, his eyes raked over my face for a moment. Heat made my cheeks flush. And then, the now niggle of irritation I'd had was gone. I was suddenly more nervous for a reason other than flying. The plane jerked, causing me to white-knuckle the arm rests again. The captain came on the intercom and asked the crew to take a seat until we were clear of the turbulence. Taking deep breaths did little in the way of calming me, so I downed my beverage. As I drank, I watched him take a deep breath then run his hands through his thick hair. "You don't want to hear this," he said while staring at his hands.

"Please, finish the story," I pleaded; anything would be better than listening to the blood that pounded in my ears. "What happened after you met?"

"We talked as we walked the strip. Didn't even care anymore about seeing the sights, gambling, none of that. It was like she was the only reason I'd come to Vegas."

I snorted but smiled.

"What?" he asked as he crinkled his forehead.

"I just . . . well . . . really? You think she felt the same way?"

"She must've because I asked her to marry me."

"And she said yes," I said as a statement, not as a question.

"Yes," he nodded emphatically.

"She must've been out of her mind." I rolled my eyes and smirked.

"Yes," he grinned, clearly proud of his wife.

I listened to his words about how much he loved his wife and how each day he tried to do something unexpected to remind her of how unpredictable life and love can be. When he was done, I had tears in my eyes, which threatened to spill over. Handing over a napkin, he smiled then chuckled when I blew my nose. I batted his arm lightly. He clutched it feigning injury.

"You liked my story, I take it."

"Uh huh, she's really a lucky girl to have you."

"You think so?" He gestured dismissively with a wave of a hand.

After the flight, I was standing at the baggage claim carrousel and felt the heat of someone standing close behind me. By the scent of his after-shave, I could tell that someone was lucky girls' husband.

My black Samsonite made its arduous winding journey around to me. I announced the bag's arrival under my breath. He leaned forward and yanked it up by the handle, but he didn't put it down. There was a burgundy suitcase already at his feet with the pull handle sticking up. "Um . . . thank you, kind sir," I joked.

Then he slowly winked at me and said, "Let's go home."

Sleeping Single—PART 3: Winter Diversions

Diane VanderBeke Mager

1:57 AM. I have got to stop falling asleep on the sofa. Every night, I convince myself I can stay awake for one more TV show. But deep down, I know I'm really avoiding heading up to bed alone. I need to get up in four hours.

Turning off the TV, I tell myself I'll go upstairs in a minute. . . .

2:32 AM. I wake. The three square windows above the sofa are filled with black winter sky, offering no solace. I rub my neck and climb the stairs in the dark, setting the burglar alarm when I reach the top. I take off my clothes, slide into bed, and roll onto my back to stretch. The outline of the ceiling fan comes into focus, and I remind myself to wipe down the blades before my dust allergies trigger. Better re-address the mold growing in the shower grout as well. I felt my nose starting to twitch this morning.

I close my eyes and contemplate counting sheep. Instead, I count down the months until Dean graduates. He already has some leads on jobs in Europe, dual citizenship being his sole reward from my failure at marriage. Helping him move seems like a good excuse for a European vacation. Maybe I'll finally make it to the Highlands—

Ta-tap-tap-tap. Ta-tap-tap-tap.

My eyes fly open.

Tap-tap-ta-tap.

Shit, it sounds like someone tunneling with a pickaxe beneath the basement stairs.

I clutch my pillow and hold my breath, hoping the sound doesn't return. Lying perfectly still, I find comfort in the beam of light cutting across my silk duvet. But it disappears as clouds cross the moon's path and my room is plunged back into darkness.

Tap-tap-ta-tap . . . whirrrrr.

I pull the covers up higher.

Okay, get real, there can't be anyone down there, the alarm system would capture all unwelcome movement.

Maybe it's the water heater! The plumber warned me the build-up of sediment in the tank might cause it to start ticking as it expands and contracts.

I focus my gaze back to the moonlight, repainting and erasing its line across the bed.

What if I play damsel in distress and run next door, straight into the arms of my elusive new neighbor?

Wishful thinking—I have yet to get up the courage to introduce myself. When Bob told me their friend Jake would be house-sitting this winter, I had no idea it would be Mister-sexy-scruff-with-dark-glasses from that mortifying moment at my bedroom window last summer.

He seems rather aloof, but I think I caught him staring at me yesterday morning as he backed down his long, narrow driveway. I was shoveling the sidewalk, earbuds in my ears, jamming out to "Layla," my namesake song, when I felt his eyes on me. Probably my imagination ... more than likely he was just focusing on the edge of the driveway, trying to avoid driving on my lawn—a level of courteousness CeCe and Bob never manage to achieve. Either way, he didn't respond to my lame, snow-covered mitten wave.

Knocking on his front door after midnight while fleeing a basement intruder would certainly guarantee his undivided attention! The perfect "meet cute" scenario straight out of a 1940s *film noir*, when the leading lady and man finally come face to face.

2:42 AM. *Ta-tap-tap-tap.*

Pushing back my jitters, I opt to believe the plumber—and to maintain my dignity. But channeling the cinematic bravado of my favorite black-and-white movie *femme fatales* might just provide the perfect distraction to end my sleep-challenged night.

Closing my eyes, I dive into a new storyline. . . .

Tap-tap-ta-tap . . . whirrrrr.
The elevator jerked into motion, rising from the basement to the

penthouse apartment. Layna adjusted the hem of her A-line skirt and checked her red lipstick in the compact Mrs. Windemere had given her for Christmas.

Cecelia Windemere was a formidable woman and a fashionable New York hostess. She had engaged Layna as her personal companion nearly two years ago, when her husband, Major Windemere, was sent over to advise the Allies. After the war, he stayed to negotiate the terms of Germany's reconstruction.

Layna returned the compact to her clutch as the elevator doors opened to a private lobby. Her new stiletto heels struck the marble floor with precision, puncturing the silence.

"Good morning, Miss," drawled Eleanor, the latest housemaid. She smoothed her red hair before returning to her dusting, closely supervised by Cleeves, the butler.

Layna had noticed him supervising Eleanor with more than just household chores of late, but who was she to criticize? Stifling a sneeze brought on by Eleanor's ministrations, Layna handed her coat and hat to Cleeves.

"Today's post is already on your desk, Miss," he stated, nearly concealing a drawl of his own.

"Thank you, Cleeves. Is Mrs. Windemere in the breakfast room?"

"Yes. She received a telegram from Major Windemere. It appears she will be meeting him in Berlin next week."

"Berlin? Next week!"

"Yes, Miss."

Layna proceeded to her small office at the back of the apartment and closed the door. Berlin . . . in one week's time? She would be expected to accompany Mrs. Windemere. Refusing would be out of the question. What believable excuse could she possibly come up with? A sudden illness? A dying parent? Not particularly helpful, considering they lived in her native Berlin—not that the Windemeres had any inkling.

She needed to speak with Erik and Evangeline as quickly as possible. The von Eberts had been her handlers in America throughout and after the war. They would tell her what to do.

■■■

Layna steadied her breath. The plane would be taking off in a few minutes. No sense in panicking.

She crossed her slender legs, tightened her seatbelt for the umpteenth time, and turned to look out the window. Tiny flakes fell from the sky, a magical snow globe surrounding the city.

A man with dark glasses and a past-five o'clock shadow took the aisle seat. He unceremoniously stored his briefcase at his feet. With Mrs. Windemere seated in First Class, Layna had hoped to have the row to herself, alone with her guilt and regrets. She turned back to the window, intending to send a clear message of disinterest.

"Excuse me, I think our seatbelts are twisted."

Layna was forced to acknowledge the entanglement. She quickly unbuckled and re-buckled her seatbelt, returning her gaze to the morning snow.

"I'm Jake . . . Jake Mackenzie. Might as well introduce myself, seeing as we are going to be stuck together for the next eighteen hours."

"Layna Casey, nice to meet you." Better to be polite. People remember rudeness.

"Is London your final destination, or are you continuing on to the Continent?"

Damn. He wasn't going to let up. Keep the answers short and simple.

"Berlin."

"Me too. I was stationed there for a time." He flicked his lighter and lit a cigarette, inhaling slowly.

She smiled weakly and reached for her book, burying her nose in it until her seatmate appeared to doze off.

For the remainder of the flight, she watched as sunlight turned to moonlight and back again. After two stops to refuel, the plane finally landed in London. She avoided eye contact and grabbed her overnight case while Jake, her interfering seatmate, assisted the woman across the aisle with an oversized bag. Layna joined Mrs. Windemere and followed the gate agent's instructions to board their next plane. Several of the other passengers had been on the transatlantic flight, but none, including Jake, sat near her.

When they arrived in Berlin, Layna arranged for the taxi to the hotel, keeping an eye out in case they were followed. She allowed the hotel porter to help her with her own valise along with Mrs. Windemere's luggage. Best to act normal, just here with her employer for a brief visit.

The following morning, she came down to breakfast alone, wearing a crisp knee-length skirt and tailored jacket to mask her inner turmoil.

The waiter greeted her, "Guten Morgen. Folgen Sie mir bitte."

He seated her at a table for two, already occupied by a gentleman, his head immersed in the morning paper. Smoke curled from behind the pages. She ordered a coffee and placed her napkin on her lap.

The gentleman lowered his paper and exclaimed, "Miss Casey, fancy meeting you here!"

Jake Mackenzie folded his paper and continued, "Imagine that, winding up at the same hotel."

"How nice to see you again," *Layna lied.*

"Are you here on your own?"

"No, my employer is taking breakfast in bed."

"I see. And who might your employer be?"

"Mrs. Robert Windemere, of the New York Windemeres," *she answered. Stick to the truth as often as possible.*

She kept the conversation neutral, making a hasty exit after the waiter took down her room number for the bill. Knocking on the connecting door to Mrs. Windemere's room, she steeled herself for the day ahead.

"Come in, I am just finishing up on the telephone with the Major."

Layna took a seat at the desk and waited for Mrs. Windemere to finish.

Cecelia Windemere squawked into the phone, "Yes, yes, we'll be there at eight o'clock. Formal attire. No, no, you silly goose." *She cackled loudly.* "Yes, dear. . . . Goodbye."

She hung up the phone and turned her attention to Layna. "Major Windemere will be meeting us at the reception tonight. He is sending a car for us at seven-thirty. I want to wear the blue silk. You will be *accompanying me of course, but the Major and I will go on to supper with the General and his wife. You can take a taxi back to the hotel. I have some letters I'll need you to take down. Let's start with . . ."*

This went on into the late afternoon until Layna was given time to change into her long, fitted gown while Mrs. Windemere bathed. At precisely seven-thirty, they were seated in a dark limousine heading to the embassy reception.

Careful not to draw any attention to herself, Layna stayed in the background until the Windemeres made their exit with the General and his wife. Despite the crisp air, Layna decided to walk back to the hotel, the familiar moonlight tracing a pattern across the nearly unrecognizable cityscape. She turned the corner and bumped smack into a tall man wearing a dark overcoat and hat. Fear paralyzed her until she heard a familiar American voice.

"We really have to stop meeting like this. It's starting to feel like a bad movie," said Jake Mackenzie with a smile. "Can I walk you back to the hotel?"

Suspicious of these "coincidental" meetings, but left without a plausible excuse, Layna begrudgingly agreed. They walked side by side, her favorite stilettos skimming the cobblestones. Jake spoke of his childhood growing up in the Midwest. Layna fabricated one of her own. His cover was broken only by the subtle bulge beneath the upper left side of his standard, government-issue overcoat, made obvious in the glow of the streetlights opposite their hotel.

Layna attempted a quick departure in the lobby, but it appeared they were staying on the same floor. They rode the elevator in silence.

Jake paused on the landing. "I'll walk you to your room."

Allowing the ruse to continue, Layna led him down the hallway. She hesitated outside her door.

"Can I see you again? Tomorrow afternoon?" he asked.

"I'm sure Mrs. Windemere will be needing me."

"Tomorrow night then?"

"I'll have to let you know," she stalled.

"Okay, you can leave me a message. I'm in room 502."

Jake inserted her key in the lock and bid her goodnight. Leaning in to kiss her cheek, his lips lingered, brushing her neck.

Grateful to be alone, Layna climbed into bed and fell fast asleep.

■■■

Ring-ring. Ring-ring. *The familiar twin tones of her former life woke her from her slumber.*

"Alena, meet us at the annex in one hour."

"Erik? Is that you? What do you mean, meet you? Are you and Evangeline here . . . in Berlin?"

"Not over the phone. One hour."

Layna dressed quickly, suspecting her past and present lives had finally collided.

■■■

Layna raced up the stairs, too impatient to take the elevator. She pounded on Jake's door. It swung open and she nearly fell into his arms.

"Layna . . . what's the matter?"

"You have to help me. I can't go on like this. Erik and Evangeline are going to turn me in if I don't get them what they want."

"Turn you in? Turn you in for what?"

"They'll call it . . . murder."

■■■

Layna took a seat in a bentwood chair on the opposite side of the thick marble column at the center of the café. They were easy to spot, seated in a plush booth, Erik von Ebert's dark, tailored suit in stark contrast to his wife Evangeline's golden hair.

Within easy earshot, Layna heard Erik order another coffee. His polite demeanor turned harsher as he proclaimed, "Alena will bring the documents. We will be across the Swiss border by nightfall."

A coffee cup clattered as it returned to its saucer. Evangeline asked haltingly, "And what about the child? Layna is never going to agree to leave him behind again."

"Alena will do as she is told. The child is none of your concern. Keep your mouth shut and stick to the plan," he replied. A newspaper rustled as the page turned.

At precisely half past nine, Layna pretended to enter the café. She took a seat at their table as instructed.

"Do you have the papers?" clipped Erik.

"Yes, in my purse."

"Take them out and hand them under the table to Evangeline."

Jake rounded the column, sat down on the bench next to Erik, and slid the nose of a pistol from beneath the folds of his newspaper.

"Stand up . . . both of you," he motioned to Erik and Evangeline. "We're going to take a little walk . . . nice and slowly . . . toward the rear exit."

Erik and Evangeline did as they were told. Layna followed the trio into the alleyway and stood beside Jake.

"Alena, what is the meaning of this?" sputtered Erik.

Keeping his gun pointed toward the von Eberts, Jake enlightened them, "I'm with the FBI espionage unit. The two of you have been on our radar since the war began. When you moved to New York, I was assigned to track all three of you and to intercept your messages. Layna—or Alena as you insist on calling her—shared the details of your latest mission with me last night. I am not about to let you get your hands on U.S. government plans."

He continued, "I give you credit for positioning Layna inside the Windemere's household, believing she could acquire the Major's access codes. But the jig is up. Your blackmail scheme is over. Tricking a desperate mother into abandoning her own son is beyond the pale."

Jake held Layna with his eyes, before turning back to the von Eberts. "And now you're going to tell us where the boy is. Layna will retrieve him while we take a ride to the embassy. I have a car just around the corner."

Erik shifted his weight and pivoted, pulling Evangeline in front of him.

"Don't get any ideas, I've had plenty of experience with spies like you and I'm not afraid to use this," *said Jake as he aimed the gun at Evangeline's heart.* "I'll give you one more chance to tell us what we want to know."

"Potsdam. Einstein's Turm," *whispered Evangeline.*

"The observatory tower! I brought Dirk there each winter," exclaimed Layna.

"It looks like we're all going for a ride," said Jake as he maneuvered them down the alley. "Get in the car."

Layna got behind the wheel and Jake took the seat beside her, facing the rear, his gun pointed toward Erik and Evangeline in the backseat.

"Alena, be realistic. What are you going to do once you have the boy? You'll never make it out of Berlin. Do you think your high-and-mighty Windemeres are going to help you once they find out you killed Dirk's father in cold blood?" hissed Erik.

"It was self-defense von Ebert, and you know it," said Jake.

"Is that what she told you? Did she come to you after our meeting last night with some sob story about the downtrodden wife putting an end to years of abuse? He was a soldier. He fought bravely for our homeland, and she killed him . . . killed him in a fit of jealous rage."

"Jealous, what does Layna have to be jealous about?"

"His mistress. The woman he had on the side while she was at home with the boy."

"Layna . . . Layna, is this true?" asked Jake.

Layna stomped her foot down on the accelerator, hugging the winding curves. She blurted out, "He was a miserable, miserable man. He deserved everything he got."

Eyes staring straight ahead, she resumed without emotion as if repeating a well-rehearsed soliloquy, "I found the note—marking the page in the book I had asked him to read. She'd thanked him for the weekend, reminiscing on how he had fallen asleep with his head resting gently in her lap. I went to the kitchen and got the knife. He was asleep in our bed. I plunged the knife into his heart . . . again and again."

Layna increased the speed of the car and her words, "When it stopped beating, I chose a clean set of clothes from the dresser drawer, took a long shower, and gathered up Dirk's belongings. . . . He was just a toddler, asleep in his crib. We took the train to my sister's. It was her husband who suggested I meet the von Eberts . . . 'A nice couple. They will help you get away—to America,' he told me."

She glared at Erik and Evangeline in the rearview mirror. "I trusted you, and you betrayed me. You got me to Washington and promised Dirk would soon follow. After a few years, you convinced me to move to New York with the Windemeres, and still no Dirk. It's been five years . . . five years since you took me away from my boy. For five years, you've held that one night over my head, threatening to notify the authorities if I refused to do your bidding or ever set foot in Germany again."

Layna fell silent. The sky darkened and snowflakes descended. She released her two-handed grip on the steering wheel to turn on the windshield wipers and heat.

Tap-tap-ta-tap . . . whirrrrr.

The icy blades bounced across the glass as the warm air forced its way through the vents.

"Layna . . . we're going to have to come up with a plan here," said Jake, wiping his brow with his handkerchief. "It was a moment of passion. . . . You can't be held accountable. We'll say he threatened to take your boy and you—"

Erik interrupted, "Don't listen to him Alena, just give us the papers and Dirk is yours. . . . He's waiting at the tower—"

She pressed the accelerator closer to the floorboard, approaching the curve at breakneck speed. . . .

■ ■ ■

The front wheels hit a patch of ice as wide as the lane, sending the vehicle into a spin. The car veered off the road, careening into a grove of purple beech—forever carving their fate into the waiting branches.

Layna collided with the steering wheel, the whiplash snapping her smooth neck in two. Erik and Evangeline were thrown from the car on impact, coming to rest in a tangle of limbs. Jake climbed his way out of the carnage, to the edge of no return.

A soft blanket of white snow covered their sins by nightfall.
THE END

Saudade

Phil Skiff

Fisk stared at the coffee cup in his hands. It had the logo of a bank, common in Phoenix. A thousand miles from here. It was stained and spider webbed with brown cracks. Fisk watched a dribble of coffee chase itself around the bottom as he rolled the cup between his hands.

Across the battered kitchen table, Angela sat. Her brown hair hung in ropes around her face, dark circles under her eyes. One hand was wrapped around a full cup of coffee, its contents long cold. The other rested on the edge of the table, the stub of a cigarette pinned between two yellow fingers. A thin trail of smoke climbed to the ceiling, twisting and curling in the stale air.

Fisk jerked, his right hand darting under his wrinkled blazer as a loud boom echoed from down the hall. A fierce growling erupted as a small figure shot like a missile from the darkness. Fisk relaxed his grip on the butt of his service weapon. *It's just the damn kid.*

The boy, perhaps four years old, tore through the kitchen without stopping. Wearing a tattered *Wolverine* Halloween mask and a pink bath towel pinned around his neck, he roared like some hellish beast and disappeared into the living room. Angela didn't react.

For the second time that afternoon, Fisk fell into a waking dream.

He pulled the 9mm from his holster and shot Angela in the forehead. Blood, bone, and tissue sprayed a crimson fan on the dirty wallpaper behind her. She remained completely still.

A moment later, Wolverine howled through the room and into the hall. His small body lifted from the ground and flew down the hall, propelled by the hollow point round Fisk put in the center of his back. Fisk opened his mouth to the hot barrel.

He jerked as the coffee cup he'd dropped shattered on the tile floor. Fisk looked at his hand. No gun. He could feel its comforting pressure against his side.

Drawing a shaky breath, he glanced at Angela. Her cigarette had burned down to the filter and extinguished itself. She hadn't moved.

Fisk slid out of the wobbly kitchen chair and stood, his knees popping. He looked around the dirty kitchen as if seeing for the first time. Reaching into his jacket pocket, he pulled out the warrant and dropped it on the table in front of Angela. As he turned and strode towards the front door, the boy made another roaring flight through the kitchen.

All This Brother Wants—Chapter 2

P.L. Middlebrook

Jabs and More Jabs

Jessica says, "Let's get out of here. Let's go outside where we can talk without anyone hearing us or looking at us."

We walk in silence through the courthouse doors and outside. The day is warm and sunny. We walk across the mall of the Daley Center, which is swarming with people. Jessica leads us to a small outdoor table with benches. We're still emotional. I can look at my mom's face and see that she doesn't feel so great.

"What the hell was that about?" I ask.

"I thought we had a final judgment," says Mom.

"Do I get to see my child?"

"It's not perfect, but it's not as bad as you may think," says Jessica.

She takes out the "Final Judgment" document. Mom has her copy open on the table. I'm looking at the first page, Darnell Wilson, Petitioner and Little Eva, Respondent. Simple stuff first, I am the natural and biological father.

"Does Little Eva have sole custody of my boy? How fair is that?"

"It states that, but in reality, the judgment reads like joint custody," says Jessica.

I'm getting a little glimmer of hope again. I read through the document, some out loud to Mom and to Jessica.

"Article I, State of Intent begins with Little Eva and I agreeing to keep the child's best interests in mind while making arrangements for co-parenting. It acknowledges that we both love our child. We cannot make comments about the other's parenting. Check."

"No derogatory remarks about the other parent. Check."

"Article II, custody and parenting responsibilities: both parties shall actively participate in raising and guiding the child. Check."

"If we cannot reach an agreement regarding a major issue, Little Eva will make the final decision. Hold up. Wait now. The court shall retain jurisdiction of this matter. I guess. I smell another boxing match, another stupid crapshoot. What chance do I have in that courtroom with that judge?" I ask, fuming.

"We'll fight back if we have to," says Jessica. "Nobody's giving up. Calm down."

"I get full weight as a parent in terms of my boy's education. Any school he attends has to have my name and contact information. They have to keep me informed with report cards, conferences, etc. Equal rights with the school. Check. My boy has never been to school. I've been wanting my son to go to nursery school at least one or two days a week. Anything would be better than nothing."

"I can't stand it that the child doesn't go to school," Mom says sadly.

"Little Eva picks the school. Don't like that, but maybe I can live with her decision. Little Eva acts like she doesn't believe in school. Our boy has never been to preschool, Head Start, or nothing. Can she get away with so called 'home schooling?' No accountability. No other children to play with or learn from. Can you hear how ridiculous this sounds?"

"It's unbelievable. The judge can't see through that? No learning experience for the child? The guardian ad litem gets paid a boatload of money and she doesn't say anything about the lack of any educational opportunities for my grandchild? When he does start school, the other kids will be way ahead, which could frustrate him or make him not like school. What kind of crap is that?" Mom's voice raises an octave.

"The parties agree that the child shall be raised in the Christian faith. Check."

"At least that part is good," says Mom.

"Lessons and extracurricular activities, both of us need to be informed. Yeah right," I say a little sarcastically.

"Medical and health related issues, both of us need to be informed. Check. I get the distinct impression Eva would never let me know if

Little Man needed medical attention. I've offered to put my boy on my health insurance plan and Eva won't allow it. I don't know anything about his health. Has he had any vaccinations? Does he go to the dentist? Does he get checkups? Come on Jessica."

Jessica just shakes her head. "We have to pick our battles. Let's get you some solid visitation established."

"Obligation to notify each other of our address and contact information. I smell trouble. Little Eva has a Lincoln Park condo and she stays at her mother's house in the suburbs. I really don't know where she lives at any given time."

"It doesn't matter as long as she brings the baby over," says Mom.

"I'm with you Mrs. Wilson," Jessica says.

"We've got other general rules like marriage responsibility and we were never married. I think some updating is called for in this directive. 'A spouse must be informed of the terms of Judgment of Parenting and Custody.' Spouse? Really?"

"Child cannot be used as a messenger. We have to use 'Talking Parents,' an online communication system through the courts. Check. Would the courts direct her to stop harassing me on my job? When she calls me, she hollers about some crap she imagines I said or did. Can the courts put her in check on that?"

"I will definitely bring up that point next hearing."

"Both parties must recognize the importance of their child spending time with both extended families and will work to facilitate those relationships. Check. I'm not the one with the problem. Eva does not play well with others."

"Love this one. 'Both parties are restrained and enjoined from threatening, harassing, intimidating, or otherwise engaging in any harmful or offensive conduct toward the other party.' Little Eva is a drama queen. I wish she would get a job or go back to school, put the baby in school, or put her mind on something else productive. I swear she's overboard obsessed. Is she so hungry for attention she has to look for it in the courthouse?

"Article III Parenting Schedule. Now I'm pissed again. I still have to have supervised visitation. At least it's weekly this time, Mondays on my day off, only for three hours. I can't afford more than that."

Mom starts going off again about how the judge denied her request to be a supervisor for visitation. Jessica tries to settle her down and I tune them both out, remembering how the GAL tried to sneak in that visitation would be one hundred percent my cost, but Jessica caught it, and the judge agreed that the cost must be shared. Like I said, it's a dirty game.

The wild part about the supervisor is the GAL said we could get a cheap one, but the supervisor would be an employee of Little Eva's mother. Do I have stupid written across my forehead? Put a jackleg in my home and all she would have to do is claim I had weed in my house. She could plant it and take a picture of it with me in the background. I wish I would be that big of a fool. No, Jessica and I continue to discuss a reputable agency with professionals like social workers.

The last supervisor I had was Linda. Linda was cool. We liked Linda, but she stopped coming regularly. I would go weeks on end without seeing my boy. I asked the "Fathers' Rights" attorneys to get rid of Linda because she was so unreliable. They didn't even write a motion for that and we paid them a lot of money. My mother, my father, my brother, my grandmother, me . . . we all pitched in to pay them and they couldn't even file a simple motion like that. Where's the shame? Incompetence, or crookery, or both? I really think Little Eva's mother paid Linda not to come. I can't prove it, but like I said, it's a dirty game.

I jump back in with, "The holiday schedule is good. Check. Everything is in black and white, easy to understand. It's divided by even and odd years and for the whole day. I get every Father's Day, and Little Eva gets every Mother's Day. Fair enough. There is a clause in the judgment that says either one of us can have additional parenting time by mutual agreement, and we don't have to go through the court. That will be the day Eva flies above the courthouse."

I get caught up in my head again. Little Eva will never agree for me to see my boy more than what's mentioned in this document now. I want to have a normal life with my boy. I want us to have breakfast or lunch, go to the park, watch TV, especially a game. How about the Cubs, the Bulls, and the Bears? That would be so cool. I want to teach him his alphabet and his numbers. We could read too and go to the park and play ball together. He loves baseball. I want to teach him how to swim. I was a Chicago lifeguard for years. I want to take him to the beach. I wonder if he'll love swimming like I do?

I have to stick a pin in that dream bubble for a while. It seems like an eternity. And sometimes a black cloud whispers that I'll never get to spend normal time with him, and I get a sick feeling.

Mom looks sad. Jessica looks a little green around the gills, and she drops that bomb again, "You have to take five consecutive clean random drug and urine tests, which must be taken over an eight-month period as verified by the guardian ad litem and then you may apply to the court for unsupervised parenting time."

"What?" I'm just about hollering at this point.

"Wait a minute Darnell, they wanted ten tests over a ten-month period, I got it down to five tests in eight months."

"Shit!" I know Jessica has done more for me than all the other lawyers put together except my brother. "Shit, Jessica, what do they think? Why are they fucking with me like this?"

Jessica is real cool. I can talk very informally with her. She's probably about thirty-eight or thirty-nine. She even has a tattoo on her arm, but nobody can see it when she goes to court because she's always dressed real conservative with the blue suits.

"And," she continues, "you have to pay for all the tests."

"They want me to pay for five more drug tests?"

"Look, I know it totally sucks, but just hang in there until March. At least the judge gave you a road map on how to get unsupervised time with your son. Take the tests. We'll go back in February, and what can he say?"

"He's got to know this is a bunch of bullshit. They haven't found nothing in four years. What's going to change?"

Jessica starts gathering her papers and gets up to leave. "It's bullshit. We know, but you can get through this Darnell. I know you can. We're going to get through this."

"Well," Mom says. "It could be worse. We've been through worse with that judge. Maybe we're finally getting somewhere."

Jessica looks up, "Hey, let's enjoy the rest of this day. At least the sun is shining."

We shake hands, say our goodbyes, and off Jessica goes. Mom and I look at each other dumbfounded. We start convincing ourselves that it's going to be alright.

"If she didn't have all those expensive lawyers, we wouldn't be going through all this bullshit," says Mom. "We may not have money like that, but we're nothing to sneeze at. You're a tough old bird. We're some tough old yard birds." Mom always has a way to make me LOL at certain things.

"They shot at us and couldn't kill us," I reply.

"They beat us with brooms, and all that happened was we lost some feathers. But we're still here," says Mom.

"They put big nails on our perch," I say, shaking my head. "And we just flew up to a higher branch."

"They're dealing with stew birds. Tough ones," Mom says. At this point we're both laughing.

Laughing to keep from crying.

"It's a dark tunnel, Mom." Just as I drop these words, I see Jessica from the corner of my eye. She raises her arm and makes a fist, bolts around, and is moving fast, fast, fast toward us. Jessica pounds both fists on our little table, startling the crap out of Mom and me.

"I've got an answer for their petition. I have a motion for them. I want sanctions against Eva's lawyers to stop this frivolous harassment and the inconsistent visitation, which is damaging to the child. It's harassment of the worst kind with an innocent child in the middle of ego and money. OK. It's like that," Jessica hisses. She raises her arm, points her finger in the direction she is going, and marches south across the mall, leaving me and Mom speechless.

Cold

Phil Skiff

The wooden wheels of the cart hit a stone and the floor smashed into Erinor's face. She clasped her hands over her mouth to keep from crying out. The two men in the back of the cart with her grunted as their bodies took the shock as well. Erinor lay still, not reacting to the pain—she wanted them to believe she was still unconscious and perhaps drop their guard enough for her to escape. A futile hope, but it was all she had.

Erinor lay on a burlap bag on the floor of the crudely made wooden cart, her wrists tied tightly together with thick hemp. Outside, the fierce wind thrashed endlessly over the barren wasteland of the outer reaches, screaming like a wounded animal. It shook the canvas covering of the cart and cut through every gap between the rough-hewn boards, stabbing her exposed skin like knives.

The men were dressed in wool-lined parkas, their large hoods pulled tight around their faces so only their eyes were visible. Erinor wore only a dirty linen smock that covered neither her arms nor her legs. The shivering had mercilessly stopped when her body temperature dropped below ninety degrees, but her skin was red from exposure and her joints ached with every movement. The end of the burlap bag she lay on was draped over her face, covered with frost from her breath.

The cart dropped like a stone into a big rut, and Erinor saw stars as her head bounced off the floor. She faded into blackness.

She awoke when she heard a gruff voice right next to her ear and felt the buzzing metal cone of a ripper pressed to her throat. The man yanked the rope off of her wrists, the flesh tearing away with it. The few drops of blood that fell transformed instantly into red crystal shards as they hit the wooden floor.

"Get up bitch, I know you can hear me. Ride's over. Now you get to walk, you filthy sow." The man laughed and leaned back, racked with gravelly coughs as the sharp air cut into his lungs. Erinor sat up, knowing it was futile to pretend any longer. It would just provoke them to hit or kick her again.

The canvas sides of the cart snapped and cracked as if being shaken by a mad dog. The roar and shriek of the wind had somehow managed to increase while she'd been unconscious. Sheets of snow and sleet slashed through the gaps, filling the interior with a stinging cloud that mingled with the fog from their breath.

Erinor looked at the two men who just stared back at her, white clouds billowing from the cones of their parkas, their violent eyes barely visible. The bigger one held the ripper in one massive gloved paw, the blue telltales blinking on the side said it was set on full power and would take her head right off of her body.

Perhaps I should provoke him to use it. A serious consideration—it would bring the easiest death she could find now. Erinor shook her head slowly. Her long brown hair, matted with filth and coated with frost, swung limply from her head. She wasn't a quitter; she was a fighter. She knew no one had survived being cast into the outer reaches, but it didn't matter. She would accept the consequences of her own actions and hope it would show everyone they could no longer just stand back and watch.

"Get up cow," the big man roared at her. "It's time to go!" Erinor stood on shaking legs she could no longer feel. "Do it!" the big man commanded the smaller one, keeping the ripper pointed at her head. Erinor smiled at him, knowing he was thinking of the last deputy who'd made the mistake of lowering his guard around her. She could still see the astonished look on the half of his face she'd allowed him to keep.

The smaller one was wary, also having seen the results of her work. He reached out slowly, and she braced for the opportunity she knew would not come. The ripper was just outside of her reach and pointed right at her face. Even she wasn't that fast.

The small man grabbed a fistful of the top of her smock and viciously ripped the flimsy garment from her body. Erinor didn't flinch, didn't give them the satisfaction of trying to cover her bruised breasts and thighs. She looked right at them. The malice and hate born of her abuse poured from her eyes. She was rewarded when they moved back towards the end of the cart.

"Out," the big one commanded. The small one undid the straps holding the cover on the back of the cart, fumbling in the big mittens he would not risk taking off. Untethered, the back cover flew up like a kite in the wind. Stinging sleet tore into the cart slashing her naked body.

The big man held the flap open with one hand and pointed the ripper at her with the other. Erinor slowly moved towards the back of the cart, her head rubbing on the low canvas ceiling. She struggled to walk. Her legs weren't working right. She steadied herself with a hand on the bench, leaving skin behind.

The small man scooted along the bench on her left towards the front of the cart. He shrank back as they passed one another and she could see the fear in his eyes even now. She stopped when she reached the end of cart and looked across the wasteland outside.

It was eternal twilight, with just the sliver of the sun appearing above the horizon. All she could see was an endless barren landscape of shale and basalt slag. Here and there were small pools and drifts of snow. This was a dry place where moisture was scarce. The uniformity was broken by large fissures and shelves of fractured stone throwing up jagged slopes scattered with glass-sharp rock shards.

Erinor felt the large man move behind her and knew he was about to push her out of the cart. She jumped to keep the decision in her hands. She hit the stony surface and nearly toppled over. The shock of the four-foot drop traveled up her legs and through her spine like a spear. She couldn't feel her feet at all and struggled to maintain her balance on the unstable carpet of rocks.

Her arms pinwheeled when she tried to move one foot out for a better stance. Several sharp flat rocks came up with her foot, having instantly adhered to the skin on the sole of her foot. She managed to stay upright and lowered her arms. Behind her, she heard the cart begin to move away without another word from the big man.

She didn't bother to look back. The wind slashed at her naked body and she could already see patches turning whitish gray. Her heart beat slowly and she felt her blood, thick like clotted syrup, pushing sluggishly through her veins. She looked at her fingers. They were now nearly all black and didn't move.

Sleep. She would sleep soon. She wanted to say something but she couldn't open her mouth. She touched her face but couldn't feel it. It didn't matter; she couldn't remember what she was going to say. In fact, try as she might, she couldn't even remember her name or why she was in this terrible place. She gazed toward the distant horizon but couldn't really see it.

She would sleep soon.

Sleeping Single—PART 4: Spring Romance

Diane VanderBeke Mager

The Saturday block party is in full swing. I rearrange trays of cupcakes and cookies, making space for more. Better to man the dessert table than wander alone from couple to couple, hearing about Spring Break family vacations and children's latest soccer successes.

Inevitably, one of the moms, forced to endure two weeks alone with the kids while her husband was away on business, will remark, "Oh Layla, I know just how you must have felt raising Dean on your own." Yeah right, fourteen whole days! Talk to me when you've made it past 7,200.

I check my phone to see if Dean has responded to my last text.

"Excuse me. Where should I put these?" asks a deep voice with a hint of Scottish burr.

I look up at an enormous platter of bite-sized morsels stacked in a pyramid and then into the eyes of Jake, the elusive next-door neighbor.

"Ooooh, are those CeCe's caramel, chocolate-chip brownies?" I exclaim. Reaching for the tray, I break off a corner and pop it in my mouth without thinking.

"Yes, she made me swear to follow her grandmother's recipe to the letter. Something about the neighbors unable to make it a full year without these."

"Mmmmmm. Aren't they amazing? We call them 'crack brownies' cuz you get addicted after just one hit."

"I don't have much of a sweet tooth." He stares down at me with a look of amusement from behind his sexy scruff and dark-rimmed glasses. "I'm Jake, by the way. And you're Layla, from next door . . . right?"

I wipe my sticky fingers on my jeans and extend my hand.

"Yes, that would be me." Gathering my senses, I add, "You've heard from CeCe and Bob then? Where are they now?"

"Halfway to the Grand Canyon."

"Nice." Not wanting an awkward silence to develop, I ask, "So what's it like house-sitting?"

"Well, the timing couldn't have been better. My lease was up at the end of the year, and they needed someone to look after the place." He added, "I'm hoping to buy in the area when the market picks up next month."

"Oh really? I love house-hunting if you ever need a second opinion." The words escape my lips before I can stop them.

"I just might take you up on that offer. CeCe said you're some sort of designer?"

"Design historian. Here, let me give you my card." I peel back my phone case to reveal a small stack of business cards covering my emergency twenty-dollar bill.

"Great. Enjoy the spoils," he responds, gesturing to the array of baked-goods in front of me.

"Thanks. I'll try to save some for the others."

I watch Jake cross the street and join the guys setting up the grill. Now that was a reasonably memorable "meet cute" to satisfy my nighttime fantasies. Seriously, it's about time I start taking some relationship risks, relishing in my freedom from parental responsibility instead of fabricating stories in my head before falling asleep alone.

I fumble my way through the next two hours, serving cakes and pies and restocking cookies and brownies. I replay the conversation with Jake over and over in my head. Finally, the last of the Tupperware containers is reclaimed, and those on cleanup duty take over. My phone vibrates and I stare down at the screen, trying to decipher Dean's cryptic message. A pair of soft lips gently brushes the base of my neck.

"I'll call you," whispers Jake in my ear.

I watch him walk away, perplexed, but excited by what just happened.

■■■

Eight sleepless nights later, and no word from Jake. I peek out my bedroom window. The lights are still off next door. I haven't heard his car pull in or out all week.

Taking out a pen and a stack of Post-it notes from my dresser drawer, I write:

Just stopped by to return something. Sorry I missed you. - L.C.

Before losing my nerve, I go downstairs, throw on my shoes, and head out the side door. I sneak across the lawn, then up CeCe and Bob's driveway, and through their side gate, taking care not to slam it—something they never bother to do. I stick the note to the screen door and bolt back home.

■ ■ ■

The butterflies in my stomach are spinning with the persistence of synchronized swimmers. There's a fifty-fifty chance that Jake will show up at tonight's town hall meeting. Standing in the lobby, I pretend to check messages on my phone, peering up every few moments to see if he's arrived. I get caught up in an actual text exchange with Dean, and when I look up again, Jake is standing in the corner near the water fountain.

It's now or never. I put my phone away and walk straight toward him. Rising up on my tiptoes, I brush my lips against his neck and say, "This is all you've ever given me, so it's all I can return." With sublime satisfaction, I stride into the auditorium and take an empty seat flanked by two couples I recognize from Dean's old school.

■ ■ ■

Three open houses, two condos, and one townhouse later . . . accompanied by two coffees, one lunch, and now Saturday dinner and a movie, I am starting to believe fantasies do come true.

Walking back from town, Jake reaches for my hand. Once beyond the glare of the streetlights, I use my other hand to surreptitiously rub the tip of my nose. The spring blossoms are already triggering my pollen allergies.

"I'm thinking about putting in an offer on the townhouse."

"Really? That's so exciting! It definitely has the best views, and the kitchen is spectacular."

"I told the realtor I'd let her know Monday morning. Do you want to—" The thundering train overhead drowns out his voice as we walk under the bridge. "—and then we could hike the forest trail. The weather is supposed to hold."

"Are we talking about tomorrow? Sure, if we're back in time for me to cut my grass."

"Okay, 10 AM then." Approaching my driveway, Jake gives my hand a squeeze. "I'll walk you to your door."

Unwilling to let the evening end with yet another kiss goodbye on my porch, I respond, "I'd rather you come in."

"I was hoping you'd say that."

I manage to get my key in the side door and turn off the alarm before Jake presses me up against the mudroom wall, crushing his lips to mine. I don't bother to turn on the lights. We kick off our shoes, and I lead him down the dark hallway and into the living room. Moonlight shines through the three square windows above the sofa. Jake takes a seat, pulling me down onto his lap, my knees straddling his thighs.

"Nice room." He cradles the back of my neck, drawing me closer.

"I like it," I murmur.

"I like you," Jake responds, turning our bodies to lay my head down upon the armrest.

Our kissing intensifies as I run my fingers through his dark, curly hair. I wrap my legs around his hips, and Jake slides our bodies down the full length of the seat cushions. My excitement mounts as he holds my wrists overhead with one hand, skillfully exploring beneath my sweater with the other.

Jake pulls the sweater over my head and it falls to the floor. His shirt soon follows. I rise up, running my hands down the smooth expanse of his back as he unclasps my bra and slides it from my shoulders, our bare skin colliding.

Time stands still as we kiss and caress. Occasional soft breezes and the rumbling of distant trains pass through the windows, triggering my heightened senses.

Jake explores the tip of my breasts with his tongue, trailing a path toward my mouth. Nibbling on my lower lip, he murmurs, "Do you want me to go down on you?"

The lilt of his voice nearly sends me over the edge.

"Yes, but—" I pull back, words rushing from my lips, "But not yet. I'm not sure I trust myself to stop . . . and maybe we should talk ab—" *Aaah . . . aaah . . . aaah . . . achoo.* "Oh, sorry!"

Smiling down at me, Jake replies, "I understand. We have time. . . . I'll head home then."

Sliding out from underneath, I take the power position on top, leaning in to kiss him one last time. Breaking eye contact, I whisper into his ear, "When it does happen, I think I'm going to like it."

"Me too."

Grinning, I reach for my sweater and pull it over my head, handing him his shirt. I stand and lead him to the side door, fingers entwined with his. He slides on his shoes and leans down to kiss me goodnight, gently tucking my hair behind my ear.

"Sleep well. Or do you think you'll lie awake all night thinking of me?" he smirks.

"Probably."

I float upstairs, toss my clothes on the floor, and climb into bed, unable to wipe the smile from my face. Jake is right, falling asleep is not going to be easy. . . . I begin to replay the evening in my head.

Ping. A text message alert interrupts my reverie.

JAKE: **You asleep?**

LAYLA: **Not yet.**

Ping. Conditioned like Pavlov's dog, my excitement mounts with each tone.

JAKE: **What are you wearing?**

LAYLA: **Only my thoughts of you . . .**

I wait. Too much? *Ping.*
JAKE: **Do they fit?**
LAYLA: **Perfectly ;-)**
Ping.
JAKE: **Mmmmmm.**
My smile grows to enormous. Best to end on a high note.
LAYLA: **G'night**
Ping.
JAKE: **Kiss**
LAYLA: **Hug**

I bury my smile into my pillow. Can this really be happening? I have met a man. Not just any man, but a patient man, one who intuitively understands and embraces the merits of my "Virgoan charms"—intellect, creativity, organization, compassion, and dedication . . . with trust issues, and a smoldering passion that simmers just beneath the surface. Translation—a controlling, know-it-all perfectionist and insecure people-pleaser . . . both dominant and submissive, able to persevere, and nearly ready to fall in love.

The light goes out in Jake's bedroom next door. Closing my eyes, I exhale, melting into my mattress like molten lava. Wanting to prolong this sense of wonder, I allow the sustained rhythms of yet another distant train to urge me forward, into a story of spring romance echoing my own. . . .

The whistle sounded as a whoosh of steam escaped the iron monster thundering into the station.

Laylee stepped from the vintage train and stood upon the platform. Her silk scarf billowed in the breeze, caressing her neck. The inn was just a ten-minute walk, and she readied herself for the steady drizzle that had danced across the coach windows throughout the long journey north.

She had booked a full two weeks, at the recommendation of a former investor. Her trip was to be part vacation, with brisk walks along the Scottish coast, and part scouting mission.

Dowager House was the latest property in the west of Scotland to be converted into an upscale boutique hotel. Neither a quaint city row house nor a massive country estate, it bridged the difference, providing in-town amenities with expansive private gardens and access to a renowned historic house tour just two miles away. The owner had agreed to meet with her to discuss the possibility of repeating the formula further up the coast.

Her confirmation email read "Past the triangular park and turn left." She rounded the corner, and there behind the stone fence and iron gate stood the imposing hipped roofline of Dowager House. The stormy skies served as the perfect backdrop to its horizontal lines and vertical, stepped chimneys.

Laylee entered the lobby, marveling at the Charles Rennie Mackintosh paneling and fixtures.

"You must be Miss Cassidy," stammered the redhead behind the front desk. Her name tag read "Eleanor." "Mr. MacMillan said to expect you. I really don't know how to apologize enough. But you see, there is a problem with your reservation."

"Really? I booked my room months ago."

"I'm afraid that's just the trouble. Your reservation was made via email, before the website went live. Your details were never entered into the system, and the hotel is fully booked for a wedding this weekend. We only discovered our error this morning when we went over the Manager's arrival calendar."

"Okay, so what am I supposed to do? Is there another hotel in the area?"

"There is a small Bed and Breakfast about twenty kilometers south of here, but Mr. MacMillan has proposed another solution. He wanted to be here to explain, but he was called into a meeting."

"Okay, what does he suggest?"

"Well, you see, your stay is intended to be for a fortnight, and the hotel is only fully booked tonight through Sunday. Mr. MacMillan would like to refund the cost of your room and host you at his estate for your first four nights. And then starting Monday, we can put you in the Royal Suite."

"Four nights on his estate? Where exactly is his estate?"
"The guest cottage is just about one kilometer down the lane."
"That sounds manageable."
"I can have someone drive you, or you can walk if you prefer."
"I think I'll walk. What's another ten minutes in the rain?"

Laylee followed Eleanor's directions down the winding lane. At the end of the hedgerow, she pushed through the cottage's low wooden gate. Turning the oversized key in the lock, she opened the front door and was greeted by a bouquet of fresh roses and hydrangeas. A bottle of sparkling water and an enormous basket of assorted teas, fruits, nuts, and biscuits stood beside it on the hall table.

Not wanting to succumb to jet lag, Laylee forced herself to unpack. She took a long, hot shower, dressed, and walked into town for lunch. At the main intersection, she was too focused on avoiding traffic coming from the right instead of left to notice the man with dark-framed glasses and a closely groomed beard staring at her from behind the wheel of his black sedan.

She found a small café and enjoyed some window-shopping after lunch. Her route took her past Dowager House. The morning's clouds had parted, and she spotted Eleanor on the upper terrace talking to a man with dark curly hair, dark glasses, and a sexy scruff. Eleanor offered a sheepish wave, and the man turned in Laylee's direction. Laylee blushed and smiled in return. With her luck, he was the bridegroom destined for the altar this weekend. . . .

■ ■ ■

The late afternoon sun was shining across the wet fields beyond the cottage. A trail leading to the edge of the forest beckoned her. When she returned from exploring, a note was tacked to the front door.

Please join us for dinner.
Saturday, at 8 o'clock.
Cliffside Manor.
- J. MacMillan

J. MacMillan . . . Cliffside Manor? The *Cliffside Manor from the guidebooks?* When Eleanor had offered up Mr. MacMillan's guest cottage nearby, it never occurred to Laylee that she would be staying on the actual grounds of the famed manor house. She was scheduled to tour it tomorrow. A complimentary pass had been included with her Dowager House reservation.

Her business contact had told her MacMillan owned and recently restored Dowager House. But it never came up, nor appeared in her research, that he also held the entire surrounding estate. Well, he certainly had an eye for design and knew how to make a guest feel welcome.

Laylee raided the gift basket, discovering some chocolates tucked near the bottom. Curling up in bed, she immersed herself in her travel novel. When she made it past the 10 PM marker, she turned out the lights, confident she would readjust her internal clock and sleep until morning.

But lying in bed, the high-pitched whistle of the night train had her reassessing her solitary nomadic tendencies. What would it be like to instead share meals and conversation, the burden of navigating new places, and more importantly, memories of architectural wonders and nature's beauty? She fell asleep musing on the merits of finding the perfect travel partner—

■■■

Saturday evening, she dressed for dinner in the only thing she had packed that was remotely appropriate, a printed maxi dress. She added a belt and sandals and headed down the lane toward Cliffside Manor. The sky glowed a fiery red as the sun set behind the cliffs.

She rang the doorbell at the entrance marked "Private," and was greeted by what she could only assume was the butler. A butler in this day and age? Then again, the house was enormous and the opportunities for entertaining tremendous. . . .

"Thank you, Cleeves. You must be Miss Cassidy. Allow me to introduce myself, I'm Jake MacMillan," said the man with the sexy scruff and dark glasses from the hotel terrace, his appearance almost as mesmerizing as the lilt of his Scottish burr.

They shook hands. "Please, call me Laylee."

Jake stared down at her intently. Laylee saw a look of contentment wash over his features, as if he was seeing something in her he had never seen before. When he released her hand, she immediately longed to reignite the connection.

"I am so glad you could join us this evening. I want to apologize again for the mix-up at the hotel. Are you comfortable in the guest cottage?"

"It's lovely, I couldn't be happier."

"Perfect. My assistant, Eleanor, informed me your name was on the list of tour guests yesterday, so I assume you've seen all of the public rooms here at Cliffside Manor?"

"Yes, they are truly remarkable."

"We can certainly arrange for a behind-the-scenes tour later."

"I would love that, but to be honest, I really can't wait to get into Dowager House. I live for early twentieth-century design. I'm afraid once I move into my hotel room, you're going to have a hard time getting me out!"

"Hmmmm . . . definitely something to consider," he replied with a rather flirtatious lift of the eyebrow and subtle smirk. "I'm looking forward to our meeting on Monday to discuss Dowager House and the potential for expansion. But for now, let me introduce you to the others. They're in the Library."

"Can I get you anything to drink, madam?" asked Cleeves.

"Sparkling water is fine, thank you."

Cleeves took his leave and Jake took her arm, leading her into the room that was undoubtedly her favorite on yesterday's tour. Her guide had revealed the library at Cliffside Manor housed over 2,000 volumes.

Two couples were seated near the fireplace, clearly eager to see whom Jake had invited to join their inner circle.

"Laylee, may I introduce you to Major Windemere . . . his lovely wife Cecelia, and the von Eberts . . . Erik . . . and Evangeline."

Cecelia rushed forward. "Jake has told us all about you. It's about time he invited someone interesting to dinner!" Laughing boisterously, she clasped Laylee's hands and kissed her on both cheeks.

"What a lovely dress," said Evangeline demurely.

Cleeves returned, presenting her water on a silver tray before announcing dinner would be served in the dining room in thirty minutes....

■■■

The sumptuous meal was peppered with lively discussion and amusing stories. After the Windemeres and von Eberts left, with promises of seeing Laylee again soon, Jake offered to drive her back to the cottage. When they reached the front porch, he kissed her on the cheek.

"I will see you on Monday then . . . unless of course you don't have any plans tomorrow. We could take the cliff walk and have a picnic at the cove. . . ."

■■■

Four cliff walks, one picnic, three business meetings, five dinners, and two overnights later . . . Laylee concluded that fantasies do come true, along with lifelong dreams.

Jake drew her into his arms. Kissing her tenderly on the neck, he asked, "Are you certain you want to move here to help run Dowager House and Cliffside Manor?"

"I couldn't be more positive if I tried. I've already extended my trip by two weeks, and I think I've seen all I need to see," *she murmured coyly, snuggling against his bare chest beneath the silky comforter.*

"And your plans for opening your own hotel?" *he asked.*

"Sharing something here with you is far more appealing than heading up the coast alone."

"Well, we both love to travel. We might just consider conquering the rugged Highlands together in the future. The damp heather, woolly sheep—"

Aaaah-achoo.

The Trunk in Grandma's Attic

Phil Skiff

"Hey, look at this!"

Levi ignored his sister's shout from across the dim attic. He was on his knees, focused on digging through the junk in the bottom drawer of a ratty old dresser he'd been searching for the past half hour. This was the last drawer, and he knew there had to be something interesting in it.

"Ah shit, it's locked," Haya complained. Levi smiled and added another tick mark to the list of times Haya had used a swear word today. *Mom will not be pleased with the report.*

Then he paused. *Locked?* That's interesting. Maybe she actually found something worthwhile. More likely she was just trying to bait him into abandoning his search of the dresser. She was still mad he'd managed to call dibs on the big dark chest of drawers before she could. She was such a brat. And another word that started with "B."

She was only two years older, but since she'd turned twelve things had changed between them somehow. When they were younger Haya had paid attention to him, stood up for him. Maybe she'd just done that because he'd taken it so hard when their dad left four years ago. "Disappeared," as mom always said. But Levi knew people didn't just disappear.

More likely, his dad had got tired of the screaming fights his mother had always caused. Haya had hidden them in her bedroom whenever this happened, covering his ears with her hands. But he had still heard it all, and it had terrified him. After his dad left, Levi had felt relieved, then guilty. The loss had made his world dark.

But that was a long time ago. Since then, Haya had become his chief tormentor. Worse even than the bullies at school. They could only hit him, and he could get over that. Haya, on the other hand, never hit him. She ripped at him with taunts and put-downs that only someone who knew him as well as she did could devise. He hated her now.

"Come help me open this Levi!" Haya commanded.

Levi dropped the old metal pill box he'd pried open, finding nothing inside, and gritted his teeth. He knew she was lying, teasing him, and when he went to look, she'd stand up, point, and laugh at him. At twelve, she was now an "adult." While Levi was still a child. Who cared that she now wore a bra and used those gross things he'd found in the bathroom cabinet. It was all just disgusting. *She's ugly and I hate her.*

"Levi!" Haya yelled and he jumped to his feet, rage boiling in him. *I'm going to hit her this time!* He marched across the creaking floorboards of his grandmother's attic, passing through the band of swirling dust motes flashing in the light from the single small, round window.

Levi wanted to swear at her, use foul words he knew would enrage her, make her face turn bright red, make her scream at him in frustration. But he held his tongue. Only because he needed to be able to tell his mom that Haya had said five swear words today, and he'd said none. He had to be able to tell the truth about this because his mom still saw right through his lies. Well, usually. He was getting better at lying.

He wouldn't test his lying with Grams though. The gnarled old woman with hands like claws was his mom's mother, and she scared everyone, including, it seemed, his mom. He and Haya both begged their mom not to leave them with Grams on the summer days she went to work. But here they were. Haya was especially offended because she felt she was old enough to watch Levi by herself now.

Fat chance! Haya couldn't even take care of herself. Couldn't fix a meal, had no idea how to work things more complicated than a spoon. She was constantly coming to Levi to fix what she'd messed up on her iPad, laptop, or even her hair dryer. That turned out to be just the circuit breaker on the plug. What an idiot.

These days all she cared about—all she thought about—was James, or Roy, or how her hair hung down over her eyes, or how a shirt showed off the tits she didn't even have. It was disgusting and stupid, but Levi always helped her, always fixed her stuff, and sometimes secretly messed up her things so she'd have to come to him for help. It kept her needing him and he wanted that.

Now that they were stuck in this nasty, dusty old house with their crazy Grams, she needed him more. When Grams wasn't napping, which she did a lot these days, she was lurking, watching, moving silently through the house in her ratty robe and slippers. Sneaking up on them. Scaring them on purpose. Levi was sure.

Levi had asked his mom about their grandfather once and was interested to find out that he had also "disappeared." Long ago, when mom was their age. Levi wasn't the least bit surprised he had run off. Who would want to be around a creaking, smelly, scary old hag like her? Grams knew Levi didn't like her, and somehow that worried him. But not enough to stop him from stealing from her.

He found Haya standing behind a row of clothes. They were hanging from a rope nailed to the rafters of the low, sloped roof at the edge of the attic space. She'd pushed some of the clothes aside and was standing between them, a frown on her face, hands on her hips, trying to imitate their mom. Pretending to be an "adult."

Levi clenched his fists at his side.

"Why didn't you come when I called you, Levi!" Haya spat, unconsciously repeating what their mom had said to him a thousand times.

Levi snapped, regretting the lapse even as the words spewed from his mouth. "Because you're not the boss of me, you no-titty piggy!"

Levi stared hate at his sister, watching her face turn crimson and her hands flutter at her sides. Amazingly, her mouth opened, but nothing came out. *Sweet.* Even though now he couldn't tell their mom about her swearing, this was worth it. He'd never seen her so angry and embarrassed. He knew he'd found gold he could mine over and over.

While Haya stood, covering her chest with her arms, her mouth opening and closing like a fish, Levi glanced down and saw the trunk. She actually had found something new. He'd never looked behind the long row of musty clothes. For one, they stank. Two, he'd just never thought about it.

He stepped over, roughly pushing Haya aside, and squatted in front of the trunk. It looked like something out of an old movie. A big rectangular trunk with large leather straps going around it like belts with actual belt buckles on them. She had already undone the straps, but the big metal hasp in the middle did indeed have a lock in it. Haya had been telling the truth. Levi didn't care.

Levi glanced up at his sister and felt a rush of deep satisfaction when he caught her trying to wipe away angry tears from her red face. She still said nothing. Perfect. He returned his attention to the trunk and the hasp. It was a really simple device with a small keyhole in the front. Levi slid a hand into his pocket and pulled out his trusty knife.

"You are a bastard Levi," Haya finally pronounced with a sniff, her voice low and shaking. Levi ignored her, selecting the slim blade he'd filed down himself. He stuck the point in the hole and twisted the blade until he found the small metal tab inside. He pushed and turned, and the hasp popped open with a click.

Hmm, easier than expected. While this wasn't the first lock he'd jimmied, he thought it would be harder to open something that'd probably sat up here a hundred years. He sat back on his haunches and put the knife away. He looked at the trunk more closely. While everything else up here in the attic was covered in a thick layer of dust, this trunk was not. It seemed somehow different from everything else. Used. Recently. That was interesting.

"Well, open it!" Haya said in a harsh whisper. *She's back to miss queen of the earth.* He shot her a withering glance. Levi pushed the lid up. It opened easily, without even a tiny squeak. Levi's face fell when he saw the piles of old trash filling the trunk—the same kind of worthless junk that seemed to be in everything up here. Stacks of papers with figures on them from banks and other things—all neatly tied together with string. Wads of cloth, also tied in string. Small cardboard boxes filled with slips of paper. "Checks" his mom told him when he found a stack of them in a desk drawer at home. Worthless. Uninteresting.

Haya knelt down beside him, and Levi dug her in the ribs with an elbow. She pushed him back, but he ignored her, his disappointment taking the fight out of him. She began rummaging around in the trunk, pulling stuff out, looking at it, and putting it on the floor beside her.

Levi sighed and shoved his arm into the trunk. If there were anything interesting in here it would be at the bottom. The trunk was deep, and he braced himself on the floor with his other arm as he squirmed through the junk. His fingers met the flat bottom, finding nothing but more papers and clothes on the way down.

Then Levi noticed something odd. He glanced over at his left hand resting on the dusty attic floorboards. Something was wrong. He felt around on the bottom of the trunk with his right hand as he looked at his left. The bottom of the trunk was higher than the floor. He felt his heart speed up.

"Hey! Stop it!" Haya hissed as he plunged his left arm into the trunk and began pulling out armfuls of junk, throwing it over his shoulder onto the floor. "Stop it Levi! You're making a mess!"

"Shut up miss piggy," Levi responded while he continued pulling armfuls out of the trunk. Haya stood up and put her fists on her hips.

"You're going to wake up Grams!" Haya scolded. *Fat chance.* She's almost deaf and usually slept all afternoon on these warm summer days while they were trapped in her house, forbidden to go outside and play while she napped.

Levi paused. Most of the contents of the trunk were now lying scattered around him on the floor. He reached in and gently rapped on the bottom of the trunk with a knuckle. The hollow sound confirmed his suspicions. He felt a new surge of excitement. A false bottom—just like in the movies. Sure enough, he saw a small strip of cloth sticking up from the floor of the trunk where it met the front panel.

He gave it a gentle tug and the bottom came up easily. "What are you doing?" Haya started, then stopped as she saw the panel open, revealing a space hidden below. There were several objects in the shallow space. Strange things. Interesting things. Haya knelt back down beside him and peered into the trunk.

The hidden compartment was a couple of inches deep. There were three things in it. Before he could stop her, Haya reached in and picked up what looked like a stack of plastic papers. There seemed to be a dozen or more clear sheets of plastic with writing on them. Levi had never seen anything like them and watched, amazed, as Haya leafed through the pages.

There were columns of strange figures on each page. They looked somewhat like the scratchy figures he'd seen on a Torah scroll his father had once shown him. But different, more spidery looking.

Haya gasped and dropped the pages on the floor. "Stupid!" Levi hissed.

"They moved," she cried in a breathless whisper, backing away from the trunk. Levi raised an eyebrow, skepticism written on his face. Haya seemed genuinely scared. He liked it. "No, really, they did move, the hieroglyphics, they moved, I swear!" Levi snarled, angry at Haya for using big words he didn't know. Trying to make him feel stupid.

He snatched the stack from the floor, but nearly dropped them himself as figures swam across the surface beneath his fingers. He watched, enthralled, as the figures scrolled endlessly across the clear plastic. He lifted the top one off the stack, turned it over, and was surprised to see a completely different set of figures there, even though the page seemed completely transparent. Very cool!

Haya's hands were curled under her chin, clearly more afraid than interested. "Put them back, Levi," she told him. Levi had been ready to do exactly that but changed his mind when Haya told him what to do, again. He shot a hateful glance at her then laid the shimmering pages on the floor in front of the trunk. He peered inside.

The second object in the trunk was a clear glass container. It was round and shaped kind of like a huge M&M. Inside it, he could see what looked like a half dozen glass marbles, shot through with colors like a tiger eye. He reached in to pick up the glass M&M then jerked his hand away. When he'd touched the glass container, the marbles had moved around inside. As they moved, the colors inside them changed, swirling, collapsing, swelling. At the same time, they made a tinkling sound like glass or chimes. The hair rose on the back of his neck.

Behind him, he heard Haya scramble to her feet. "What was that Levi! What did you do?" She'd heard the strange sounds as well though they seemed very faint. Levi was embarrassed at being afraid, and it made him angry. "Shut up Haya," he commanded, and for once, she had no retort.

He decided to leave the strange container of marbles alone and turned his gaze upon the last item in the trunk. A shiny silver cigar. At least it had kind of the same shape as the nasty cigars his uncle Efraim used to smoke all the time. His mom had hated them and left the house when he lit them, yelling at their dad to make him stop. Dad had just laughed at her, but he'd coughed too.

It wasn't exactly like a cigar though, Levi thought. One end was wider and kind of flattened. He shoved down his fear and reached into the trunk. He picked up the silvery cigar, surprised by how heavy it was. It slid into his palm and he almost dropped it when he felt it seem to move and change shape, fitting itself perfectly to the shape of his hand.

Levi stood, entranced, wrapping his fingers around it. The end of cigar stuck out between his thumb and forefinger, the wider part flowing into his palm as he closed his fingers around it. An indent formed and his index finger slid into it. Levi felt the thing warming in his hand, and somehow, he knew what it was. He smiled and turned toward Haya.

Haya stood, a few feet away, hands back on her hips, her face red again. "Put that thing down this very instant Levi Gersham," Haya commanded, stamping her foot on the floor. Levi's grin grew broader. Haya lifted her head and arched her eyebrows, trying to look like their mom. "If you don't put that back right now, I'm going to go tell Grams you're into her stuff," she said, obviously forgetting that she was the one who'd found the trunk in the first place.

Levi said nothing and just stood looking at his sister, feeling a light vibration in his palm as he raised his arm to point at Haya. He squeezed gently with his index finger.

A dozen strands of intertwined blue lightning shot from the weapon, hitting Haya right in the chest. She threw her hands in the air, a scream emerging from her mouth, her face lit from below. Churning red bloomed where the blue lightning seemed to impale her. It looked to Levi like lava, red underneath, boiling, wrapped in dark ash. In an instant, the lava spread and consumed Haya, cutting off her cry.

Levi, breathing hard, a sharp acid-sweet tang filling his nostrils, lifted his finger from the trigger. A gray figure, the same shape as Haya, hung in the air for a split second and then fell to the floor, leaving a pile of smoldering ash.

"What the hell have you little brats gotten into now?" The attic door flew open and Grams stood on the threshold, her cane held over her head in one claw hand. She stopped in mid-stride as Levi turned towards her, her eyes fixed on the object in his hand. She froze, looking up at Levi, clearly seeing what was in his eyes. Slowly she shook her head side to side. "Levi," she croaked.

"Hi Grams," Levi replied quietly. "I think I know how my dad "disappeared," he said, making air-quotes with two fingers. He gently squeezed the trigger and the attic filled with blue light.

Swan Lake
Peter Banks

"And give me one good reason why working for my family is such a bad thing," she argued ferociously, and her usually graceful face contorted into something reptilian. "There are way worse ways to spend your days and this being broke all the time is killing me."

"Ve- lo- ci- rap- tor," he mumbled to himself as she continued ranting.

"I missed that. Did you say something?" She pressed on and he wisely stayed silent, keeping this a one-sided debate.

He just wasn't up for the fight, not now, not tonight. Staring at the empty wall behind her, he fished for a focal point, needing an anchor for his energy, to calm himself, weather the barrage. The gnawing at the base of his skull had grown as he felt the bite of her invective. He was numb but felt like he was being eaten alive. There must be a name for that type of ambivalence. Now he was lost and stared out the windows into the darkening sky, in his mind floating away with the clouds. Drifting, out of body, out of his own existence. The less you care about yourself kills the ability to care about anything else. There must be a name for that subtype of ambivalence, he just couldn't recall it right—

"Are you even listening to me?"

∎∎∎

Driving up to the lake alone would probably kill the chance of resolving their issues anytime soon. Leaving was only fuel for the next fire, if this one ever stopped burning. He needed to be away right now. Away from her, away from people, just to collect himself. He remembered the cabin as an afterthought—a few days getaway during the holiday. At least until this latest volcano stopped spewing.

A jukebox in his head accompanied everything he did. Feng-shui for the soul, the right mental music usually fixed even the worst of days, but right now only one song was on repeat and it wasn't working: U2's depressing "With Or Without You," just the intro, just the instruments. The rumbling bass line and wailing guitar deepened the darkness outside and in his mind. It was stuck right now and was not the music he needed. Wrong effect. Dark and distant—but slowly approaching, he felt it growing, filling up reality until he was no longer certain it was only in his head. He drove on, but the night was not his friend. The sun was just burning the edges off the morning mist when he reached the cabin. Exhausted, he collapsed into a sound sleep until well past noon.

■■■

The cabin was comfortable, even luxurious as far as cabins go, but he hated it. A "gift" from the future . . . potential . . . in-laws. More like bait dangled to keep them in Michigan once they got married. Who gives a damn cabin as a *pre*-wedding gift anyway? Another exercise in excess. How much can one family have? How rich is just obscene? Maybe that was the point. To them the money didn't matter. They probably bathed in it, and besides, they had another cabin up near Grand Traverse, way more exclusive as far as necks-of-the-woods go.

■■■

Solitude creates an intellect unto itself and he always felt like Walt Whitman when he camped out at the cabin. Rustic and tuned-in to nature, he struggled to remember even a fragment of old Walt's poetry. He was refreshed after sleeping so soundly and scrounged around the cabin for some food and old hunting clothes before going out to soak up some sunshine. Muskegon in the fall is cool but beautiful. Crisp. Nature's full palette on display, pure sky and leaves changing hues: from the normally monotonous green into unexpected rainbows. He was dumbfounded by the beauty and couldn't resist, "I sing the body electric," he gloated loudly to the trees.

The lake itself is midway up Michigan's western coast, a small inland lake near the immense Lake Michigan. Natives point to the palm of their upturned hand to describe the location of their getaways. Usually seconds before the uninitiated ask, "Where's Muskegon?" Hand maps are just a *thing* in Michigan.

He wandered a ways up the trail, hoping to find a spot where it broadened out into a more idyllic view of the lake. The trail weaved through the woods a while before opening onto a small outcropping, a bluff jutting from the forested overgrowth. Slightly elevated above the beach, he'd found a place where he could see most of the lake surrounded by the full spectrum of autumn chromatics. Impressive and inspiring, he forgot every year how beautiful the fall colors truly were and was held in awe again by this picturesque vista. "I sing the body electric," was still all he could manage, but it fit perfectly.

Rejoicing in the autumn aesthetics, it would have been easy to miss the body lying in the sand near the water. Just above the reach of the lapping waves, half blending in with the beach, she was nude and unmoving. Unsure at first, he paused a moment before acting, afraid he'd stumbled upon another lost soul seeking solitude or a late season nudist just catching some rays. The cove was perfectly concealed with only the sun and sky bearing witness. Despite the scenery, the figure in the sand became the new center of the universe; it was all he could see and ponder. Human beauty trumping nature's sublime bounty.

After only seconds that stretched into a breathless eternity, he scrambled down from the outcropping and jogged over to investigate more closely. Offer help if he could. With hope, she might still be alive, more ready for a rescue than eulogy.

How had this happened? Her upturned face was struck in a half-smile, the ambivalent look of passivity and wonder, a paradox that did nothing to dim the brilliance in her face. And she was perfectly posed, as if sculpted by the master himself, Rodin, or painted there by Boticelli: Danae, La Primavera, La Giaconda. His mental reflexes only supported the theory that Da Vinci had captured Mona Lisa's death mask, that's why he couldn't get the smile quite right. It dampened his sense of guilt somewhat, thinking this broken ballerina had died with grace and in some apparent peace. Enough so that there was some eloquence in her repose. But had she truly died breathlessly, without agony or indecision? Die young, leave a beautiful corpse . . . beauty for beauty's sake . . . like roses, even in death she lay undiminished.

He'd seen a dead girl before, but never this close, freshman year in college, drowned after an overdose. Certainly a suicide, they'd finally concluded, but innocence killing itself just increases the remorse. But why, doesn't all grace eventually end in sadness? He hadn't known her, no one had, not there on campus at least. They'd only guessed she had a family somewhere out there in the real world. Crowded out by all the detectives detecting, it was the first time he'd felt the shame and embarrassment of being abjectly out of place, "behind the line please."

Back then, his cohort of friends would gather in the campus quad after dinner to "verbalize" in the spirit of their new surroundings. He'd jokingly called them the *Platonic Dialogues*, ironic because the platonic and the dialogue only lasted until the drink and the smoke ran out. After that, the group would split off into pairs to "explore the night air."

He wondered if those nights had been even remotely intellectual. They'd found the dead girl after one such gathering. She'd been there the entire night, right by the pond. They could see the spot from the dorm windows when daylight broke. He'd settled in at his own dorm window to a front row seat of the proceedings. Obsessively, he'd observed evidence collection and the taking of statements for days on end. Devoted to his vigil, he'd skipped classes for two weeks, claiming grief, while the counselors still fell for it. Even to the point of nabbing a script to "calm his nerves" as if his nerves could've been any calmer after all his other recreational indulgences.

This time was different though, but why? The proximity? The solitude? He grappled for context but could only draw empty impressions. Her skin's insistence was a blank slate for anything his logic conjured. Reflexively, he organized everything into little equations, A or B, figuring anything binary at least suggested choice. Nymph or naiad? Siren or Medusa? Venus or Aphrodite? He couldn't quite nail it down, killing one argument as he created the next, with no true solution in sight. Before one argument could fully settle, he'd rephrased the equation. He would only realize much later in life that his habit of pigeonholing beauty was futile, like expressing the ineffable or drawing the face of God. It is what it is, but he stayed there all day pondering.

There's a reason they say a picture is worth a thousand words. The first five hundred don't count. It's that last five hundred where words begin to fail as photographs just begin to describe. Even memory is subservient. His eyes oscillated over the entire scene, committing every nuance to memory.

He returned to the outcropping above the lake and communed in vigil until well after sunset. Once darkness had reclaimed the world, denying sight of his new friend, he somberly thought Jane Doe was insufficient and so he dubbed her Ophelia. Jealous nature succumbed to a new focus and grudgingly the autumn air expanded to contain something more, higher in clarity, but still ungraspable, never quite his to fully understand. He never listened to opera, but his mental jukebox somehow thought it best. And before long, that was the only thing rolling around in his head. A soprano swooning in song.

Despite himself, he didn't stay at the lake and drove home the next day. He only recognized the poncho as a mistake afterward, utterly useless. It was transparent and did very little to preserve her final dignity. Besides, her presence was a bit more profound veiled in translucence. It also occurred to him too late; he had clumsily created evidence. At least he did know enough to not call and report what he'd found. Facts aside, he was just a suspect without an alibi and didn't have the stomach for that type of trouble.

■■■

She argued ferociously, his shrewish new bride. But of course he was unaggrieved, smiling even, because he knew that even if he never visited the lake again, Ophelia was somewhere smiling with the flowers. He was confident she could stay silent and keep all their secrets safe and sound.

The Declaration

Phil Skiff

Amy sat on a bench against the curving wall, one heel tapping an anxious rhythm on the marble floor. The sound of her tapping was lost amid the noise of the crowd ringing off the high walls and dome overhead.

Her gaze was fastened on a young couple standing on the far side of the broad rotunda. She squirmed, twisting and leaning, to keep the two in sight as tourists wandered around the room gawking at the huge paintings and other art on display.

She's touching him!

Amy leaned forward, staring at Penelope's back who seemed oblivious of Amy's burning gaze. Penelope stood close to Ahmed. Thin and lithe, her perfectly sculpted arms and legs were on display in a sleeveless blouse and short skirt, one hand rested on Ahmed's shoulder, the other pointed at the painting in front of them. Across the room, Amy's heel tapping became a staccato and she ground her molars, biting back a scream.

"Afterwards, they asked Trumbull why he included several men who didn't sign the declaration," Penny explained.

Ahmed jammed his hands into his pockets to keep them still. He could barely concentrate on what Penelope was saying, feeling the warmth of her hand on his shoulder. He was also keenly aware of Amy's surveillance from across the rotunda. He knew the depth of her jealousy.

"I thought you said this really isn't a painting of the signing of the declaration, even though that's what it's called."

"Right." Penelope cooed, giving his shoulder a squeeze, then letting her hand drift down his back and casually brush over his ass. Ahmed shuddered.

Across the room, Amy leapt to her feet. Without taking her eyes off of the pair, she plunged her hand into a pocket on the side of her purse, her fingers closing over the cool metal there.

Penelope pushed a lock of curly hair from her face and studied Ahmed. From the corner of her eye, she saw Amy standing, her face red with fury. A tiny smile lifted the corner of Penny's mouth. Ahmed continued to stare at the painting, refusing, or unable to look at her. Penny's smile grew.

"There is this conspiracy theory that the others mysteriously included in the painting were the real power behind the new government. Interesting, huh?"

"Um, yeah, I'd never heard that." Ahmed coughed, his throat suddenly dry. He risked a glance at Penelope and felt his skin flush finding her close, eyes locked on him. He coughed again and looked away.

Penelope licked her lips, rising up on her tiptoes. She leaned against him, whispering in his ear, her breath warm and moist. "You know Jefferson hated John Adams. That's why Trumbull painted him stepping on Adam's foot." Her voice was soft and husky, filled with the promise of a different kind of congress.

"Wh, what?" Ahmed asked, confused.

A shot rang out, booming off the walls and the high dome above.

All This Brother Wants—Chapter 3

P.L. Middlebrook

Chance Encounter

I grew up in Detroit and graduated from Cass Tech High School. The "D" is cool, but I had this idea in my head to go away to college. Between scholarships, grants, and student loans, I figured it's doable. Chicago is alluring to say the least. It's far, but not too far, and it's easy to get to from Detroit. When I got my acceptance letter from DePaul, that was it.

DePaul has this unique course that all freshmen must take. It has to do with seeing many parts of Chicago, studying the architecture, the unique neighborhood hubs, and city planning. I learned the history of the neighborhoods, how they developed, and how gentrification plays a part, especially in a city like Chicago.

Some Chicago neighborhoods are desolate and on the brink, but many neighborhoods have turned for the better. Chicago has a lot of interesting ethnic neighborhoods too. Downtown Chicago, the Gold Coast is fascinating, lots to do, very expensive, tons of tourists, just a sweet place to be. DePaul is in Lincoln Park, not far from downtown. It reminds me of what Brooklyn, New York must be like with million-dollar brownstones.

If you're a student living in Lincoln Park, rent is expensive, and apartments can be more than a little grimy. Actually, there are two Chicagos, one is luxurious and exciting and the other one is an underbelly of homelessness, gangsta life, and crime. My motto is "look over your shoulder." Nighttime Chicago is fun though.

I lived in the dorm my first year. Basic small room. I had my computer and good music beats to listen to any time of the day or night. Everybody, at least everybody I knew, was into rap music. I even listened to old school Tupac. I had an interesting group of friends to hang out with. Two of my good friends were from California, around LA. It seemed like everyone I met was from somewhere else, not Chicago. I did have this one good friend, Leroy, born and raised on the South Side of Chicago. He always knew what time it was.

My LA friends and I decided sophomore year to rent a house in Lincoln Park together. There were four of us renting a four bedroom flat. Four dudes in one crib. Housekeeping, food, I don't remember how we managed, but we did. The place was on the funky side.

There were a bunch of super rich kids at DePaul. My roommate Don's father was a major player in LA. He produced a number of major TV shows on network and cable for years. He wrote and developed the shows too. That's how he became wealthy. His own private jet, stupid rich.

On one of our breaks, Don's father invited me and another of Don's friends to work on a popular cable TV show he produced. It was an amazing experience. We learned so much and got paid for it. I especially liked the set design part. I even did an acting part, you know, the background acting stuff. I don't remember having any lines.

I was a Chicago lifeguard most of the summers. Actually, it paid pretty well. Without a doubt, it was a strenuous Red Cross program, but I enjoyed the challenge. One time, I had to search Lake Michigan for a homeless man they thought had gone under. That was real tough. Another time when I had public pool duty, I was in a Hispanic neighborhood and my biggest challenge was to make sure everybody had a proper swimsuit on. Girls had to wear a for real bathing suit top. You would be surprised how creative folk can get when they want to swim on a hot summer day. When a dude strut into the pool area in seriously cut off blue jeans with his booty cheeks out, I had to put Chico in check. I picked up a lot of Spanglish over there.

I kept a job during the semesters too, and I enjoyed my classes for the most part. My friends and I always had a blast, probably too much fun at times. You could feel the music through the floor. It wasn't cool unless it made your feet vibrate. Sometimes we would play dumb-ass drinking games to see who could get wasted first. Frat boy shit but I never pledged a fraternity. I don't recall any of my friends pledging either.

We were always looking for girls to hang out with. Don eventually got real serious about a girl and kind of stuck with her. The rest of us, in and out of relationships, I guess. Not too many.

Nothing out of the norm, just nothing stuck. Halcyon days in retrospect. I was content.

Days, weeks, months, years, they went by fast, but I liked being busy. Eventually, graduation day was on the horizon. I wrote papers on top of papers, took exams, and when the counselor said I had all my credits in order, I just about jumped for joy. It was nice while it lasted, but after a hard earned, tough row-to-hoe journey, it was time for me to get my degree and move on.

My family came to graduation, not just my mom and dad, but my grandma too. My roommate, Brian, and I had a couple of weeks left on our lease. We had gotten lucky senior year and found a dope apartment at a great price in Lincoln Park. But Brian was getting his accounting degree and going back to Detroit, so I had to start looking again.

My family stayed at a little Lincoln Park hotel and came and picked me up about an hour and a half before graduation. Everybody was in a good mood until a few miles down the freeway; traffic came to a snail's pace halt. Chicago traffic is horrible. The graduation arena was way out somewhere, outside of Chicago, a suburb.

After about a half hour of this pace, we came to the realization that we just might not make it. I had on my gown and held onto my cap. Grandma was in the back seat calling on the Lord and fussing about everybody and everything. Dad did some creative driving and used the commuter lane.

When we finally arrived, I jumped out of the car fast as I could, scared I would be late. The family could come in after they parked the car. It was a long walk, but lo and behold, I made it.

I couldn't stand in my assigned spot. I had to stand in with the late comers, but at least I made it and was actually going to walk across the stage with my class. Because I was late, my family was seated not so far behind and could fortunately see me a little better. I was so happy, I struck up a conversation with the girl standing next to me.

"I'm so late, I was afraid I wasn't going to make it, but look, they haven't called the first name yet," I said smiling. I immediately thought she was real pretty.

"I'm late too. My mom and I almost couldn't find this place. I was supposed to be way up front."

"My name is Darnell, last name Wilson, and you are?"

"My name is Eva Atiana." She smiled.

"I think I've seen you before Eva Atiana, around campus. I noticed you in the Student Center." I was grinning like a Cheshire cat.

"Why didn't you say something?" she asked.

"I don't just go up to women I don't know and start talking." My laugh was easy at this point. "What did you major in?" I inquired, truly curious.

"Philosophy."

"Whoa, interesting, I've never met anyone who majored in philosophy."

"What did you major in?" she asked.

"Public policy. I would love to have a job in my field. Maybe do some political stuff. Work for the mayor or an alderman. If I could parlay this into urban planning, that would be seriously awesome. I might have to go back to school, I don't know. What about you? What does one do with a degree in philosophy?"

"Search for answers."

Her hand ever so lightly brushed up against my hand. I couldn't help but look. And then I looked her in the eyes. "If you're searching for answers, what are the questions?"

"I'm not sure," she said looking down.

"Whoa, that's deep," I said. "What kind of plans do you have for the future?"

"It's started," she whispered. "We better quiet down."

"Where do you live?" I whispered back.

"Lincoln Park."

"I live in Lincoln Park too. What a major phenomenon," I smiled again. "Why don't we get together and have some coffee at Starbuck's or something? There're a ton of places in Lincoln Park."

"Yeah, I would like that," she whispered and looked ahead.

I could have been on time, and I never would have met her. I could have arrived five minutes earlier, and we never would have met. I could have been thirty seconds earlier and we never would have met. I could have been thirty seconds later and we never would have met. That's how I met Little Eva, and we were on a wild ride from that moment on. Have you ever driven a car with no brakes?

Saudade (Redux)

Phil Skiff

Fisk stared at the coffee cup in his hands. It had the logo of a bank, common in Loveland. A quarter mile from here. It was stained and spider webbed with brown cracks. Fisk watched a dribble of Diet Pepsi chase itself around the bottom as he rolled the cup between his hands.

Across the battered kitchen table, Cynthia sat. Her blonde hair hung in ropes around her face, dark circles under her eyes. One hand was wrapped around a full cup of Diet Pepsi, its contents room temperature. The other rested on the edge of the table, the stub of a Cuban cigar pinned between two yellow fingers. A thin trail of smoke climbed to the ceiling, twisting and curling in the stale air.

Fisk jerked, his right hand darting under his wrinkled blazer as a loud rumble echoed from out in the living room. The hair stood up on the back of Fisk's neck. He hadn't heard a sound like that since, well, since before his ex left with the Subaru. Down the hall, a door slammed and a small figure appeared out of the darkness. Fisk kept his hand on the butt of his service weapon.

The boy, perhaps four years old, stopped near the end of the hall and looked at Fisk. He was wearing a tattered *Wolverine* Halloween mask, now shoved up on his head, and a pink bath towel pinned around his neck.

"What was that, Uncle John?" He stared at Fisk, his eyes big, but didn't come further down the hall. Another sound, a thump, from the living room. Fisk pushed himself to his feet, a glance finding Cynthia hadn't moved a muscle.

"I don't know, kid," he said, pulling the Sig Sauer P320 partway out of his shoulder holster, but keeping it under his jacket. He turned and took two careful steps across the cracked linoleum towards the living room. He glanced at the kid, putting a finger up to his lips.

As he leaned against the wall, another low rumble came from around the corner. Then a breathy sound, like an exhale. Fisk felt his heart hammering in his chest and saw the kid take a couple steps backward in the hall.

Fisk pulled the Sig out and held it down by his side. He leaned forward and peered around the corner.

"What the hell!" Fisk blew out the breath he'd been holding and blinked several times.

The unicorn standing beside the ratty couch wagged its head up and down and stamped a hoof. It had a long pink mane and a matching tail it swished lazily. Its body was covered with multi-colored stripes. The long spiral horn sparkled with glitter.

Fisk twitched hearing a sound and found the kid standing next to him, his mouth hanging open. Fisk closed his own mouth.

"Uncle John?" the boy asked, not taking his eyes off the animal. Fisk shrugged.

The unicorn's eyes closed and it lifted its tail in the air. A loud grumbling started somewhere inside its torso, moving towards the back. A short squeal was followed by a blubbering wet sound usually only heard in the Greyhound bus terminal bathroom. A billowing rainbow cloud shot out of the south end of the unicorn and floated towards the ceiling. It joined three others hovering there. The unicorn blinked, its eyes watering, and stomped again.

"Oh, hell no," Fisk said, raising his pistol and emptying the clip into the animal. The hollow point rounds blew holes all the way through the wallboard and aluminum siding. A dozen shafts of late afternoon sun speared through the pink cloud that hung in the air where the unicorn had been.

In unison, Fisk and the boy both covered their mouths with their hands. The boy gagged, spit on the carpet, then pulled the *Wolverine* mask down over his face.

"Thanks Uncle John, that's nasty."

"Don't mention it, kid," Fisk said, popping the empty clip with his thumb. He pulled a fresh one from his belt, shoved it home, and pushed his jacket back to holster the weapon. Drawing a shaky breath, he looked back into the kitchen at Cynthia. Her cigar had burned down to a stub and extinguished itself. She hadn't moved.

Fisk sighed and reached into his jacket pocket. He pulled out the warrant and held it out to the kid. "Give this to your mom, would you?"

"Sure, Uncle John," the boy said, taking it in his small hand. Fisk turned and strode towards the front door. The boy let loose a roar and flew into the kitchen, his cape flapping behind him.

Sleeping Single—PART 5: Summer Slayings

Diane VanderBeke Mager

At last, a man is sleeping in my bed.

Defenses eliminated, I stare in awe at Jake's glorious torso glistening in the summer heat and ask myself again, what have I, Layla Cascia, done to deserve the sexiest, most trustworthy, and generous soul on earth? I was never one to believe the old adage, "Good things come to those who wait," but I am starting to reconsider.

The bedtime stories have served their purpose. I can finally fall asleep to the sweet rhythm of my lover's steady breath. Fantasy is now my reality.

The ceiling fan cools our flushed skin, making tiny ripples in the silk sheets. The manly scent of Jake's cologne wafts in the air. My nose tingles in response, but I hold back my sneeze. He is so worth it.

Jake rolls onto his back. I close my eyes, blissful and content.

His breathing slows. Then it falters. Sublime satisfaction turns to restrained fury as the sound of a struggling turbine engine emanates from his nostrils . . . inhaling, *kwaa-kwaa-kwaa* . . . exhaling, *woooosh* . . . inhaling, *kwaa-kwaa-kwaa* . . . exhaling, *woooosh*.

In quiet resignation, my mind begins to plot. . . .

Jake's bare torso is the perfect real estate.

Layla plunges the knife with precision and purpose. Blood pools, and the smell of his cologne takes on a sour endnote, no longer thrilling her senses. She repeats her actions until the sound of his pulsing heart matches the deadness of her own. . . .

CONTRIBUTING AUTHORS

Peter Banks

"For the sake of a single poem," Rilke wrote, "you must see many cities, many people and things." This fragment is Peter's mantra—for the infinite inspirations arising from daily life. His charge and challenge is to receive and record these daily gifts. Peter has learned to thrive under the chaos caused by this openness in collecting and interpreting these welcome interruptions.

For Peter, the greater challenge is in making sense of the miasma of information gathered. One side effect of this organic approach is that he is seldom seen far from writing or formulating dialogue from dreams. Peter would say that this experience, this thing we call life, is all just more material for writing. What some would dub "the muse" is a very real thing for him.

Peter embraces the dying art of great literature by reading and writing what some disparage as "difficult texts." When the way gets rough, Rilke reminds: "It is not yet enough to have memories," but that, "in some very rare hour the first word of a poem arises in their midst and goes forth from them."

Peter occupies his time between bouts of writing as a "Shelving Strategist" at our favorite local library. Stop in and say hello sometimes, it inspires him.

This photograph is of an officially commissioned graffiti in Detroit. For me, it visually refines one elusive aspect of all art—anything you pour your heart into succeeds, but only to a point, and forever remains an incomplete composition. Artists are never completely satisfied with their works—or grow to wish they could expand the dimensions of those works. Thankfully though, artists are constantly inspired by this to create and recreate, furthering their vision. In that regard, this photograph will probably remain "untitled" because no definition can quite capture its continually shifting meaning for me.

Diane VanderBeke Mager

Diane is a published decorative art historian, museum educator, and children's historic fiction author. She holds a BA from Kalamazoo College, an MA from the Cooper-Hewitt Smithsonian Design Museum/Parsons School of Design, and an MS Ed from Bank Street College. "Sleeping Single" represents her first romance short story.

A reflection of her penchant for creating short stories and films in her head in order to fall asleep, her five-part story within a story is interspersed throughout the Anthology to reflect the seasonal passage of time and the arc of the narrator's journey. Diane hopes that her readers will see a part of themselves in the character of Layla, whether they currently or once upon a time slept alone.

When not staying awake all night writing or editing other authors' work, Diane is immersing herself in television, film, and literary plotlines; pursuing her passion for travel, politics, and wellness; and sharing her fascination for art, architecture, and design with her son, Lorenz, and her engaging program patrons.

Photo credit: PD Rearick

P.L. Middlebrook

P.L. Middlebrook believes the best literature is provocative and enriching.

Born and raised in Detroit, Middlebrook graduated from Cass Tech High School and went on to the University of Michigan to receive a Bachelor of Arts degree in history and English.

Middlebrook earned a Master's degree from the University of Detroit/Mercy while teaching. Prior to Middlebrook's career in education, Middlebrook worked at MGM Film Company for eight years in the Story Department at the old studio lot in Culver City, California. Both careers were extremely interesting and as an educator most enriching.

What drives Middlebrook's motivation to write is a passionate belief in her topic and the characters to which the story unfolds. Middlebrook believes an artist should be reflective of the times with glaring honesty.

I walk by faith, not by sight. And a good cup of coffee.

A.J. Norris

A.J. Norris is a romantic suspense and paranormal romance novelist. She began writing as a way to dim down the voices inside her head. She enjoys being able to get inside someone else's head, even a fictional one, and see what they see. Watching how her characters deal with difficult situations or squirm with the uncomfortable ones make the hard work of writing all worth it. She is a movie buff, especially book adaptations. She loves to watch her son play baseball and to commune with other writers. A.J. lives with her family who is extremely tolerant (at least most of the time) of all her late nights behind the computer.

Website: www.ajnorrisauthor.com
Twitter: www.twitter.com/AJNorris_Author
Facebook: www.facebook.com/alisajnorris
Goodreads: www.goodreads.com/author/show/14888581.A_J_Norris

Tim Patrick

Tim enjoys writing slice of life stories about ordinary people in extraordinary circumstances. Setting characters in uncomfortable situations and watching how they react and come of age has always fascinated him. Writing credits include articles in trade publications, advertising copy, short stories and essays, writing contests, newspaper articles, grant writing, and academic research.

His business travels and experience in advertising, marketing, and aviation have provided an ample supply of characters, places, situations, and ideas. Tim is an independent business owner and a graduate of Oakland University.

D.M. Patton

D. M. Patton is a writer living in Bloomfield Hills, Michigan. She is a graduate of the University of Michigan. She enjoys reading, writing, long walks with her dog, and gardening. To relax, she started a blog.

Blog: kibasgarden.com

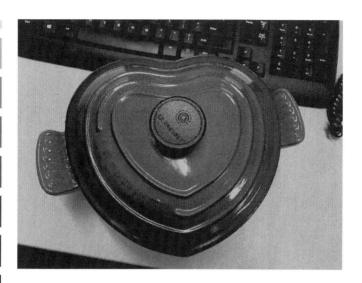

The picture represents love. The pot symbolizes love of food that nourishes our bodies. The keyboard represents the stories of the lives of the people I love. These are simple things everyone can relate to, but it's the feelings associated with the food and stories that make us special. Food feeds the body. Words feed the mind and soul. Love is what unites us and creates the memories that allow us to live forever in the hearts of those we touch.

Theresa Shen

Theresa has been interested in writing ever since she was a child and was often good at it. After years of education in the Republic of China, Europe, and the United States, her writing style varies, mostly focusing on short stories and poetry. Her short stories, be they biographical or creative, are often perceptive and humorous. Her poetry, visual and philosophical.

Writing is also therapeutic to her well-being. In 2010, Theresa was diagnosed with lung cancer; her life expectancy was unknown. However, after all the treatments, she turned to creative writing, which, indeed, has been the best medicine she has ever had.

As an adjunct, she taught at Wayne County Community College District, Lawrence Technological University, and Oakland Community College. Her teaching experience has enhanced her writing.

Theresa will continue to write as long as she is alive, if not for fame, for joy. Her other interests include art, music, languages, and travel.

My writing reflects my life, cultural experiences, philosophy, and sense of humor. Whether they are short stories, memoir, or poems, I always try to capture a moment of sensitivity and jot it down on paper, so the reader will share with me my feelings and thoughts. Furthermore, my writings are very visual. When someone reads my writings, they can experience being there with me.

Phil Skiff

Phil is a third-generation writer. He has several published essays and short stories, but his passion dwells in suspense, sci-fi, and romance fiction writing. The long nighttime hours spent hunched over a keyboard are funded by his secret daytime life as an IT Consultant. Phil lives in Michigan with his patient wife and ambivalent man-cat, Max.

The terrific book, The War of Art, *by Steven Pressfield, made a real impact on me as a growing and learning writer. There are so many key concepts in there to help you grapple with the passion and process that is creative writing. Lots of people are compelled to write. Many do it well. A few have real skill. And an even tinier percentage make the leap to success— however you may define that for a writer. Steven's book, for me, points the way to that success. I'm working on that.*

I'd also like to mention the inspiration and courage given to me by my father and his mother—both also writers. Thanks Dad!

The other objects in the picture are just whimsy—an homage to my sisters who inspired "Saudade (Redux)."

Anthony Stachurski

Anthony is a Michigan Poet whose poems primarily deal with the existential questions of life. Along the way, there have been poems about nature, love, and romance; his early years in England and Canada; and some funny stuff too. His goal is to get people thinking about and questioning their attitudes and beliefs about the way life works.

Anthony is a retired high school and community college teacher who, when not writing, is icing down a sore knee or shoulder from playing handball. He is, also, an avid reader and musician.

Crows are inquisitive, thoughtful, and independent birds, who mind their own business, standing apart from society, preferring the solitude of woods. They must laugh at all the superstitions about them. If for no other reason, I love them in the fall when they gather in the cornfields cawing, flying in the wind, free spirits, too unbeautiful to be caged. In many ways, I see myself as one of them.

Awards & Works Previously Published

"The Great Equalizer," by Theresa Shen, published in *Bald Eagle Stew*, an anthology by the Michigan Authors Syndicate, 2014; a Memories, Memoir Writers' selected work, Bloomfield Township Public Library website, 2015.

"The Outsider," by Theresa Shen, winner of the Cranbrook Writer's Guild short stories competition, 1991.

"The Green Beans," by Theresa Shen, published on the Bloomfield Township Public Library website, 2014; a Memories, Memoir Writers' selected work, Bloomfield Township Public Library website, 2015.

"The Declaration," by Phil Skiff, published by Mashstories.com as a shortlist selection, July 2015.

"Saudade," by Phil Skiff, published by Mashstories.com as a shortlist selection, January 2016.

Also by

A.J. Norris The Dark Amulet Series:
(Limitless Publishing, LLC):
Her Black Wings
Her Black Heart
Her Black Soul

The Tattoo Crimes Series:
(Limitless Publishing, LLC)
Tattoo Killer
Inked Killer

Phil Skiff "Learning to Purr"
(Amplitude Magazine, March 2016)

Anthony Stachurski *Under Salvation*
(Writing Hands Press, 2014)

Acknowledgements

As most projects do, creating this anthology took longer than expected. It was also quite a bit more work than perhaps any of us anticipated. But in the end, we got it done.

I'd like to thank all the dedicated authors who put up with my clumsy first attempt at leading an anthology project. They all patiently submitted to my constant barrage of complaining and cajoling emails, reviews, revisions, and changes of direction. Their work is what makes this book so spectacular.

We also had a small ad hoc team assigned the task of overall design for the anthology: structure, formatting, pictures, and of course the cover. This team accepted the role with grace and amazing patience as we endured round after round of changes, critiques, and conflicting opinions. In the end, I think this work speaks for itself!

Diane VanderBeke Mager invested countless hours working with me on the final review and edits of the entire manuscript. The overall design of the anthology also has her fingerprints all over it. Her detail-oriented and meticulous approach made a huge difference in our final product.

Lastly, I'd like to thank Tim Patrick, our leader and facilitator of the longest running writers' group I've ever come across. It takes incredible dedication to keep something up and running for decades. It's been incredibly valuable to me as a writer and I'm personally deeply grateful.

Phil Skiff
Editor in Chief

Made in the USA
San Bernardino, CA
11 March 2018